WRATH OF THE CAVE-BEAR!

Conan jabbed with his spear, then again, once narrowly missing the creature's face and once striking its shoulder, to little effect. He avoided the batting paws, which would splinter his crude weapon to matchwood . . . and the jaws, that could easily shear through wood and stone alike. The shaft's fighting-reach was scarcely longer than the bear's massive arm, so he had to leap in and dodge back to protect his own skin. Seeing an opening at last, he drove his spear at the monster's hairy flank . . .

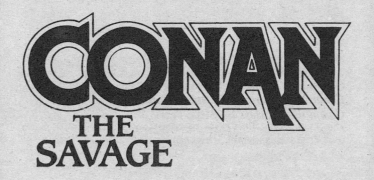

CONAN
THE SAVAGE

—— BY ——
LEONARD
CARPENTER

A TOM DOHERTY ASSOCIATES BOOK
NEW YORK

CONAN THE SAVAGE

Copyright © 1992 by Conan Properties, Inc.

Cover art by Ken Kelley
Maps by Chazaud

A Tor Book
Published by Tom Doherty Associates, Inc.
175 Fifth Avenue
New York, N.Y. 10010

Tor ® is a registered trademark of Tom Doherty Associates, Inc.

ISBN: 0-812-51412-2

First edition: November 1992
First mass market printing: August 1993

Printed in the United States of America

0 9 8 7 6 5 4 3 2 1

To Robert E. Howard,
creator of Conan,
and to the dream:

The Howard Memorial House and Museum
P.O. Box 534
Cross Plains, Texas 76443

Donations gratefully accepted

PROLOGUE:

The Trap of Darkness

"Well, now . . . a haughty Priest, a Prince, and the King himself!" The gambler's voice rang out exultant over the click of draughts on the marble-topped table. "My royal entourage sweeps all before it."

The dealer arrayed in front of him the white stone tiles engraved with regally costumed figures. He himself, clad in silk and grimy lace, smiled with the arrogance of a slumming noble. "Play if you think you can, barbarian, or else yield up your bet!"

"Nay, Caspius." The player opposite him shook his black-maned head. "Sure as I am Conan of Cimmeria, I have vanquished mightier hosts than that." Hunching his strong neck between muscular shoulders, he peered at the row of tiles he kept concealed beneath a thick, sun-bronzed hand.

"You would do well to yield," the bushy-bearded gambler to his right whispered to him. "Rich as these stakes are, a Royal House is nigh impossible to beat.'' He slid his own handful of stone draughts forward, blank sides up. ''I, of a certainty, have nothing that can match it.''

''Nor I.'' The gambler on his left, a lean, mustachioed officer of the Brythunian cavalry, retired his hand likewise with a glance to Conan. ''Once again I must yield, as any seasoned player would.''

''Hmm.'' His advice was met with only a grunt from the frowning Cimmerian.

''You would be wise to heed them, Conan,'' murmured the tavern wench who sat at the Cimmerian's elbow. ''Stem your losses now, while you can still afford my night's hire, at least.'' As she spoke, she massaged his thin-shirted back with lithe arms whose coppery bracelets sparkled. Meanwhile leaned low in an effort to glimpse his hand.

''Nay,'' the one called Conan decided, ''I shall purchase one more lot.'' Digging into the pouch at his waist with his free hand, he produced an unmounted ruby, pear-cut. Held up between his thick fingertips, the gem glinted in the dimness, drawing an appreciative sigh from the woman at his side.

''This bauble should suffice, as you can see. Taverner, more light here!'' the bettor called impatiently over one burly shoulder. ''It grows accursed gloomy in this musty corner of your cellar!''

''Very well, barbarian,'' the dealer proclaimed. ''One lot for you, and one more for me as well.'' Reaching to the stack of tiles before him, he dispensed two with expert ease. ''And what is mine? Ho-ho, the Sorcerer, the mightiest servant of the House of Maces!'' The lace-garbed aristocrat laughed imperiously as he filled in the row of

2

draughts. "You may as well throw up your hand, out-lander. Nothing beats this combination!"

"Does it not, then?" the northerner grumbled. "What of this august gathering of Kings?" So saying, he flipped over four of his tiles, including the newly purchased one, advancing them as if to claim the prize. "Their might would prevail in any encounter on the field of battle."

"Why, nonsense," the aristocrat said. "A full Royal House beats four of any rank! Every fool knows that, even a barbaric one!" He stretched his lace-cuffed arms forward to rake in the accumulated treasure.

"Not in this affray, lordling—since your Sorcerer is as false as you are, drawn from your foppish sleeve rather than the deck!" With lightning swiftness, the Cimmerian's hand shot out, striking aside the soiled ruffles of the dealer's arm, and laid hold of the stack of tiles. "True, 'twas hard to see in the dimness—but here is the proof!"

So saying, he spread the draughts out on the tabletop, exposing the sneering face of a second Wizard of Maces.

"Are you saying our friend Caspius is a cheat?" the cavalry officer cried out. "Sully his name at your peril!"

"Aye, truly!" The bearded gambler, scarcely glancing down at the table, spoke swiftly in defense of the dealer. "You could have palmed that second Wizard tile. How do we know you are not the sharpster?"

"What? Are you three in league, then, that you defend his thievery?" Conan shifted on his wooden stool, getting his legs beneath him as he eyed the trio. "You and the tavern-keep too, perhaps, with his low-guttering candles?"

The ruffled noble made a sudden movement in his place, reaching toward his other sleeve, and Conan caught the flash of a knife—a short, heavy blade it appeared to be, made for throwing. The dealer's motion halted abruptly as the Cimmerian gripped the tabletop and threw his full weight against it. His powerful lunge slid the heavy marble slab forward on its trestle into the dealer's chest, driving him back against the stone wall.

"Uh-urk!" the false noble gasped, finding himself suddenly deprived of wind. He tried to draw breath, and coughing shallowly, stared down in amazement as drops of bright blood dribbled from his lips, pattering on the white wafers of the playing tiles before him.

Conan's own view of the scene was jarred at that moment, and damned by the rain of baked clay fragments of a heavy wine jar the tavern wench had shattered over his head from behind.

Dully, doggedly, he shook off the blow. Only half-feigning stupor, he hunched forward across the table and raked the gold and jewels of the game treasury toward him with one hand, drawing open the pouch at his waist with the other.

"What! Seize that devil, he's taken the whole pot!"

Conan bounded back from the table, waylaid only by the tavern-trollop's tenacious grip on his sword-arm. Failing to pry her loose, he lifted her up bodily and flung her heels-over-head at the pair of gamblers who were rushing toward him, drawing their weapons. She and the bearded henchman tumbled to the floor in a tangle of limbs and curses. Meanwhile, Conan's heavy-bladed shortsword rang out of its scabbard to clash with the cavalryman's scything saber.

Parry, cut, kick, and thrust; Conan fought the man back swiftly. The officer was a skilled fencer, but hardly equal to the Cimmerian's ferocious strength. A hammerlike stroke of

Conan's heavy blade, lashing down as from nowhere, broke both the cavalry sword and the wrist that upheld it. Following that, a blow across the face from Conan's hilt-guard was enough to send the officer sprawling senseless to the floor.

The other tavern patrons were exiting through the kitchen, and an outcry had risen. As the bearded gambler recovered his sword, Conan strode for the exit.

Once up the stone stair and onto the landing, he turned—and saw no pursuers framed in the tunnel-arch of the stairway. No surprise, that. With two of his henchmen down or dead, the bearded man would be unlikely to follow their vanquisher—at least not too closely—into narrow alleyways smothered under the dark canopy of Brythunian night.

Satisfied, Conan sheathed his weapon and turned. He pushed out through the heavy curtain that served as a door—straight into a band of armored figures waiting silently in the dark.

Here were city proctors, he knew at once, the guards assigned to keep order in this Brythunian capital. The Cimmerian's sudden blind dash for freedom was halted by three of the burly, black-clad guards. Two pinioned his elbows tightly beside him, while a third crooked a mailed forearm around his muscle-corded neck.

"What ho, then . . . a late roisterer, is it? And a foreigner!" The fourth proctor, a bronze-crested sergeant, spoke low and gruffly in the dimness. "Say, stranger—in the name of the city of Sargossa and its ruler, King Typhas—what can you tell me of theft, and of foul murder? For know you, screams and sword-strokes were heard in this vicinity mere moments agone."

"By Bel's purse, I saw nothing and I heard nothing!"

The Cimmerian bucked and strove against the clutch of his captors' iron gauntlets. "Unhand me, or I'll teach you all I know of murder in one simple lesson!"

"Oho," the guardsman cannily said, "do you expect me to believe an oath sworn in the name of the God of Thieves? And speaking of purses, what of this fat one here at your waist?" Bending forward, the proctor hefted the thick reticule and made it jingle, meanwhile dodging a low kick from the captive. Then, with the lightning flick of a hidden knife-blade, he slit the thong that bound the pouch to its owner and bore it away into the light of the tavern archway.

"Oh so, a trove of gold and gems, is it?" the proctor said with dire humor in his gruff voice. "Very dubious, outlander. These would appear to be stolen goods. What say you?"

"Aye, stolen they are," the angry Cimmerian growled, "but only this very minute, by black-cloaked cutpurses lying in ambush, and taken from their rightful owner—myself!" His words were punctuated by another savage lunge in the alley gloom, almost breaking his captors' hold. "By Crom and Mitra, I'll have them back or I'll have your rotty gizzards for breakfast!"

"Now, now, outlander," the rough voice cajoled him, "calm your struggles. If you want your rightful property back, tell me how you came by it—for know you, if it was duly taxed on your entry into the city, there will be record and remembrance of it." The proctor cleared his throat meaningfully. "If you came by it honestly since you arrived—why then, simply tell us how."

"By Gwanatha's hairy tail," the prisoner cursed. "But then, I suppose your question is fair enough. I came here to Sargossa yesterday with a fraction of that wealth. The rest of it is one night's gambling winnings.''

''What, you mean you have gambled for profit? Here in Sargossa, during our hallowed Feast of Amalias?'' The sound of the proctor's gruff amazement covered, until too late, the clank of iron shackles, which Conan now felt clapped about his ankles, presumably by an unseen fifth man who had crept up behind him in the darkness. ''For know you, this is a high holy day, on which all such vices are forbidden! Do you mean to flout the harsh penalties for profaning a high festival?—aside from the forfeit of any illegal gains, I mean.''

''Curse you for a hellhound's three-tailed whelp!'' the Cimmerian roared, kicking out against the shackles and almost toppling himself and his captors. ''Do you mean to tell me that this open sewer, this foul stew of dives and brothels, has renounced its vices for this one night? Nay, 'tis just another form of legalized theft, like your city's confounded entry tithes—''

''Enough riot and seditious talk!'' the proctor barked at the struggling Cimmerian. ''Such an ill-mannered ruffian as you has no rightful business in Sargossa. There is none here who could speak for you or plead your case, I suppose? No person of high status?'' He cleared his gravelly throat while waiting for the prisoner, who now writhed sullen and wordless amid his captors. ''No, I thought not. No matter, we can find a suitable place for you.'' He jingled the purse in his hand. ''You have a liking for gems and gold, it would seem. Good, then. You may yet acquire them beyond your grandest wishes!''

ONE

Plunderers from the Border

"Tamsin, daughter of mine, where are you? Come and help your mother, child. It's time to feed the chickens!"

The voice rang out across the meadow, chiming melodious in the early light. But small Tamsin, where she crouched inside the burned hollow stump a stone's cast from the cottage, gave no answer. She did not stir or smile. She sat hugging her rag doll, watching her mother's sun-bright shape through the bark crevices and a screen of pale, dewy grass blades.

"Tam dear, come and help spread the grain. I know how you love to feed the rooster." The woman's voice sounded patient and untroubled as she scooped meal into her apron from the earthen granary in the cottage yard. "If I thought you had wandered away, I would go and search the forest. But I think you're somewhere nearby, and I know you would love to come and help me." The sound of her voice receded as she turned and moved gracefully past the dwelling, toward the slatted wooden coop. "After that, Tam, there is bread for us to roll out. And if you want to make some tarts . . ." The squawks and flappings of the half-wild fowl obscured her words at that point.

Still Tamsin did not stir, but watched the cottage pensively. She felt vaguely bored and discontented. She would not have known how to put it into words, but the very grace and patience of her mother somehow seemed a burden, a weary trial that a stubborn part of her sought to resist.

Crouching in damp shadow, she hugged the makeshift doll tight against her side, whispering to it. "We don't want to go back now, do we, Ninga? When Papa comes home from the fields for midday dinner, then we will go. But not before."

The chickens' raucous noise must have drowned out other distant happenings, for at that moment old Higgin came limping out of the ox barn, calling out something and looking toward the head of the meadow beyond the house. And one of the dogs commenced barking; it was soon joined by the other two, the trio of them raising up a defiant clamor at the edge of the meadow beyond the barn. Even Velda shuffled out to wait behind her husband, staring in the same direction.

Than at last Tamsin saw what it was. From beyond the trees that formed the meadow's angle there emerged a lofty banner—bright yellow, a flapping triangle of fabric. Painted all in black at its center was the silhouette of a strange animal. It had the body, tail, and hinder paws of a lion, attached to the head, hooked beak, and flaring wings of a bird of prey. Its forelegs, one of which was raised high, were large, birdlike claws, resembling those of the rooster Mama was feeding.

The banner was borne at the end of a long pole held upright by a rider astride a beautiful reddish-gold horse.

The man, Tamsin saw with wonder, was black-bearded and gold-helmeted, dressed in horseman's leathers and high black boots. He rode with five other men on similarly splendid mounts of different colors. All of them approached the farm at a trot, reining up in the space now abandoned by the snarling, slinking dogs.

At that moment, Tamsin's mother emerged from the fowl roost. Obviously still ignorant of the arrivals, she brushed feathers and seed husks from the auburn braids of her hair and her brief, patterned shift. On her sudden appearance there was a stir among the halted riders, which was cut off by a sharp command from the flag-bearer. Startled, the young mother stood looking up as the black-bearded man spoke in gruffly accented Brythunian.

"We are of Einholt's Nemedian mercenary troop, riding to the aid of King Typhas in the southern wars. As you can see, our banner bears the gryphon, your country's royal sigil. By your king's authority, we are warranted to make our way through the countryside."

Old Higgin spoke up staunchly in his drawling, cracked voice. "The king's High Road is back that way, half a league or less," he said, pointing down the meadow. "Just make your way through the glade and follow the stream's course. You are sure to find it."

"We know that, old man," the leader said over the laughter of his troops. "We are a foraging party, instructed to gather supplies for our march." His eyes rose to fix on Tamsin's mother. "Our needs are to be filled, by order of your king."

Old Higgin coughed to regain the mercenary's attention. "Well, I know not—ours is a poor farmstead. But if you will tell me what you need, I can try to fetch it."

"Old man, we need provisions for our march to the Corinthian frontier. Food, stock, cattle fodder—carts to carry it in, and dray animals if we can get them. We need things you cannot possibly fetch," he added with a curt laugh.

The old retainer scarcely seemed to hear him. "Alas, we are very poor here. A bite of bread, to be sure, and a sup from our kettle—you are welcome to what we have, within reason."

Tamsin heard her mother's voice ring out abruptly. "Higgin, give them anything they want."

"Well, yes, I suppose, by the king's command," the old man muttered, looking from his mistress to the horsemen, "but for what recompense, I ask you."

The standard-bearer laughed, lowering his pole. "Old fool, do you really suppose it makes a trollop's-fart of difference to great King Typhas in his palace at Sargossa whether we strip this miserable place or raze it to the ground? Will it matter to him, when he needs mercenaries to bail him out of a war on the other side of his empire?"

"His Majesty's royal collops are in a sling in Corinthia!" one of the mounted soldiers jeered.

"Aye, but this Brythunian kingdom of his is a hospitable land," another mercenary cried. "They do not hide away their women!"

At this remark and the hooting laughs that followed it, Tamsin's mother turned one brief, frightened look toward her daughter where she crouched inside the stump. For the merest instant their eyes met; then she turned and bolted away in the other direction, headed toward the forest—to be followed by an explosion of hoofbeats as the riders broke out of their loose formation.

As they charged forward, they rode straight over Higgin

and Velda. Tamsin watched it happen with amazement; one moment the old couple stood there, then their gray heads could be glimpsed bobbing amid dust and hooves. Then they were not to be seen anymore.

Meanwhile, the foremost rider leaped from his saddle directly onto the little girl's mother, dragging her down and rolling with her in the meadow grass and flowers.

Tamsin crouched there for a long time, clutching her doll beside her. The two of them watched as one man after another dismounted and went to where Mama was, behind the grazing, idle horses. The rest of the mercenaries, when they weren't doing that, went into the cottage and the other buildings, bringing out things in sacks and leading off the cow and the ox. Two of the men went into the fowl pen and after a lot of squawking, came out with big bundles of quiet birds. The dogs had stopped barking; they were lying in the farmyard with arrows sticking out of them. Tamsin thought she saw Higgin and Velda lying there, too.

Then one of the mercenaries yelled in a foreign language, and some of the others got up on their horses. Someone was coming. It was Papa, Tamsin saw, returning from the fields on the other side of the stream. He was running now, carrying his long, straight-bladed hoe in one hand. Tamsin knew he would chase the bad men away and fix everything back again; she raised up her doll Ninga so that she could see too.

When Papa got near the farm and saw what they had done, his face twisted up and he began yelling strange, loud words that were hard to hear. He raised his straight hoe in one hand like a spear and ran toward the men.

The leader with the flag had gotten back onto his horse

and kicked its sides to make it run forward. Then the worst thing happened. The leader lowered his pole with the flag on it, and the end of it went right through Papa.

It was like a spear too, but longer than the hoe. When it went into Papa, he bellowed like a bull and fell over on his side. The yellow flag was all crumpled against his chest, and it began to turn red.

Tamsin screamed when she saw it, but no one heard, because the bearded man's horse screamed too, and all the mercenaries were yelling and cheering around their leader. After that, she understood that she had to keep quiet. She watched as the mercenary pulled his spear out of Papa, straightened the bloody flag, and raised it over his head again, without even getting off his horse.

After that, the mercenaries took more things from the cottage and loaded them into the ox cart, driving it and the other animals back up the meadow. The last thing they did was to take fire out of the kitchen hearth and spread it onto the roofs of all the buildings, laughing all the time. They had found Papa's wine, and one of them raised his bottle, calling out, "A toast to King Typhas and his generous subjects!"

As they rode away, the buildings roared with fire and began to cave in. Tamsin hid Ninga's face against her side so that the doll would not have to look.

Two
The Treasure Pit

"**W**ork, you mewling, miserable wretches!" The Brythunian guardsman's taunts echoed down from the catwalk high above the rocky chasm. "Dig and grovel, and send the fruits of your toil up in yonder baskets! Else there will be no rinds and crusts to gnaw for your supper tonight!"

The mine was a crude open working, a broad, deep quarry yawning like a pale grave under the chill northern sky. Its walls were steep, formed of brittle, ragged shale. Its shape was irregular, because the vast pit tended to widen itself informally as its sides were undercut, either in planned cavings or unexpected landslides.

Such occurrences, whether foreseen or not, were ever a threat to the miners who toiled below. Even so, since every laborer was a convict, the many deaths and injuries were regarded as unimportant. The products of the mine were in any case so prized, its raw gold and varieties of gemstones so valuable, that any amount of death and suffering would have been deemed worthwhile in obtaining them.

"I tell you, Conan, do not cut too deeply into the base of the south wall. The cliff will require stoping. This rotten stone will not sustain a tunnel, as many have learned to their sorrow."

The warning voice was that of Tjai, Conan's fellow prisoner and toiler in the quarry's depths. He was an Ilbarsi hillman, hailing from far to the southeastward; having made the mistake of traveling to Sargossa to find his fortune, he had found more than he could have wished. As fellow foreigners from remote but equally savage tribes, the two convicts had discovered a mutual bond, apart from the others—the dregs and sweepings of Brythunia's town gutters, who made up most of the mine's labor draft. Crom only knew how Tjai had come to wander so many hundreds of leagues from his home; but the hillman's canniness and lean, wiry toughness rivaled the Cimmerian's own fierce stamina.

Conan himself was not quite sure where in the world he was, and exactly how he had been brought there. After his arrest and imprisonment in the capital, the world had changed; scatterings of white lotus dust cast into his face by his warders had temporarily blinded and paralyzed him. His captivity after that had become a hazy, drug-slaked stupor.

He knew only that, chained together with a half-score other drugged captives, he had traveled countless leagues in the hold of some wooden conveyance, either a wagon or a barge. None of the prisoners had known much, or been lucid enough to tell it, except that they were bound for a slave mine in the north of the country: a remote place of fantastic wealth, from which none ever returned.

Conan now rued the dim awareness that even while lying in a groggy, paralytic state, he had found those rumors tantalizing. He cursed himself, along with all the fickle bitch-fates, because on the one occasion when he might have escaped—when he was being strapped across the back of a mule for a night passage over rugged mountain trails—he had lacked either the strength or the spirit to break free of his captors, slay one or two of them, and drag himself away into the brush. Instead, his weak, bleary will had been lulled by the notion that because his destination was a mere work camp and not a prison, escape would be possible at any time. After all, he had temporized, it might pay to learn the location of the mine and, over a period of days, pilfer some of its wealth.

In truth, knowing the whereabouts of such a rich lode—or even the transport routes by which its product was carried to civilization—would have been a boon to a skilled and daring thief. But without any real knowledge and the freedom to exploit it, the advantage melted away to nothing. The mine was a well-kept state secret, and had proved more escape-proof than any prison cell Conan had yet been shut up in.

"Conan," Tjai now exclaimed, "your ox-brained northern zeal places us both at peril! If we undercut this cliff face much farther, it will slump down of its own weight. It will bury the two of us for our trouble!" Resting his pick-head on a jagged chunk of shale, the Ilbarsi leaned against the handle letting perspiration wash dark runnels down his thin, dusty-olive limbs. "Besides, there is no gold here! If you so crave the sight of the stuff, go help them strip out yonder pocket.'' He nodded toward a sunlit corner where a half-dozen ragged prisoners worked with feverish, pointless intensity amid the sparkle of rich yellow ore and watery-pink crystal.

''No, Tjai,'' Conan grunted, ''bear with me a while longer. Come and help hew away this buttress that so cramps our space in this little cubbyhole. At least we are out of reach of the guards, with their infernal pelting and pestering! Arrh, Crom blast these cheap bronze tools! They lose their edge and scarcely do more than bludgeon the stone!''

The convicts, in their unremitting toil, never left the pit They worked, slept, ate, and voided in its dusty depths, preferring the chill shadows of the southern half by day and the sun-warmed northern side after sunset. Never in Conan's experience was a ladder used, and never did an outside guard or worker descend into the hole. On the rare occasion when the Cimmerian found a rope hanging unattended, he knew better than to swarm up it seeking escape, lest his playful captors cut or unreel the line from above. Tjai had told him of prisoners being dropped to their death or crippled by such wanton tricks.

''Nay, Tjai, you Ilbarsi hound! Do not dig so near that other pillar! It is narrow and fragile, as you can see. Why, a good, hard levering of this timber prop might crack right through it—and see, it supports this whole overburden that looms so massively over our heads! Dig with care, as you yourself have wisely cautioned.''

The mine guards, outfitted with the yellow-tan tunics and fur-trimmed iron caps of elite Brythunian troopers, lived and patrolled along the pit's lofty rim. Catwalks—

narrow plank rampways secured by ropes—ringed the quarry's perimeter and made supervision of the work easier. There were also cabins set at intervals along the edge—porched dwellings that could be hauled back from potential landslide areas on wooden skids.

The guards' role was to occupy and maintain these structures, and without overmuch concern for any rocks and debris they dislodged on the heads of the toilers below, to watch the prisoners, dispense tools and food, and oversee the hauling out of ore and rock tailings. This latter work was performed by the convicts from beneath, using the rope pulleys and open metal baskets controlled by the guards.

The warders could direct the digging too, if they saw fit, by means of commands shouted down through speaking-trumpets, or by hurling or slinging stones and filth to enforce swift obedience. This kind of close supervision was seldom necessary, unless the workers seemed to be sabotaging the dig.

In actual practice, the guards' supervision of their prisoners was lax and arbitrary. They could easily speed up labor by controlling the food supply, throwing down grain and hardtack only in proportion to the amount of ore and tailings that were hauled up. Water, too, would doubtless have been controlled, had it not been naturally available in the form of an underground stream that flooded a lower fissure of the digging and ran out by an unseen channel. As things stood, a good part of the guards' time was spent in gambling, whether at lots and dice or on the fall of small pebbles that were slung or tossed at convicts as they toiled in the quarry's depths.

"Now, Tjai, we must leave this spot." Stretching his

massive shoulders, Conan wiped sweat and dust from his tanned, grimy face. "You were right, 'tis foolhardy to work in such a cloistered hollow, with the paunch of the earth sagging over our heads. I thought I heard the mountain shift just now, didn't you? Come, fellow, let us flee!" Tossing down his pick-hammer and taking up the end of a spliced, knotted rope that he trailed after him, he led the way out of the broad cul-de-sac the two of them had burrowed into the cliff.

"Ahoy, you dogs, get clear of the wall!" At the Cimmerian's shout, the nearby workers, without stopping to look or question, threw down their tools and bolted with him. "Tjai and I have heard grumblings, and yon cliff is sure to fall! Come, fellows, save yourselves!" The running, leaping fugitives soon numbered a score and more—bearded dusty hobgoblins, shouting and scrambling over the rock-strewn floor of the chasm into the bright sun at its center.

"I see no sign of a cave-in," one of the hairy troglodytes declared at last. "What is it, then, another false alarm?"

"The northman lost his nerve," a miner jeered at Conan through gapped, broken teeth. "Get your wits about you, fellow, or you will be climbing these walls in madness— and clawing them down on your head, as better men have done!"

"Pulling them down?" the Cimmerian countered, scowling. "Aye, 'tis an idea. If you dogs want to help, lay hold of this rope!"

Conan held up the rope end he had brought along, drawing it hand over hand to form a taut length running straight into the hollow at the base of the cliff. He threw his whole weight against the line, and Tjai, suddenly grinning, followed suit. Others joined in, until a dozen or more of them had braced their backs to the task, chanting as they would for the daily ore lifting.

"Steady, ready, heave!" Conan shouted, and the team followed through with a lusty cry, making the rope strain and oscillate in the half-shadow.

The result of their effort could scarcely have been foreseen: a creaking of timber, a grating of stone, and then an abrupt slackening and collapse of the line, all resistance gone. Its haulers staggered and cursed, regaining their footing on the broken quarry floor while still gaping backward at the cliff.

There followed stirrings and rattlings from the base of the overhang. A grating shock occurred, sending a man-tall puff of dust jetting out of the hollow, followed by creakings and small rivulets of stone from far above. Then, with a trembling roar, the whole cliff face began to slump down and forward.

The rope-haulers raised their fists and issued a cheer, which was instantly drowned out by the tumultuous din of clashing, fracturing stone; then the miners leaped and scrambled farther away as the slide sent rubble tongues and jagged boulders trundling toward the spot where they stood.

The avalanche roared and thundered, filling the air with its tumult, reverberation, and acrid-smelling dust. Then it ceased, leaving the group of miners cowering at the foot of a broad rampway formed of loose, smoking rubble stretching up and out of sight into the pall of rolling gray.

"Now upward," Conan cried, "before the dust settles! Fight your way to the top, and to freedom!"

Leading the charge, he started up the talus slope in great,

leaping bounds. He was slowed by the rubble, which gave underfoot and caught at his loose, ill-mended sandals, vastly increasing the effort needed for every step. Seeking out the larger chunks of stone awash on the sea of gravel and shale, he began to leap from one to the next. As he progressed upward, the way grew firmer, if steeper.

Yelling and jabbering on either side of him, seized by the novel and half-forgotten notion of escape, Conan's fellow convicts swarmed desperately forward. Some of them—the leanest, wiriest veterans at rock-scrabbling—even raced ahead of their leader. Ragged and long-bearded as they were, waving their arms with excitement, their charge resembled more the disgorging of a madhouse or a graveyard than a prison break. The convict Tjai stayed close by Conan's side, clutching his shoulder for mutual balance in difficult spots, his face alight with hope at the sudden opportunity.

" 'Tis a brilliant idea, Conan!" the Ilbarsi gasped along the way. "I did not think you knew the stone that well, to shave things so close—and after such a short time in the pit!"

Conan turned, clasping his comrade's arm in the legionary double handgrip, the better to haul the smaller man up a cottage-sized boulder. "When I was a lad, I hunted mountain sheep through the alps of my native land. I learned to read the rocks even as the hornheads do."

"You learned well, Conan," Tjai affirmed. Slit-eyed, the Ilbarsi pointed forward and upward. "There, see, through the dust . . . it looks as if this slide of ours stretches clean to the quarry's rim!"

"Aye, Crom thump me," Conan swore devoutly. "But

21

now the thrice-curst guards have guessed what we are about. Our work begins in earnest.''

Ahead, they could see where the landslide had cut into the mine's defenses. A catwalk was down, one end of it trailing in the sloping rubble, with what looked like the broken body of a guard lying in the stony wrack a little way beneath. Two more guards crouched on the last, sagging horizontal reach of catwalk, outlined against the bright, welcoming sky as they peered down through the roiling dust. Above them, one of the cabins had been partly undermined. Its rounded log-skids sagged out over the precipice, yet it had not fallen.

"Ho there, you prisoners, get on back!" a voice came down to them, funneled through cupped hands. "Do not venture near the rim, on pain of death!"

"Aye, rascals, take your stenchy hides back down into the pit," the other guard called less officiously. "You lackeys have a sorry mess of stone to clean up!"

As Conan climbed, hard, round pebbles began to shatter near him: slung stones, each one easily large enough to kill or maim. Slingers could be seen on the balcony of the guard cabin, with more now appearing at the unbroken edge of the quarry. Their barrage intensified, and just ahead, a crunching, despairing cry rang out. One of the white-bearded convicts clutched his shoulder and fell, rolling a dozen man-lengths down the rubble slope to lie moaning, his arm bloodied and one leg twisted crazily beneath him.

This, however, did not halt the others. It only hastened their climb. Some, with wild eyes set on the cliff edge, scrambled past the dangling end of catwalk and its two

22

defenders; but Conan headed straight for it, with Tjai following close behind him.

Slipping and scrabbling in the rubble, the Cimmerian grabbed hold of a trailing end of rope and used it to haul himself up all the faster. When he reached the hanging wooden slats, he gained some protection against the bombardment of stones; they smote and dinted the thin planks, thudding down heavily at his feet.

The two catwalk guards were armed only with long daggers, which they now used to saw at the thick, tarred cordage, working to cut away the dangling portion of catwalk where it trailed into the pit.

"Tjai, grab hold! Stoutly, now!" Seized by a sudden, devilish inspiration, the two tugged and swung on the slack ropes. The men on the unstable footing above clutched for their lives, and one of them, taken by surprise, overtoppled. Flailing and calling out piteously as he fell, he ended in the netting just above Conan's head, while his long, sharp poniard tumbled almost into the Cimmerian's lap.

"Aha, fellow, and welcome!" But the man was dead, his neck twisted in cordage. Hauling the corpse down, Conan laid hold of the makeshift ladder. "Now we must climb, and fast!"

Clamping the weapon in his teeth, oblivious of the stones that still cracked and thudded onto the scree around him, Conan set his toes into the narrow interstices of the dangling catwalk planks. He scaled it spiderlike, mounting toward the level section and the lone guard who now gaped down at him in fear.

"Mount to the rim, and freedom!" the shouts from the other convicts rang down. "Onward, fellows! Fight! Aiahh!"

The cries and screams of the escapees echoed from the cliff as they charged the summit, wading into the thick hail of projectiles. A few lay slack or twitching on the rocks, while the surviving score or so straggled toward the last, man-high crest of the slope, which was topped by a dozen or more vigorous defenders.

Conan, meanwhile, swarmed the catwalk like a ship's rat following the scent of rancid beef. Tjai flanked him, creeping up the loose netting with equal agility. The guard above paused in sawing at the ropes, as if debating whether to bolt from his station and flee up the sagging span. Conan's snarled curses were unintelligible, issuing as they did from knotted lips clenched around a sharp steel blade.

Of a sudden, a new turmoil broke out along the cliff side. Barely stopping to crane his neck, Conan saw the desperate guards trigger a new avalanche. Its keystone was the guard cabin, cut loose from its moorings and toppled over the side by a group of Imperials who now stood waving and cheering. Made of beams and light timbers, the wooden hovel sagged and split apart on its sliding journey. But in its wake, shaken loose by the impact, came a slather of loose stones that no climber could dodge or resist. Those convicts at the center of the rush were bowled over by a tide of shifting rubble; some of them were knocked sprawling, others vanished entirely from sight.

The guards, howling in exultation, turned to face the few remaining prisoners. It began to seem that none would escape the pit after all.

Snarling his inarticulate rage, Conan hauled himself up the last few planks of the ropewalk and seized the tunic collar of the remaining, wide-eyed Brythunian—

—just as the man's dagger finally sawed through the rope at the side of the catwalk, causing the web of cordage to sag free and reshape itself. Conan's one-handed grip was broken; he fell backward, losing his hold on the dagger but not on the guard. Bowling Tjai loose as they tumbled, the two enemies rolled off the sagging netting at the bottom and pitched headlong into the sliding, churning avalanche.

"Ah well, it was a worthy effort," Tjai reflected. "At least, if those guards had not been lucky enough to die, we might have gained hostages."

To Conan, seated on a flat stone nearby, Tjai's words did not sound genuinely comforting; in truth, they sounded even more glum and disconsolate than the drab innermost hues of the Cimmerian's own sullen spirit. In reply he only grunted, yielding the conversation to the moonlit silence and the gurgle of water in the rock crevice.

"It would have been well worth dying for," the Ilbarsi tried again moments later.

"Aye," Conan snarled, "but most assuredly not worth living for—or through!" Impatiently he flexed his shoulder, then halted himself, emitting a low, reluctant breath of pain. The thews of his back and side, exposed through the rents in his shredded shirt, were one large and vivid bruise.

"Nay," the northman ruefully said. "My attempt cost the lives of a dozen hopeless men. Now the bitter survivors shun me—shun us, that is, since you insist on casting in your lot with mine—and the pox-ridden guards pelt us from the catwalks every chance they get, and aim quarrels at me because of my reputation as a troublemaker."

"True enough," Tjai agreed glumly. " 'Tis a real misfortune. I had my groin-stash with me—" he patted a pouch of cloth at his waist "—the tidy fortune of gems I have set aside for the chance of escape. Have you seen it, my friend?" Removing the twisted rag from his clout, he unfolded and spread it on a stone. Its grimy folds contained raw jewels and nuggets that glinted dimly in the moonlight: gold and turquoise, amethyst and jasper, chrysoprase and ruby. "Not a man here but has one, and carries it with him at all times . . . haven't you?"

"Um," Conan grunted. Taking a packet from his lap, he twisted it open and emptied it carelessly on the stone beside him. "Not as well-chosen as yours, since I have had less time here—but that will come, doubtless." Again he shook his black-maned head. "Crom," he cursed, "is there no future for us but to rake and shovel up all the rock we toppled down, and hoist it up in basketloads out of this wretched hole—after gleaning through it for any pittance of gold and gems our slave-masters may require?"

" 'Tis hard, I know," Tjai murmured, gathering up his hoarded treasures and returning them to his belt. "Day by day one gets used to the routine, toiling and sleeping, handling the gems. But then, when the hope of escape is dangled so near, so vividly, and is just as suddenly snatched away—" He shook his head. "The thought of freedom, of returning to one's homeland and seeing one's family . . . why, one begins to wonder if this life is worthwhile."

"Aye," Conan grated, shaking his fist out toward the throat of the crevice at the beetling walls beyond. "It is ranklesome to me, a climber trained since birth! None here can mount sheerer, smoother scarps than I. But the coarse, rotten stone of these hills is hard enough to abrade a man's flesh, yet scuffs or crumbles away at the weight of his step. Even solidly bedded, it patters down and gives warning. I daresay that if I made the climb, I could not get within a dozen paces of the edge without calling down a rain of stones, arrows, and offal upon myself!'' Settling back and resting his elbow on one knee, the Cimmerian fisted his chin grimly.

"I may yet try an escape again, but if I do, Tjai, I warn you, it will be alone.'' He regarded his slender Ilbarsi companion balefully. "I want no more innocents to share the bitter fruit of my scheming!''

Some days later, Tjai stalked Conan down the dusty ramp to the stream crevice. He watched as his quarry waded out into the pond, bent, and bathed his face and upper body in the chill water.

Then some animal instinct warned the Cimmerian. He splashed to the bank and seized hold of his pick-hammer.

The lean Ilbarsi laughed and stepped forward. "Tell me, Conan—the time is near, is it not? What is your plan?''

"Tjai, what are you raving about? Are you mad, to creep up on a man this way?''

"Mad, Conan? Nay, not I. You are the hag-ridden one these past days, hulking about and brooding . . . ready to crack other men's heads on the least provocation, and answering none save in grunts and snarls.'' The hillman cagily eyed him. "You are hatching some escape, Cimmerian— I can tell it, and I want to go with you! It cannot be far off now. Tell me, what is your scheme?''

Squatting beside the pond, dripping and goose-prickling, the northerner somberly shook his head. "It matters not what plan I may or may not have, since if I have one, it is for myself alone. 'Tis me the guards are trying to murder, not you. You cannot follow where I would go, nor could any man here, even if I chose to let him try. So just leave me alone!''

"Tell me, knave!" Hefting his own battered pick, the olive-skinned man took a menacing stance. "For you were right: I am half-mad, and will be wholly so if I cannot escape this filthy hole!" The dark hollows around the Ilbarsi's eyes seemed to echo his words, as did the shadowy recesses of the crevice they stood in. "Another week here will be the death of me, Cimmerian. Do do me a kindness . . . let me die seeking freedom!"

"Nay, Tjai, hush now. 'Tis nonsense," the larger man said. "Listen, though. If I do escape, I promise you I will be back to fill a wagon or two with this wealth—" he patted the pouch at his waist "—and to avenge myself on these ape-fisted guards. See here, fellow, do you really believe I could pass up such wealth? Or take the abuse these louts have heaped on me, without exacting full payment? Just sit tight, and when I return, I'll slit a few slandering Brythunian gullets, free the lot of you rogues, and make us all rich in the bargain. Now, let us have no more of it!"

Tjai stood unmoving before him, weapon in hand. "You have three choices, Conan. Watch me go to the center of the mine and scream out that you are plotting an escape, or slay me to prevent it, or else tell me your plan. Now, speak, and truthfully, without your false promises!"

Conan raised his pick in menace, but then cast it down to clatter sharply on the stones. "All right, then, Tjai, and curse you for a wheedling hillman! I'll tell you, if you swear to say nothing of it to the others. Once I tell, you'll see why I cannot take you along.''

"After you tell me," Tjai put in, "I will be bound to go along—"

"Enough!" Conan rapped at him. "Ilbarsi hound, can you swim?"

That stopped the hillman flat. "Swim?" he marveled after a moment. "What do I look like, Cimmerian, a man or a fish? What man can breathe underwater?"

The northman grunted. "I thought not," he said. "Your folk are ignorant of the skill. I myself, when raiding Vanir trading-posts by canoe in the far north, picked up the knack of it. It comes in handy from time to time."

Tjai shook his head. "Conan, be not a fool! If you are thinking of throwing yourself into this underground stream, I warn you, it means sure death. Legends say with certainty that it runs straight to Tartarus, the kingdom of the dead— the one place under heaven that is worse than here!" The convict folded his arms, accepting the story with total faith. "Anyway, there is no air beneath, so you will smother first in the black, boiling depths of the earth. Other miners, crazed with despair, have tried that route of escape, and none was ever heard from again."

"And what does that prove? That they died, or that they had good sense?" Conan shook his head impatiently. "Nay, Tjai, I would not wish to persuade you of it, since you cannot accompany me. But I tell you so that you will have faith in my survival: there is air, caught in pockets in the roof of such water caves as this. And light too, for a little way at least, let in through crevices in the quarry wall above us."

"How do you know that?" the Ilbarsi asked sullenly.

"I have explored downstream in secret—three, no, four times now, and each time I practiced stretching my lungs to go without breath a little longer. I have swum to the extent of fifty paces or more. So far into the cave, one can still find air—enough for one man to fill his lungs, anyway, if he does not tarry too long and waste too many breaths. I know there would not be enough for two." He laid his hand gravely onto his friend's shoulder.

"Beyond the farthest point of my explorations, the fissure narrows, and the stream grows swift. I do not think I could make my way back against the current." The hulking Cimmerian shook his head. "That is the spot I intend to pass today. A rope would be of little use, for eventually I will have to swim free and trust the river. So, likely you will not see me again—until I return with a band of cutthroats to free you," he added to reassure his listener.

"Conan, take me with you!" the Ilbarsi pleaded, laying aside his pick. "Wait another few days, and teach me to swim and breathe underwater. I can learn too!"

"Not in this fish-bath, Tjai, and not in cramped darkness. It would be impossible. The chill of this water by itself is enough to knock most men senseless. Who here of the miners swims in this pool—or even bathes in it, I ask you." Stepping into the pond knee-deep, he resumed the slow process of inuring his body to the cold. "No, my friend, you must wait and preserve yourself. I shall return, I swear it—only for your sake, since these others dogs mean nothing to me."

"Conan, I must come along! Having once smelt freedom—"

"Nay, enough!" The Cimmerian slung a handful of water at Tjai, who shrank back in dread from its chilly touch. Meanwhile, Conan strode deeper into the pond until its lapping mirror-surface ringed his waist. "If I die, your death would be in vain. If I live, I can win your freedom. Either way, you will do better to wait and have faith."

A moment later, Conan eased in deeper, letting the water lap around his chest and shoulders. He had to incline his head under the low overhang of the rock wall, and his voice echoed with the trickling water. "Wait here a while if you will," he told Tjai, "and learn whether I am turned back by some unknown obstacle. If not, then farewell." He took a deep breath and ducked his head underneath the water.

The cold was sharp enough to enforce brisk physical activity. It bored in at the nape of Conan's neck and gripped the top of his skull like an icy helmet. Yet even as he cringed from it, his skin numbed. Kicking and breasting through the water in frog-fashion, he dove down under the hummock of stone that crowded the pool's sandy bottom.

Beyond, the cavern widened into dim reaches that offered the faint glimmer of light to his wide-open eyes. Pacing himself, Conan added the force of his kicks to the smooth trending of the current. He covered the distance efficiently but unhurriedly, only occasionally scraping his back against the cave ceiling and the pointed stone icicles that hung fanglike from above.

Below him, blurred and barely discernible in the dimness, was the eerie showplace Conan had forborne to mention to Tjai, lest the hillman's supernatural imaginings be goaded to madness. Tangled and half-buried in the dimness it lay—an underwater garden of bones, with here and there the gape of a hollow-eyed skull or the sparkle of gold and

gems from a rotted purse. These were the remains of convicts who, over the centuries of the mine's operation, had
flung themselves, well-ballasted with treasure, into the underground stream, vainly questing freedom or oblivion.
Presumably, having made it only this far, they lacked the
skill of swimming, or of finding air; in any event, Conan
hoped for better luck than had been vouchsafed them.

Ahead, a thin screen of flowstone jutted down toward
the thicket of bones, presenting a difficult obstacle; just
beyond it, Conan remembered, lay a large air pocket where
he could thrust up his face and fill his lungs decently. A
little way farther ahead was the place where the light entered: a mere crevice, alas, and one so narrow it didn't
afford a likely breath, much less a potential exit.

He bellied down toward the cave floor, feeling a superstitious reluctance to brush against any of the algae-slimed
bones. His head nudged the lower fringe of the stone curtain, more felt than seen. Then of a sudden, he felt real,
corpselike fingers brush him as a sodden bulk bore up
against his nether parts.

In a flurry of panicked motion, expelling most of his
hoarded, near-depleted breath, Conan turned to face the
menace—and saw only a dark, looming form, spectral and
man-sized, pressing forward against him in the gloom. Its
pallid fingers did not clutch or tear; in fact, the attacker
appeared driven onto him mainly by the current, its gestures slack and random-seeming as it groped for his face.

Kicking out again in dread, and ramming the back of his
head against the stone outcrop, Conan struggled beneath
the overhang. Then he dragged himself upward, scraping
his face in the open stone cavity as he gulped air. A mo-

ment later he ducked down again, laying hold of the slender, drifting shape—which he now identified in the brighter cave light as Tjai's. He dragged the Ilbarsi upward, to thrust his face into a pocket of precious air and hold him there as best he could.

But what, in Crom's name, could he do? He could hardly tell the fool to breathe or, in that confined space, pummel him into doing so; neither could he breathe for him. It soon became obvious, from the bluish-pale hue of his flesh and the unchanging slackness of his limbs, that the hillman—having plunged after Conan in desperation and ventured too far in the paralyzing chill—was already dead.

Conan, leaving off his battle with the corpse and laying it aside, was close to being the same. Coughing, he tried to suck new air from the cavity, yet found his attempts unsatisfying, the air having been depleted of its vital power. Thrusting away, he found another remembered pocket, a shallow one that choked him with water droplets, barely justifying the effort of reaching it. At a third breathing place, lunging desperately to fill his lungs, he rammed his head against a stone outcrop and saw stars explode in the dimness. He must have drifted senseless for a moment; he wakened to the tickle of spent air bubbling upward from his slack mouth.

Deprived of breath, sight, and direction, the Cimmerian began drowning in earnest. He lashed out blindly . . . and felt himself sucked by the accelerating current into lightless, airless depths.

THREE

Dark Protectress

"Tamsin, Tamsin! Freckle-nose, Tamsin!"

The singsong noise of the children swirled and scattered through the houseyard. Frequently it boiled over into the muddy lane adjoining the huddled stone cottages of the hamlet. The noise of the urchins rose and dwindled with their pell-mell scamper as they played in turn at being warriors, animals, or nobles. Only intermittently did they swarm at the back of the cottage and bedevil the young girl who sat alone on the kitchen stoop, quietly grooming her doll.

"Tamsin, head of flax! Get the ax, Tamsin!"

In truth, the little child was fairer-colored than the rest, coming as she did from a family only remotely related to the village folk—a proud, standoffish family who had insisted on staking out a croft in the distant woods, to their sorrow. The children, mistrustful of outsiders and quick to seize on any visible difference, made common cause against this stranger who intruded on their sleeping space and supper table.

"Don't you mind their teasing, Ninga," the little girl comforted her doll, ignoring the unruly stampede. "Your hair is the same color as mine—I know, because it *is* mine! Papa saved some and used it when he made you. I think you are splendid, no matter what they say."

"Why do you always play with that stupid doll?" a brisk, boyish voice intruded. "You act as if you're talking to it, but you never really make any sound!"

The wave of children had changed direction and rushed back to the doorway, with nut-brown Arl leading the pack in his ragged, oversized shirt.

"Why don't you answer when I ask you things?" he demanded. "You used to talk when your parents were alive. What's the matter, have you forgotten how?"

To a chorus of laughter, small Ulva piped up: "Look at that doll, it's so ugly! See, its head is falling off!"

"The awful thing!" another girl-voice chimed in. "We ought to throw it in the well!"

A small, mischievous boy, creeping from behind Arl, made as if to snatch the object from Tamsin; but her quick clutch of the doll to her bosom, combined with the look of utter terror on her face, made him veer away.

"A plague on you urchins," a strident, brassy voice overruled them all. "Must you do your prating and screeching here by the kitchen? Off with you! I won't have you cluttering up my dooryard." Quick sweeps of a broom sent dust and grit pelting at them from the threshold, scattering the mob—all except Tamsin, who remained hunched on the stoop.

The broom-wielder was great old Gurda in her soiled, greasy bonnet and apron, her face as seamed and puffy as one of her overcooked turnip pies. In the fleeing children's wake, she stood muttering distractedly. "Enough it is that I must feed you, boil your foul laundry, and cater to your mother's idle vanity," she declared. "I will not be your wet nurse too!" Indignantly she turned back toward the kitchen.

"As for you, young missy . . ." The clumping slattern abruptly paused, looming over Tamsin. "You hold no privileged place in this household—what, you rascal, have you been into my rag bin, stealing brightly colored scraps for that hideous doll of yours? Take care, my girl, or you will have your fingers seared as a thief!" The beldame made a perfunctory snatch at the doll, though her middle was too thick to allow her to bend over far enough.

"All right, then," she declared at last to the crouching child. "If these whelps will have no part of you, why then, you can be my playmate. Go find an old shingle and scrape the ashes out of yon fire grate—" she pointed to a scorched heap in the middle of the yard "—so that when I render down the pork guts this noon, the fire will flare up crisp and bright. Off to work now," she goaded, aiming raps with her knotty broom handle at the doorjamb near the child's head. "You can begin earning your keep around here!"

Later that morning, Tamsin huddled behind the tanning shed, dressing and primping her doll. Using a bone needle she had taken from the dry chest, and purple threads laboriously unraveled from a berry-stained fabric remnant, she attached a collar and sleeves to a small, crude shirt she had already fashioned from the same cloth. It did not occur to her, perhaps, to remove the garment from the doll; as she worked, the figure sat bobbing in her lap like a real, gnomish creature whom she mentally addressed in her silent, crooning way.

"There now, Ninga, you will have no more chilly drafts on your neck. And your sleeves are elegant! When I am finished, you will have the finest suit of clothes in the village. Only the best for Ninga, my one true friend!"

The pinkish-gray gourd that formed the doll's head had dried rock-hard; as it lolled, the loose seeds within rattled and shivered with a sound almost like a whispered rejoinder. Its shape was bulbous and somewhat tapering for a human head, it was true—but the inked scratchings that sketched in the eyes, nose, and mouth gave it a convincingly somber and only slightly fish-eyed expression, while its rag body was stuffed and seamed so as to dangle realistically where it sat, like a slack human form.

"So, little missy, this is how you repay the kindness of your cousin's household!" From around the corner of the shed, old Gurda was suddenly upon Tamsin, striking and swatting at her with the rough, bristling end of her broom. "For shame, ingrate! Instead of doing the one simple chore I ask of you, you sit here playing and idling the hours away!"

Tamsin bolted, but the housekeeper planted a heavy-clogged, wooden-soled foot on the hem of the girl's outsized dress, pinning her to the spot as she tugged and struggled to escape. Switching her grip on the broom, Gurda belabored her victim's head and scrawny back with its knotty handle, striking hard enough to produce audible thwacks. "Believe it, missy, that hearth will be well-cleaned by you—if not today, then tomorrow or the day after!"

By a desperate lunge, Tamsin managed to pull free and escape, running with her doll clutched to her chest. Gurda stumped a few paces after her, shaking her broom threateningly and hurling oaths. Then, muttering under her breath, she went back around the shed and returned to the task of stoking the fire under the great copper vat of steaming entrails.

Tamsin, meanwhile, ran around the side of the house. When she saw that she was not pursued, she crouched down beside the trunk of a great gnarled oak, breathing heavily, yet neither crying nor whimpering. Her pale-glazed blue eyes stared out unfocused over the farm fields . . . until a soft voice caught her attention.

"Got a beating, didn't you?" It was young Arl; he asked the question almost shyly, keeping both hands out of sight behind his back. "I am sorry, really. Gurda is an old she-bear. My father would make it hard on her if she ever touched me! But I guess you have no one to protect you." Slowly he moved nearer—walking alone, though the rest of the children stood behind him in a giggling row at the corner of the house.

"I shouldn't have teased you before," he told her with boyish earnestness. "I have something for you . . . to make it up. Here, look. It is a bracelet."

Stopping a few paces from the crouching girl, he took

out from behind his back something that glinted dully in the noon sun. The small band of scalloped and speckled beads turned and twisted, its baubles clicking together in his careful fingers.

"They are seashells, look—from the Vilayet Sea, far away from here. The small creatures that live in them die, and then they wash up on the beaches. But they contain the magic of the southern lands. If you have a bone chill, or the ague, they will cure it." He thrust the bracelet toward the girl. "Here, Tamsin, take it. It's for you."

He held out the trinket toward her, patiently waiting. The young girl gazed on it with obvious fascination; she turned the face of her tightly clutched doll toward it as well, in an unthinking gesture.

At length she straightened from her crouch, careless of the nervous giggles of the waiting children . . . and yet she hesitated, watching the charm. Then at last she came forward and reached out, her fingers closing on the dangling beads.

"Now! Grab it!" His hand snaring hers in a taut grip, Arl lunged against her to seize her doll—but Tamsin twisted away from him, shrinking and cringing to escape his one-handed clutch.

"Get it, throw it in the well!" the rest of the children cried as they swarmed around Tamsin. They darted at her, trying to pluck the toy from her stubborn grip. At last the small, mischievous boy-child Asa succeeded. He hurled the flailing effigy overhead to Arl, who bore it toward the stone-curbed well.

"Aha, run, Arl! Keep it away from her!"

"Drown it, the ugly thing!"

"Maybe when we drop it in, she'll finally talk to us!"

Tamsin, by some miracle of acceleration, darted across the hard-packed earth to converge with the older boy as he reached the well. Seeing the taut, silent determination in her lunge, he tossed the doll out of reach, back to the elfin boy.

"Now, throw it in!"

As he spoke, the gourd doll whirled overhead, to bounce with a hissing rattle off the angular wooden crane of the well. The agile lad leaped up and seized it in midair. At the same moment, Tamsin spun and launched herself at the boy, both hands extended to clutch the doll. She collided with Asa and knocked him over backward; an instant later, boy and doll disappeared from sight over the high curb of the well.

The children froze in their play. Mere instants later they were roused by raucous, frantic screams echoing from the mouth of the well.

Running to the curb, they found the boy-child caught a mere arm's reach below the rim. Through luck, the heavy wooden bucket had been left in its raised position, and the rickety crane had jammed tight instead of unwinding. The boy's arm, caught in the vessel's metal strap, appeared broken. Yet he lived and still bellowed loudly. Promptly Arl and the other children hauled him out, trying to calm his moans and cries.

Tamsin, meanwhile, retrieved her doll, which had landed in the dry bucket. Plucking it out, disregarded by the others, she darted off around the house . . . only to run straight into the wet, smelly apron of Gurda, who was just leaving her fire to see what the tumult was about.

"Here, now, my little hellion! What new mischief have you been stirring up? What happened, tell me—no, don't try to pull away from me, or this gutting-fork will play a serenade on your hard little skull! Just what are you up to, missy? Get back here—no, ah, aieeee!''

Moments later, when others came hurrying from house and yard, it was clear what must have happened. One of the cornerstones of the broad hearth, sustaining the weight of the great copper kettle, had split in two from the heat, allowing the vessel to topple and empty out its boiling contents. At the same time, one of Gurda's wooden clogs must have turned under her, throwing her to the earth in the path of the foaming torrent.

The entire village was soon gathered round the cottage, puzzling over what might be done. It was exceedingly difficult to speak or think, they all agreed—because of the noise made by the scalded victim, who did not scream her last hoarse, agonized scream until late the following morning.

Arnulf the Good returned home from the groat fields with a slow, weary step, slower and wearier than normal. Thoughts weighed heavy on his mind, thoughts far heavier than the weight of the soil-caked hoe propped over his bone-weary shoulder.

It was a hard thing running a farm, he told himself. There was the seed, the furrowing, and the planting—things that should never be done too late, or too early, for that matter—the rain, the crow-chasing, the weeding, the harvesting, the threshing and tithing and selling, and then the seed all over again! And it was all upon him. His elder son Arl was but a child; it would be years before he could lend a hand. Meanwhile, there was the question of farm helpers, of getting them but not giving them too much for their grudging labor. And on top of it all, the household.

The household was in its way the hardest thing of all. This new problem, now . . . it had been coming on for some time, ever since the death of old Gurda. For a month, two months, or more, it had been working its way into his awareness. But now it was time; he had to talk to the girl, had to tell her something. Things couldn't be allowed to go on this way. He must talk to her; there was nothing else to be done about it.

Scuffing his dusty boots on the doorstep, he was careful not to knock the drying earth from his hoe as he set it inside the door. Keep the soil, that brought good luck. He grunted to the new housekeeper, Ina. She was a young, shy neighbor girl, too bashful to look at him, much less to reply. His boots shuffled on the bare dirt floor as he went to the sleeping closet and paid his respects to his ailing wife. Then, shutting the door behind him, he went into the Great Room.

There before a low-guttering fire were his children, the four of them, two boys and two girls. Three sat in a quiet circle on the hearth, playing jackstraws or some such game. The other girl, Tamsin, sat in the chimney corner, watching them but not taking part.

"Children, you must go outside now. No, not you, Tamsin. You can stay behind. But you others, go and find some new game. Go and play with the neighbor children—you never seem to do that anymore. Ina will call when it is time for supper."

The flock obeyed him wordlessly, banging the plank door shut after them. They were strangely subdued, he realized. Normally they would have been wild and restless, would have squirmed and protested at such an order, and crept back in a dozen times to eavesdrop. He recalled the joyous, contentious uproar that used to greet him when he returned from the fields.

"Tamsin, stand here by the fire. I came home early today, before dusk, so that the other children could play outside and I could talk to you alone." Seating himself on the rough-hewn chair that he favored, the one draped with doe hide, he waited until the little girl came and stood silent before him.

"Tamsin, I have wanted to talk to you because . . . things have not been the same lately. Not as they once were, and not as they are in the other houses of the village. I know you never talk, but you seem to understand what we say. So I will tell you, and you can answer in words or by sign, as you wish." He shook his rumpled head with the awkwardness of it all.

"It has been hard on everyone, I know. You, coming here after that awful thing . . ." Arnulf's timid soul hardly dared to mention the murder of Tamsin's parents. "Pray the gods nothing like that will ever happen in this village!" He shook his head devoutly, humbly.

"And now, since that terrible affair with Gurda, Amalias rest her, things are even more changed. It has been very hard on my wife—your stepmother. She was never healthy, and now with all the kitchen work since Gurda died, it is much more to handle. Thank Amalias we have Ina. And that terrible screaming at the end . . ." He turned his gaze

away from the patiently watching girl, casting a heavy sigh.
"Since it happened, your stepmother has hardly come out
of her bed, as you have seen. She is so unwell that we have
had to treble her dose of lotus elixir on the instructions of
old Urm the physician. That medicine is not cheap to come
by in these parts, nor was the cost of his services to mend
Asa's bent arm easily met."

Looking up again, encountering the mute girl's gaze, he
felt compelled to look back at the fire.

"Relating to that, there is the matter of the seashell
bracelet. I know how you came by it. It was a foolish
prank, and I see that it has made a fine necklace for your
doll." Looking up again, he nodded at the brightly clad
effigy that rested in the crook of Tamsin's arm, adorned
with the beach shells and other odd trinkets. "But you
know, it belonged to . . . belongs to . . . my wife. If ever
she should miss it, I fear she would be greatly upset. So,
if you could return it . . ." He stopped short of extending
his hand for the bauble. "I know you will . . . but enough
of that for now." He cleared his throat awkwardly.

"We took you in out of kindness, you know, because of
family duty to my wife's cousin. If the gods had not decided to strike your parents such a terrible blow . . ." He
shook his head again, the anxious words clotting in his
throat. "But they did, for whatever reason. There is no
knowing, and certainly we would not hold it against you."
He sighed deeply. "It must have been a very hard thing
for you. You have not spoken a word since that day, except
for mumbling to your doll, which is the only thing you
have left . . ." He shook his head again, his eyes roving
furiously about the room.

"You must know, we all pity you so." He managed to look at her at last. He extended one gritty hand for a vague pat on Tamsin's shoulder, which she twisted away from.

"But you know," he went on, "this silence of yours is not right. I don't know why you persist in it, since it does no one any good. The neighbors do not like it—it makes rumors, and rumors can be a very hard thing in a small village like this.

"There are rumors about the doll, too." He looked up again doggedly at her. "And you know, it could be that the doll and the silence are connected. It seems to me that something is very wrong here. With all the terrible things that have happened—and the doll, the silence, and the children—" he kept his gaze on hers "—a curse has fallen over this household. It is not right.

"So I think you should give me the doll," he told her at last. "It is from before, a reminder of everything you have lost, which ought to be put behind you. Give it to me, and then maybe you can play and speak like a normal child." He extended one open hand toward her. "I will not hurt it, do not fear. I will bury it in the fields where we put our offerings for the blessings of the gods. Give it to me, and everything will be right again." He leaned forward in his seat to take the fetish from her grasp.

The child did not flinch away from him; she did not relinquish the doll, either. Instead, she grasped it in one hand, darting it to arm's length and shaking it a mere handsbreadth from his face.

"Touch me not," the voice came forth. To Arnulf the Good, it seemed to issue from the doll, though in fact it may have been a combination of the hissing rattle of seeds

45

in the leering gourd head and the cracked, rasping notes of the girl's rusty voice.

"Profane me not," the voice spoke on, "lest your bloody bones be laid in the fields as an offering for the blessings of your gods!"

Returning the doll to its place in the crook of her arm, little Tamsin looked calm and unshaken, as if waiting for a reply.

Her stepfather had fallen back into his chair, one hand visibly trembling. "I see," Arnulf the Good managed to choke out, sweating and pale-stricken. "As you wish."

FOUR
Escape to Nowhere

Conan came to awareness in warm sun, on a beach of coarse sand lapped by wavelets of a talking, gurgling river. His nether limbs trailed in the tepid waters of a slow, shallow eddy, and he lay naked, divested of breechclout, treasure pouch, all.

Between the weight of the sun and the damp sand in which he lay, he felt both scorched and chilled, a discomfort that he sought to correct by turning over. His joints felt strained, bruised, and scuffed . . . but intact. As he tried out his stiff, abraded limbs and rolled himself to a sitting position, he noticed furrows behind him in the sandy bottom of the clear pond; there he must have staggered or crawled ashore. Hours ago, it felt like, though he had no recollection of it.

His surroundings were unfamiliar and primal, without sign of human presence. Immediately beside him was a tangle of driftwood, bark, and other flotsam lodged by some recent flood in the bare, undercut roots of a tall evergreen. Beyond this, atop the chest-high embankment, stretched a slope of scattered trees and brushy undergrowth. Before him, the rocky river cut through forest, bare stone ridges, and patches of coarse meadowland some way upstream. Where he sat, the course of the stream leveled and pooled to a middling-sized river, too deep to be forded easily, and broad and swift enough to carry a weakened swimmer far downsteam.

Because it wound past hills, stone outcrops, sandbars and cascades, with its upstream reach curving sharply in Conan's sight, it was difficult to say in what map direction this river flowed. Judging by the height of the sun and the angle of Conan's shadow on the sand, the time was noon, more or less, and the trend of the channel at his feet was southward. That told him little of his relationship to the Kezankians or any other mountains, since the general course of most waterways in this part of the world should likely be toward east or west. Furthermore, there were no high peaks in sight whose snows might give birth to this freshet.

Crouching on the sand, after peering around him for beasts or lurking enemies, the Cimmerian dipped his face into the water, filled his parched mouth with its delicious coolth, and splashed water over his gritty head and chest. Shaking his wet mane and bending forward once again, he tasted. Did the water bear the chill astringency of the Hyperborean snows? The peaty redolence of tundra land, or the sulfur taint of the Kezankian Mountain springs? He could not say; the cool drafts were pristine, tasteless . . .

as, come to think of it, had been the waters of the Brythunian quarry pit's underground stream.

Where in the world was he, then? How far had he been carried, and from what mysterious source? If the mine's location had not been such a hoarded secret, it would have been an easy guess—or a likely probability, at least—to surmise his whereabouts, since Conan's knowledge of the Hyborian map-scape was the equal of any man's, and a good deal more firsthand than most.

Yet his former slave-masters—by drugging him and carting him to an unknown quarter of their vast empire, and by keeping him there in cloistered ignorance—had posed for him an imponderable riddle. If, say, he should follow this watercourse downstream, would it lead him straight to the stately Danibos River that watered lush Sargossa, the Brythunian capital? Or would the stream dwindle and die somewhere in the trackless Zamoran desert, a hundred leagues short of Shadizar's palmed oases? Or mayhap, would it lead him on a thousand-day trek eastward to the salty shallows of the northern Vilayet Sea? Or to Corinthia? There was no knowing.

To attack the problem another way . . . how far could he have been carried downstream? The river was swift, yes, as was the underground flume that must have fed him into it, but how long could he have been dragged down its rocky course before collapsing here in the sand? Not for an entire day, certainly; it had been late morning, after all, when he set forth on his desperate escape from the slave pit. Could he be very far now from the site of his former imprisonment?

As he crouched in the warm sun, his eyes came to rest

on a wooden snag floating half-lodged against the sandbar in front of him. More than man-sized it was, a thick torso of red-barked pine with a few stubs of branches still projecting. It was darkly damp all around, he saw; its exposed surfaces were still drying in the day's heat.

Did he not have some memory of clinging to those worn, blunt limbs amidst a watery chaos, after having been swept in a timeless, sightless rush through echoing subterranean gulfs? Was there not a faint recollection in his mind of clutching for the snag and clinging to it in a mad grasp at survival? Thoughtfully he probed a sore spot on his chest, a chafed bruise that may have matched the contours of that same log. Abruptly then he shook his black-maned head, more to banish the memory than to recapture it. If indeed he had entangled himself in that jagged float, why then, he could have floated downstream for hours, even through a whole day and night.

For the moment, anyway, more pressing matters loomed. He arose to his feet, hunger drawing into a sudden, insistent knot in his belly. As he straightened, he maintained a cautious watch around him, but the only untoward noise was the flap and whir of a startled peafowl, its flight curving away across the water. At this, his empty stomach twinged him; had he but known before of the bird's nearness . . . He began to watch his surroundings more carefully.

All around him the day stretched still and warm, its passing seconds counted by the buzz of insects, the easy banter of falling water, the twitter of songbirds. Further along, the streamside showed signs of other life: bird tracks, snake and turtle furrowings, and the lobed hoofprints of antelope or goat. This latter sight gladdened Conan's heart; yet he knew that where wild game abounded, flesh-eaters might also lurk. He was not equipped to deal with such, at least not yet; without steel, he was truly naked. He judged it unsafe to linger near the steep bank.

Wading into the shallows, he chose a place where a boulder diverted a clear channel of water against a broad, weedy sandbar. This stream had fish aplenty. Even as he watched, he saw a blue fisher-bird dart down near the far bank and pluck a gleaming tidbit out of the water. Nearer at hand, almost underfoot, he could discern dim shapes hovering and flitting against the pale sand.

Crouching waist-deep in the lazy current and choosing his place carefully, he extended one hand palm-up beneath the water's surface. Getting used to the river's chill, he let his feet settle into the soft bottom; then, gently, he began waving the fingers of his poised hand in a slow, undulating motion.

The fish, he knew, liked to idle facing upstream, twitching their fins only occasionally as the water flowed past their gills. He watched them—or rather, their darker shadows on the bottom—keeping stock-still himself to let them forget his presence.

In a matter of moments, there came a response. A silver-blue trout, full and supple, swam up out of the shadows and positioned itself over his hand, enjoying the tickling currents his fingers directed upward at its belly.

After a brief, lulling moment, Conan moved. His arm arched strongly upward, its splash trailing a curve of sparkling drops in the sunlight. At its apex, the trout twisted and writhed, to fall flopping on the sandbar.

In mere heartbeats, Conan was upon it, seizing its thrashing, wriggling form in two hands. He raised it to his mouth, teeth poised, then thought better of it and groped around him to find a stone. He took time to smash the creature's feeble brain and end its suffering before tearing into its scaly back and devouring the raw, succulent flesh.

Though sizable, the fish only whetted Conan's appetite. Returning to his place in the stream, he waited patiently, interminably. No more fish came to his beck.

At length he sought out another spot, where, in the course of the afternoon, he enticed two more fish, the first and larger of which wriggled out of his too-eager grasp. When he finally finished wolfing down the second trout, he was cramped and shivering, his teeth a-chatter in the descending afternoon shadows.

Swamp onions grew in a muddy place near the side of the stream. Conan dug some of them out and, to warm himself, sat gnawing them in the cleft of a southwest-facing rock, partly in shadow but retaining plenty of heat from the day's sun. Now that evening was nigh, he cursed himself and all the gods for having let his food quest become so miserably lengthy after his initial good luck. He had no way to make a fire with which to warm himself and fend off predators, and the approaching night would be the prowlers' best stalking time.

Creeping downriver—wading, or traversing bare rock, where possible, to lessen his spoor—he at last found a crevice that looked defensible amid dry, jumbled boulders. It opened out through a man-sized notch at one end; jumbled rocks barred the other, and a steep cliff loomed above. Tall firs stood nearby; their fronds, stretching overhead, would keep out the dew. Any hunting creature that tried to approach him within the confines of the crevice would face a cornered and dangerous foe.

He tore pungent boughs from a nearby cypress shrub and spread them on the ground for a bed. Then he laid in a good supply of rocks for throwing and obtained from the riverbank a knotted club of dry, hard driftwood that would serve to punish any attack at close quarters.

On his last trip down to the water, he heard a rattle on the far bank and peered across to see, in the deepening gloom, a young stag emerging from the brush to take a drink. Conan crouched, selected a fist-sized pebble from the shallows, and with a smooth, supple motion, sent it arcing through the air. But it was an unlikely shot; it only glanced off the stooping animal's antlers. The elk wheeled, and some moments' crashings in the brush signaled that it ran far away. He could have swum the river and pursued it, but he saw little use in hunting the dangerous animal, wet and unarmed as he was.

Returning to his lair, he curled onto his scratchy heap of fronds, half-closed his eyes, and in moments was asleep.

His slumber was deep, scarcely interrupted by brief, nervous alerts at night sounds heard over the murmur of the stream: the hoot and flap of an owl nesting nearby, the forlorn howling of wolves or wild dogs somewhere downriver, and from an even farther and loftier remove, the mating roar of panther or hill tiger. Conan's wilderness training was such that he could register these noises, identify them, and dismiss them as harmless to him without even fully awakening—whereas a civilized man in the same situation would have been shocked awake, to wait out the night in sweating fear.

This night, however, it was smaller things—the river damp, the night chill, and the prickling creep of insects across Conan's bare skin—that caused him to stir and thrash himself awake in darkness after the heaviness of his first sleep had passed. His stony den, he realized, was damp and unhealthy, colder than a Hyperborean tomb. Through the dank crevices formed by the tumbled rocks at its head there poured drafts as chill as the currents of the river in the canyon bottom. Weakened as he was by enslavement and near drowning, not to consider his more recent exposure, Conan had no wish to arise in the morning sluggish, stiff, and feeble from nightlong shivering. It was difficult to summon thought, much less to move. Nevertheless, gathering himself into a crouch, he ransacked his numb brain for tricks of woodcraft. Then, taking up his club from beside him, he set his bare, half-numbed feet on the tumbled rocks and began climbing.

In mere moments, he was out into the open, where the light of a crescent moon dusted the cliffs and treetops with silver. Already the faint breeze that tingled across his bare shanks and back felt feather-dry and warm.

Finding footholds was easy with the aid of the moon's stark light. Soon, following a crevice that angled up the fractured slope, Conan came to a shallow ledge screened by the boughs of one of the tall pines standing close underneath.

Here, instead of the dank drafts of the canyon floor, mild air from the sun-warmed slopes yet lingered and drifted. The aerie appeared safe and afforded adequate room.

Brushing aside the rocks and small, barbed pinecones, but conserving the softer, decaying needles that carpeted the ledge, Conan curled himself behind the screening boughs and returned to sleep.

Morning brought a warming dazzle of sun, a twittering chorus of newly awakened birds, and an insistent pelting of pinecone teeth from a chipmunk breakfasting high overhead. Conan sat up and stretched, brushing embedded grit and tree needles from his scalp and hide. Edging into the warm, golden rays, he surveyed the dawn-shaded landscape visible from his perch.

The river here emerged from its broad canyon to continue roughly southward, as the station of the sun at his left showed. The land before him was gentler, rising toward low, rolling hills to the eastward; there lush meadowlands stretched between belts of dense-shadowed forest. The routes of tributary streams could be picked out as trails of dissipating vapor, along with the occasional pale gleam of sky on ponds and lakes. He saw no glimpse of any or habitation—no smokes, plowed fields, or other signs of settlement.

All the better, some part of Conan's feral nature whispered to him. Survival should be possible here, perhaps even more congenial without the interference of civilization.

To the right, across the murmuring river, the land rose rocky and steep. Cliffs were in view, yet there were no true mountains, none that could be identified with any prickings on the war maps and caravan maps he had seen. As he pondered this, one question rose uppermost in his mind: had he, then, crossed over the jagged barrier of the Kezankian Mountains? Had his captors, or the lightless torrents of the underground river, somehow borne him to the eastern watershed of those high, snow-crested peaks?

If not, then he was still in the Hyborian world as he envisioned it, albeit in some wild, untamed fringe of its charted and settled lands. But if so—if these streams and valleys before him ultimately spilled eastward—why then, they opened on fates stranger and more diverse than anything he had known in the past. It might be years, or even a lifetime, before he could make his way back to any place he had heretofore seen.

As he sat there on the cliff, basking like a lizard in the morning rays, the question began to fade in importance. Where had he been, after all, that he so longed to revisit? Where would he be welcomed, not hunted as a black sheep, a foreigner guilty of past nonconformities? The boon friends he had made in his wanderings were, most of them, as footloose as he. Had he not, during his few and turbulent years, ofttimes started life afresh?—though hardly as naked and misplaced as he now was. But was there anything worthwhile in his past that carried over to this lean, desperate present?

Thinking of friends, his last sure memory was of Tjai, of his drowned face, thick-tongued and bulbous-eyed, floating in the ghost light of the skeleton garden. The grim fact of Tjai's death was certain . . . and with the little hillman gone, why look back to his recent captivity at all? The mine was there somewhere, to be sure; he might forfeit his life seeking it, or suffer a worse fate once he found it. Why trouble over it at all, then? For some petty revenge or the promise of riches? In this new land of urgent necessities, he could neither sup revenge nor gnaw riches.

Nay, to mount any such project, or to find his way to anyplace scrawled on a mortal map, would require long, careful preparation. Greater adventures, he guessed, lay nearer at hand, and to face them, his mind must be clear.

So the feral northman, shucking his past like a spent lizard skin, climbed down from his ledge.

His morning spoor he buried, to avoid drawing predators to his track. Again he tried fishing, before the river surface was clear of early shadows, and his luck was good; in a short time, he tickled up two trout, one small and one large, and crouched to gnaw these without ceremony. He followed with a vegetable course of bulrush roots and crisp waterweeds dredged from the river bottom. Most congenial of all, he ended the repast with ripe berries that he found in a prickly hedge above the bank.

As he foraged, he kept his eyes sharp for usable rocks in exposed cuts and pebble bars along the watercourse. Flint, or a speckled bluish stone reasonably near to it, he soon found; this made him doubly curse his lack of a knife. With a steel shank to strike sparks from, he could have had fire by nightfall, and with it, new possibilities of food, warmth, and protection. Without it . . . well, even so, there were more urgent matters at hand.

Kneeling atop a flat rock, he struck at the flint pebble with a hammerstone of tough granite. The dark, heavy stone fractured easily with the blows. Its freckled blue proved to be superficial, concealing a uniform, glossy-dark interior that flaked away in rippled crescents with each careful, glancing blow of his hammer. Where two of these flaked edges intersected, they formed a blade edge sharper than any steel; it could easily scrape callused skin from Conan's thumb tip, he found, though it was more brittle than civilized metal.

Conan worked his way carefully around the end of the stone, chipping with gradually less force, trying to recall the deft movements he had seen the village grandsires make in his boyhood—wizened men whose youth extended into Cimmerian old-time, before steel and the art of smithing had come north from Aquilonia. They had worked with effortless skill, he remembered; in a trice they could freshen the surface of a worn tool, or fashion an adze or ax bit that would hew through bone or heavy hide.

His own labors were slower and far more painstaking. In their course, the lopsided butt of the flint pebble slid against the base rock, causing Conan to nick his hand— and, incidentally, to shear away almost half of the keen working surface of the hand-ax he was shaping. With muttered curses against all the gods, yet with surer, swifter motions than before, he dressed down the angular, inadvertent break.

Then he examined the tool, hefting it in one hand. Somewhat unwieldy, to be sure, and now more of an adze than an ax—still, it might serve. Using it as a weapon, he would have to strike true with the first blow; the bulky base would be hard to grasp once slimed with blood. He looked wistfully at the driftwood club he kept beside him; yet without any thong or ligature, he had no way of attaching his razor-sharp stone to a serviceable haft.

He took up his ax and his club; also a thumb-sized, curved chip of flint that might later serve as a knife. Given only his two hands, this was all he could carry, a limitation that he hoped soon to correct.

Stalking downriver on the more open, grassy side, he met a variety of game. A large-footed rabbit cropping herbs near the meadow's edge let him draw near, his approach covered by the noise of the stream. His club, propelled by hunger, was already hurtling through the air when the rodent disappeared with a series of leaps, leaving only weed tufts and petals drifting in its wake. Further down the meadow, a blue-plumed peafowl was less fortunate; its plump body, knocked from the air and battered into oblivion by Conan's club, furnished a raw, succulent lunch for the slayer.

His hunt, however, was far from over. Proceeding to the lower edge of the meadow where lay a broad, muddy riverford, he found along the bank many tracks and spoor indicating a miscellany of game: antelope and mountain buffalo, wolf and foraging bear; the hair-tufted, bone-filled droppings of small predators, and the blunt-padded prints of mountain cats. All seemed to pass here, so Conan made his way through the open swiftly and with careful alertness.

Then, in the forest margin beyond the beach, he found what he sought: a trail of animal droppings, dark-greenish pebbles still soft and warm to the touch, and fragrant to his nostrils. These signaled, not many moments before, the passing of good-sized deer or elk. Scanning the branch-littered turf, Conan picked out faint marks and disturbances there, as well as the subtle trending of a game path that any large animal unaware of danger might use.

Filling his lungs with mild forest air, Conan set off in pursuit. He started at a jog, slow enough to read the forest markings in front of him, but with no particular effort at stealth. A healthy man, he knew, could outrun any deer, but only by dint of a sustained effort, conserving his strength and relying on superior endurance. The deer would outpace the man time and again, expecting to lose its pursuer in rugged terrain—but it would flee in short bursts, exhausting itself and pausing long enough to let a determined hunter overtake and frighten it again. Eventually it would tire and fall, or turn at bay; then the hunter's courage and weaponry would face a test.

Meanwhile, Conan's task was to stay on the scent, to watch for hazards, and above all, to keep from injuring his feet. Toughened as they were by roughshod travel and the jagged stone of the Brythunian quarry, they were yet vulnerable. The prospect of a barefoot chase headlong through branch-littered forest, rocky wilderness, bramble and slippery stream-course, posed a considerable risk. Every part of his mind that was not reviewing the broken twigs, crumpled blades, dark earth-turnings, and other signs of his quarry's passage had to fix on where to place his feet and how best to negotiate the shrubs and fallen trunks that hindered his passage.

He heard his prey before he saw it. The deer must have sensed him as well, for the sudden cracking of twigs and thrashing of foliage in the forest glade ahead indicated sudden alarm. When Conan plunged through a stand of bushes into the open, he found himself pursuing, not any visible animal, but a receding thrash of hooves and the twitching of foliage at the far side of the clearing. The scuff of the creature's weight over roots and stems sounded reassuringly heavy.

He pressed on, keeping to the track. Some moments later, the beast paused to rest, looking backward as Conan ran into view. It was a fine four-point buck, broad and muscular in the neck and shoulders, standing framed between massive trees at the base of a forest slope. As the huntsman pelted forward, the prey started off again. It bolted up the hill, plunging with agile leaps through shallow undergrowth and over fallen logs. Conan, skirting the worst of the tangle and judging which way the animal would turn, followed as best he could.

At the hill's rocky crest, he lost the trail. On a guess more than by any sign, he vaulted a gap between two stone hummocks and bounded down the far side. There, on the right, came the scrabble of cloven hooves over rock. He angled toward the sound, letting the downhill course speed him along. Then he had to slow and negotiate an expanse of jagged, broken scree.

At the bottom there was no clue. A broad, sunny glade spread before him, grass-tufted but without discernible track. The prey might have entered the trees at any point along the farther side; to search for traces would cost time, enabling his quarry to rest or lose itself. He scanned the bright, blinding forest edge in vain.

Then came sharp trillings. A pair of birds fluttered from the trees, scared up by his quarry, no doubt. Breaking into a run, he headed straight for the source.

When next the buck paused to rest, sweat dripped from Conan's damp, tossing mane, streaming down his heaving chest and his long, unobstructed flanks. He was winded, his heart hurling itself at his ribs like a frantic prisoner trying to escape from a barred cage. But his quarry had weakened too. As it sprang yet again to flight, it caromed sideways against a sapling, and its leaps through the foliage were more deliberate and less tight-sprung than before.

To be sure, Conan had doubts about the eventual confrontation. The buck's antlers were keen weapons. Its neck muscles were massive, not to mention its granite-honed hooves and goatlike teeth. He almost wished that his quarry were a less worthy one, or that he had somehow fashioned a spear with which to harry and cripple it before closing in for the kill. Yet he had downed such creatures in the past with little more than sword and hatchet; surely he could do the same now with a club, a hand-ax, and a far keener hunger.

The animal mounted a stone ridge just ahead; its hind legs faltered and scrabbled pathetically at the top of its lunge. Conan could smell its desperation now, the rank, musky scent of its fear. He almost flung his club at the creature's slender shanks as he clambered up close behind, but was himself delayed by the steepness of the rock. He felt exultation overcoming fatigue as he hurled himself after the buck where it passed out of sight over the rise.

From just ahead came a crunching sound accompanied by a quick, bleating gasp. Something large passed, signaled by a stirring of foliage and a flurrying of scattered leaves. Conan thought he also sensed a faint tremor of the earth under his bare soles, as of some great weight shifting.

When he pelted into the open space at the crest, it was empty. There was no quarry, no sign of it at all—except, across the faint trail underfoot, a spattering of blood. Red and rich, it glistened from the grass blades and dark loam in sufficient quantity to tell him that he need not chase his prey any farther.

But where had it gone? Wary, scanning the broken slopes around him, he saw no more blood on the nearby rocks, and no scuffs or drag marks across the turf. Could the buck have been carried off by some huge bird, he wondered? If a predator, how far had it stalked the prey—and, presumably, him?

Or was this the work of man? Some tree-sprung snare perhaps, that whisked its victim far out of sight? No. Sorcery? Mayhap.

No prey, no marks, not even a scent . . . except for the faint, coppery tincture of blood. And, of course, the smell of his own runneling sweat, mingled now with a faint odor, rank and distinctive, that he soon recognized: the smell of fear—his own, wholly in keeping with the sudden change of his status from hunter to hunted.

Fear. It would not do to let any stalking creature smell that scent on him, and mark it, and remember it. He scanned the treeline carefully, wondering if something lurking in the forest might have paused to watch. Then he turned and jogged resolutely back toward the stream, to bathe himself.

FIVE

Divinations

It was in the fourth year of her stay in Sodgrum hamlet, at the farmstead of Arnulf the Good, that the child Tamsin regained her speech. Most fittingly, it occurred on her Naming Day, a high holy observance of the Sargossan church. Likely it would have been considered a sacred boon of Amalias, chief god of the Brythunians, if things had worked out differently.

In the years following her parents' death, Tamsin had grown taller and straighter, but not yet ripe in a womanly way. She was exempted from daylong labors in barn, kitchen, and farm field that the other village children inured themselves to; doubtless this exemption was because of the kindliness of her foster father. Further, she was hardly of a temperament to ride, hunt, or play childish games during her long, idle days.

Thus she was spared the callused, sunburnt skin of most

rural maidens, as well as their shambling, clog-footed gait. In her twelfth year, the child Tamsin remained a slim, ascetic-seeming maid whose flaxen hair had darkened to the deep-auburn hue of clotted blood. She dressed most often in long, flower-painted robes and flimsy slippers handed down from her stepmother. The latter parent remained during all those years a nervous invalid who seldom touched her foot to the floor.

"That wife of Arnulf's is not truly ill, but drunk on lotus potions," some of the villagers would whisper. "Aye, and the fool is too deathly afraid of that little slut Tamsin to give her chores," others agreed. Yet even so, it was seen that those who spoke against Arnulf's household tended to be stricken by neck boils and stomach cramps, and so the whispering was stilled.

Inherited garments, and coarse ribbons for binding up her long hair, remained Tamsin's only affectations. All other adornments that came her way were lavished on the doll she carried unfailingly at her side. Ofttimes the quaint effigy would make its appearance draped in garlands of herb and thistle, strings of beads carved from stone, wood, and bone, and more costly ornaments borrowed from the dowry chest of her ailing stepmother. Though others in the village at first ridiculed the doll, experience taught them to regard it with acceptance and subtle fear.

Lucky it was for young Tamsin, residing in such a remote, uncultured district, that she was not of a stolid or idle disposition. In spite of her lack of speech, she took a lively interest in the world around her—in the growth and uses of plants, the lore of animals both domestic and wild, the origins and mystic significance of stars, seasons, and elements, and the devious will of the gods as expressed in the daily affairs of mortals.

The child's dearth of words was more than made up by her increased powers of observation. Scarcely an hour passed when she could not be found standing at a window or a doorway, before the fire, or in the cool shadow of some forest oak, her blank-faced doll clutched at her side. Mutely she would observe the unfolding patterns of natural life or the coarser rhythms of human play and work, and solemnly eavesdrop on the conversations of her elders. In time, the village folk accepted the slim orphan's watchful habits; they even welcomed her presence, largely for the sobering, intimidating effect it had on their unruly children.

Tamsin's principal ally in her quest for knowledge was old Urm, the local physician and spell-caster who attended the community's needs. From her first days in the hamlet, the child was drawn to him, watching as he ministered to Arnulf's wife and paying frequent visits to his thatched hut at the bottom of the town path. Faintly, for hours on end, he could be heard muttering to her his magic lore, cantrips, and mnemonic rhymes, until it seemed that she must have absorbed every bit of his supernatural knowledge. The two of them—or rather the three, if one counted the child's doll—often seemed inseparable, brewing up strange-hued fires in old Urm's oven, catching odd fish and insects from streams and swamp-holes, and ranging the countryside to gather potent earths, herbs, and bones for his spells.

Whether Tamsin made utterances for Urm's ears only, and so preserved the habit of speech, or whether they employed some more mystical means of communication, none could say. But it was clear that the girl learned much from the old witch-man, and that he was more a friend to her than any of her adopted family or age-mates.

Thus it was seen as one more stroke of tragedy in the child's life, another baffling whim of the gods, when Urm's hut caught fire and the old physician perished in the blaze. Tamsin may have been with him when it started, or she may, through some premonition of doom, have come running to the scene. The nearest neighbor saw the cottage explode in flame; on approaching, he found the girl standing helpless in the blaze of firelight. Dry-eyed from the scorching heat, she stood watching expressionlessly, shielding the face of her beloved doll against her shoulder.

"It was the wicked lass that done it, don't ye know?" one village crone was heard to gloat. "She sucked out all his wisdom like a leech, then roasted him in his own thatch, the old fool!" But that same winter the old woman was done to death by a pox and a quaking ague, and so once again gossip was stilled.

After the fire, little remained of the witch-man's science and arcana. Touchingly—since the rest of the villagers hesitated to enter the blackened ring of his once-feared abode—it was Tamsin, with her doll tucked into the blouse of her robe, who was honored to gather up Urm's charred bones. These she laid most respectfully in a fragrant cedar chest to preserve his memory. The shrine was on display long afterward in the small magical dispensary that she established in the shed of Arnulf's cottage. One other relic of her predecessor—the tarnished and blackened copper reliquary locket Urm had worn around his neck—was henceforth seen dangling from the doll she always carried with her, another perpetual tribute to her mentor.

As it happened, the thaumaturgic skills conferred to her by the old man were sufficient for her to take up his duties in ministering to the town. When a farm wife needed a lung cure, Tamsin could mix up the stinging plaster, ably wielding the pestle in the blackened stone mortar salvaged from Urm's ruined house. She would even apply the medicine to the sufferer's back, working deftly one-handed, with the jingle and hiss of her gourd-doll substituting for the soothing incantations the old warlock would have intoned. Or, if a cottager required a weasel remedy for his poultry roost, she possessed all the necessary herbs and powders; she would hand over the poison bait with grave, silent assurance of its potency.

Her methods differed from Urm's in one respect: in all such cases, to the villagers' mumbled surprise, she would give the cure time to work before making a visit to collect payment. More particularly, in regard to her stepmother's continuing malaise, her services were rendered without charge. Using only ingredients gathered from the local swamps, without the costly powders purchased from traveling vendors that her predecessor claimed to rely on, she simmered and fermented a new healing elixir. To everyone's surprise, it quieted the poor woman's plaints and maintained the peace of the household, at a saving that Arnulf the Good found gratifying indeed.

Throughout the countless hamlets of the Brythunian hinterlands, the relation between such small rural practitioners and the Temple of Amalias and his pantheon of gods was an uncertain one. The great church laid claim, of course, to all the healing and divining powers that touched common mortals in daily life; whatever their talents, Amalias demanded his servants' entire worship and fealty. But since the priests' most vital and profitable concerns unfolded on the largest scale—that of wars and droughts, plagues and aristocratic marriages, and interpretation of the visions and deliriums of King Typhas when steeped in his cups—their priestly interests centered on the capital and the main district temples. The priests of Amalias were hardly so many and so humble as to have daily contact with low, common serfs and tenants of the remotest, backward districts.

Therefore the efforts of local shamans and healers were tolerated as being adequate for the ignorant denizens of forest and rural mud-bog, who were ever reluctant to let go of their old gods and superstitions. Some of these spellcasters made crude obeisance to the high church, using Amalias's name in their chantings, or wearing rough imitations of the holy charms and symbols that adorned the Imperial priests and officers. Other practitioners did not yield even so far; in consequence, they might—when the need arose for a handy scapegoat or for some distraction from regional political problems—find themselves hanged or pilloried as witches by officers of the central church for their failure to conform.

What contact there was between the high church and the common herd took place during annual festivals, whose dates varied locally for the convenience of traveling priests, and similar ritual events. One such was Naming Day, when a circuit priest appointed a date to visit a locality, bless all the virgin children of a mature age, and name them in the registers of the church, thus permitting their marriage banns or sale to desirous nobles.

When such a day was announced in his district, Arnulf

the Good, revered as a pious man, submitted his step-daughter Tamsin's name for the ceremony, along with those of his elder children. Since the young girl did not yet speak, it was not likely done with her approval; yet the villagers observed that when the ritual was discussed, she showed no sign of displeasure at the action.

The head priest of the church district encompassing Sodgrum and half a hundred other wretched hamlets was one Epiminophas. His affected southern name, and his olive-oiled hair that crowned a somewhat chubby, tallow-faced countenance, proclaimed his desire to merge with the ruling elite of his country and church, who were mostly descended from noble Corinthian blood.

The demiurge Epiminophas paid scant attention to those faithful who dwelt out of hearing of the massive bronze bar-chime in his district temple at the provincial capital Yervash. As his tenure and prosperity increased, he certainly did not intend many more toilsome rides to local festivals. And yet, just lately, there had come to his ear a somewhat unusual rumor of a village healer more youthful than any before seen. A mere child, but skilled enough at nostrums and hocus-pocus to astound the bumpkins and enjoy local fame, and with talent and showmanship whispered of in a spreading circle of a dozen or more hamlets. On top of it all, Epiminophas heard with interest, she was a maiden . . . and one of exceptional, delicate beauty.

To the temple authorities, such a local sensation was a familiar issue—an opportunity to confront the self-styled holy man or prophetess and demand submission to the High God Amalias. Either the rural quack would kneel to church authority, thereby reaffirming his or her oafish admirers in their fealty to the high temple, or the trickster would refuse and be made an example of, thereby helping to accomplish much the same end. The story tended to play out over varying time periods, with greater or lesser soul-searching on the part of the upstart prophet. And depending on the depth of his or her self-delusion, it occasionally involved the regrettable eventuality of torture. In past cases where the witch was female and stubbornly recalcitrant, Epiminophas had nevertheless found cause to experience deep personal gratification from his holy work.

With this in mind, the plump demiurge made a point of appearing personally at the ritual site on Naming Day. He was borne thither on a gilded palanquin shouldered by eight acolytes, husky lads chosen and trained not just for burden-bearing, but for rough duty as bodyguards and riot troops.

The ritual was to be held at midday in the Abbas Dolmium, a holy place located centrally enough for families from all the villages of the district to hie themselves hence on foot. Though not the site of any permanent habitation—doubtless because of its deeply hallowed reputation—it resembled any other dolmium in the eastern kingdom. It stood high on the windswept fell above Abbas hamlet, a ring of massive, crudely chiseled pillars connected by crumbling stone lintels and covered by a low, conical roof of poles and rushes to keep out the icy sleets of the rocky height. Though its stony skeleton had been reared in a past aeon—likely, it was rumored, by some faith older than the Imperial church—it was now part of the network of shrines and temples of the high cult of Amalias. As such, it made a suitable place for seasonal devotions and sacrifices.

The head priest was carried into the temple forecourt,

passing amid a procession of virgins and their families just arriving from their long morning's walk. Others, called from more distant hamlets, had spent the night in the sacred shelter of the temple, warmed by a fire of peat and bones laid at its center. A layer of new green rushes had been stitched by the worshipers atop the damp thatching, and fresh-cut grass was strewn on the floor inside. Now the acolytes set to work erecting a brightly figured canopy at the altar end of the enclosure, behind which Epiminophas could don his second-finest robes and prepare the ritual.

The ceremony got underway smoothly. One by one the virgin boys and girls, clad in sackcloth or coarse linen, were brought forward to the altar by their elder relations, some going proudly, some in halting shyness. Their names were called and affirmed as they went to the altar; then their right hands were brought forward, clutched firmly by a cowled acolyte, and their forefingers slit by a sacred copper knife in Epiminophas's skilled grip. The fresh blood that dripped into the altar basin was used by a second acolyte to pen their names onto the sacred scroll, thus affirming each child's place in eternal slavery to almighty Amalias.

The witch-child, of course, was reserved for last. She arrived late, shortly after Epiminophas himself, but the looks and murmurs attending her appearance confirmed her reputation. Indeed, her wan, blank gaze made an eerie impression even on the arch-priest. As the girl's cringing cousins and siblings were led awkwardly forward by the family's moon-faced patriarch to receive their name-blessings, the deep, expectant silence proved how well the red-haired girl was known and feared by these ignorant clod-lumpers.

At last the little witch was brought to the gory, blood-crusted altar, which yet was scarce redder than the tangled coils of her hair. She did not wear the gray-white jerkin that was customary for the ritual; instead, Epiminophas saw, she affected a most garish attire. Her floor-length robe was of faded green, loose and oversized about her slender wrists and hands, with just a wedge of flat, pale breastbone visible at the neck. Even more outrageous was what she carried in the crook of her left arm: an ugly child's-doll, grimy-looking and crudely made, yet clothed and adorned in tailored garments and ornaments—necklaces, wrist-bands, diadems, and badges, most of them garish in design, though a few were of middling value.

After a moment's thought, Epiminophas determined not to challenge her trappings. The doll, it would appear, was a part of her wizardly show. If she chose to single herself out thus and aggrandize her meeting with the Imperial church, it could only redound to the temple's greater credit as well as her own. If, on the other hand, the two sides ended in opposition, it would still magnify the church's glory; only the charlatan's downfall could be made any worse.

"Name, child?" the priest roundly intoned. During the long pause that followed, Epiminophas sternly surveyed the watchers for any mutterers and fidgeters; most of all, he regarded the sweating, apprehensive face of the stumble-footed fool they chose to call Arnulf the Good.

"Your divinity," the farm oaf ventured at last, "I will

have to speak for my stepdaughter. Since the day her parents were slain, she has not uttered—"

"Tamsin," a firm, clear voice interrupted him. "Record the name Tamsin."

It was the girl. As she spoke, she extended her hand submissively over the altar. From the stir and murmur in the thatch-covered gallery, the priest could guess that something remarkable had happened. An instant later, he understood; she had been playing mute all these years, and had handed him a miracle.

"Tamsin—" he affected a weighty pause "—do you swear eternal obedience to the High God Amalias?"

Epiminophas added the question as a further prod, to remove any doubt in the onlookers' minds as to what had happened.

"I swear obedience to the High God."

Again a sigh of wonder swept through the assembled worshipers; there was no question who had spoken. By the bell-like resonance of the child's voice, it was hard to say that she had not been schooled in temple oratory the while. Yet Epiminophas knew better; here stood a gifted performer. At his nod, the girl's extended arm was steadied by the waiting acolyte. The priest himself grasped her frail hand in one of his own, with her palm upraised, and brought the copper knife down to her fingertip.

Was it his imagination, or did the pale, soft skin begin to bead with thick, ruby drops even before the razored edge had touched it? Could the lass have palmed a blade somehow . . . or did she possess the power to will such stigmata? Or was it only the steady gaze of those green eyes, momentarily distracting him from his task?

"Tamsin, of Sodgrum hamlet." He made the declaration less firmly and resoundingly than he would have liked. The hooded scribe bent forward, ritually dabbed his quill-point in the spot of fresh blood on the altar, then transcribed the name with a special flourish to the parchment resting on the nearby scroll-rack.

"May you live in Amalias's blessing," Epiminophas proclaimed. Hearing the sigh of gratification from the audience, he felt vaguely relieved that this youngster, vexingly pretty as she was, would now be leaving his sight.

But she did not turn away. Though the acolyte had released her arm, she continued to stand before the altar expectantly, fixing him with that greenlit stare.

"You can go, child," he condescended quietly, glancing with meaning from Tamsin to her stepfather.

The farm dolt hovered nervously over the girl. Though obviously eager to leave, he seemed afraid to touch the little enchantress and guide her away. Epiminophas turned his gaze back to her, sternly.

"The naming rite is over."

"No, it is not," she assured him with a compelling steadiness in her look. "There is one more."

"One more?" Epiminophas shot a quick gaze around the crescent of gawking onlookers. He followed with a glance to his scribe, who frowned in the negative.

"—my friend," Tamsin was saying. "Her name must be recorded too."

The witch-girl's meaning became obvious as she raised her unbloodied hand before her, holding forth her preposterous doll in all its garish finery. She shook it imperatively with a practiced motion of her wrist.

"Ninga," the word came then in a flat, rasping voice, one that blended eerily with the sibilant rattle of the dry gourd and the jingling of trinkets; it sounded as if the doll itself were talking. "Name me Ninga, please, Epiminophas!"

The demiurge had heard of witch-dolls being used in primitive magic, but they certainly had no place in the enlightened worship of Amalias. This pantomime struck him as moronic and shameless. And bandying his own name thus . . . why, it was nothing but a sly, sacrilegious jape.

"Ingrate," Epiminophas began. "Lord Amalias did not grant you a tongue to mock him with!" He gathered breath for a fuller denunciation, yet stopped when Tamsin spoke once again in her own voice, soft and clear, but with an oddly compelling tone.

"We had best talk." The girl's eyes flicked to the bright red canopy that hung behind altar and priest, swaying slightly in the draft that blew in off the moor. "Alone," she added, "just the three of us—" and folded her grotesque fetish back into the crook of her arm.

On further reflection, Epiminophas saw the value of a parley. It might serve to intimidate this precocious child, who, as mad as she seemed, did not entirely lack sense. Or, elsewise, it might tempt her into further heresies and defilements that would justify a swift, spectacular punishment before the throng. At the very least, it would make him appear in control—a useful step after his authority had been so evidently shaken.

Even so, the notion of granting the wench and her doll a solitary audience was an outrage. When Epiminophas led her behind the canopy, he was accompanied by four of his officers, including the scribe. As the girl departed, her unlucky relative Arnulf the Good prostrated himself before the altar, quaking in obvious apprehension.

"Now see here, you young charlatan," Epiminophas began, "you must render all due fealty to Amalias." The priest spoke openly, trusting his acolytes to prevent anyone beyond the curtain from eavesdropping. "You can conduct a rich magical trade here in the provinces without paying a heavy tithe to the temple. We let the peasants follow their local heresies, within limits. 'Tis not as if you were setting up shop in Yervash, working in direct competition with the state church. That would be something else again."

Epiminophas settled onto his folding stool, lowering himself to the maid's level to give an appearance of reasonableness. "All we ask of you is superficial obedience and decent respect. Understand, child, we cannot grant the authority of the church to sustain your conjure tricks and illusions, such as naming that doll of yours in our sacred rolls—" He waved impatiently at the effigy still nestled under the girl's arm. "That would be putting the plow before the horse, so to speak, making the servants of mighty Amalias subservient to you."

The girl Tamsin regarded him as if in naive surprise. "You speak as one who lacks faith . . . not just in your own church law, but in all magic and holiness as it springs from the earth and air all around you." The words themselves, Epiminophas thought, sprang amazingly glib and fluent from one who had been believed mute.

"Come, child," the priest laughed. "Do you mean to tell me you believe in your own tricks and foolery—the mumbles and smoke-puffs you use to bedazzle the local bumpkins?—such as that doll, or your own supposed lack of speech?'' He shook his head sagely. ''If so, you are more innocent than I would guess.'' His stare into her unblinking eyes bore an insinuation as well as a threat.

''Nay, think not to trick a trickster, child, nor mock those wiser and more cynical than yourself. The result could be most . . . painful. The benefits of respect, on the other hand, and proper submissiveness, could be great.'' Leaving the hilt of his ceremonial knife, which hung sheathed on its copper chain around his waist, the priest's beringed hand moved forward to caress young Tamsin's green-robed shoulder.

''So,'' came the sudden, rasping, rattling doll-voice in return, ''you think our magic as false as your own?'' Epiminophas, in spite of himself, recoiled from the leering witch-doll that was thrust up into his face. ''Let us try a test!''

After Tamsin and the priests passed out of sight behind the vestry curtain, Arnulf the Good prayed and groveled before the altar. He feared the wrath of Amalias and the shame and harsh penances Tamsin and her peculiar ways might bring down on all their heads. Yet a part of him feared Tamsin even more. He hoped that father church would take her firmly in hand and curb her worrisome power over his family and his entire village.

Tamsin and the priest had not been behind the canopy long when a sort of hush occurred. The chirping and cooing of moor-birds from the thatched eaves ceased, and all the virgins and their families waiting in the Abbas Dolmium looked around in a sort of expectancy. Then the shaking began: soft waves in the hard-packed turf underfoot, building to deeper undulations that made the joints of the heavy lintel-stones grind and shift in their places.

The quaking might well have scattered the worshipers, except for the design of the place. They were more afraid of passing out through the massive, top-heavy stone columns that ringed the ancient temple than they were of the flimsy pole-and-straw roof falling in. Thus they cowered together at the center of the stone circle. The kneeling Arnulf, and even the four waiting acolytes, rushed to join the throng as dust and straw sifted down onto their heads from the unsteady ceiling.

In moments it passed, the vibrations receding like the footsteps of some wayward titan. There came a brief, confused murmur. Then from behind the vestry curtain, one corner of which was now collapsed and trailing on the earthen floor, came the six who had retired there before the quake. Solemnly they resumed their places: the priest behind the altar, his acolytes at either side, and Tamsin standing respectfully before the red-rimed stone. As Arnulf hastened back to join her, he saw that her doll was clutched in the hand she now stretched commandingly over the altar. The old farmer knelt in mingled thankfulness and fear.

"Ninga," the eerie, rasping voice proclaimed, and the priest affirmed it . . . "Ninga" . . . to the scribe, who bent over the altar, dipped his pen, and recorded the name on the sacred scroll before him.

The blood that dripped on the stone from the small, sewn fist, old Arnulf saw, and likewise the entry it made on the scroll, were of deepest black. He also noticed, along with the others, that when Tamsin turned imperiously from the altar, the effigy at her side bore a new, bright ornament granted by Epiminophas. Chained about the doll's neck, in its small copper sheath, was the sacrificial knife ritually worn by a High Priest of Amalias.

After Naming Day, the fame of Tamsin and her doll Ninga spread farther and faster. The two now bore the church's blessing, firm and uncontestable. Accordingly, they were called on to perform healings, hexings, exorcisms, and other priestly rituals, some involving long trips away from their home village.

Such was the demand for her magic, indeed, that Tamsin began to school her stepbrothers and stepsisters in the more rudimentary procedures that could be carried on while she and Ninga were away, such as child-purging, well-purifying, and pest-baiting. Young Arl, in particular, became known as an adept healer of livestock, while his youngest sister Hurda was found to be unequaled at causing cheese to ferment.

One highly portentous call for Tamsin's services was from the elders of Phalander-town, who had sought throughout the land for the aid of a water-witch. The young woman had never, to anyone's knowledge, tried out this skill; even so, it was thought to be one she certainly possessed. Therefore, summoned by a courier dispatched by the town fathers of Phalander, she and her doll were led off on donkey-back several days' ride southward, lodging at the finest inns, performing small miracles along the way, and—though saying little—generally spreading her mystical reputation.

Phalander, as it happened, was the largest settlement Tamsin had yet seen, grander by far than Sodgrum and the puny hamlets of the northern district. It was no fortified city, though the interlinking walls of the rich estates high on the hillside formed a sort of defensive bastion. There was even a stone gate-arch reared across the main avenue, where it led down to the tradesmen's stalls and the more humble dwellings at the foot of the hill.

The town fountain before the archway, however, yielded sparse and brackish draughts for shorter seasons of each passing year. The cisterns were near dry, and the rich citizens of Phalander were faced at last with abandoning their lavish villas and retiring to some neighboring city far from their birthplace and landholdings.

"We have tried prayer, as commanded by the district temple at Yervash," the grayheaded old burgomaster explained to Tamsin when they met at the inn. "Our local priest has blessed the well, as have the high church officers we import all the way from Sargossa." He shook his head, clutching to his chest the gold-plated medallion of rank that dangled on a ribbon from his ermine-collared neck. "They all say it will pass in time, that mayhap it is divine punishment for some great sin of ours, and that our devotions and support of the temple must accordingly increase." The old man looked across the inn table at his two fellow councillors, both of whom rasped bitter laughter from dry, elderly throats. "If you ask me, they seek payment without a guarantee of results."

"Aye," the balding city treasurer agreed, grinning through his gapped, discolored teeth at the young girl and her spangled doll. " 'Tis an ill investment to pour more of our commonwealth's drachms into. That would scarcely be a bargain for us!''

''You, on the other hand, Tamsin,'' the fat shire-reeve spoke up, ''have a reputation for besting the temple authorities at their own game, so to speak. You have more magic in one of your pretty young fingers, I would wager, than a whole palanquin-load of their mumbling, droning priests.''

''Yes, in sooth,'' the burgomaster said with an unctuous smile. ''Therefore, young lady, if you . . . I mean, you and your idol there,'' he added as a polite afterthought to the doll, ''can achieve what these temple prelates have not, you stand to profit richly. Replenish our town spring to year-round flow, or conjure us up a new and ampler one, we pray you! We are prepared to reward you with the grand sum of—''

''Nay, that is enough!'' the girl Tamsin declared in her new, fresh, resonant voice. ''You complain of priests who wheedle for payment without giving you any result. It is my custom to resolve the problem first, then the matter of pay. Come, has your man brought what I requested?''

The city fathers, never indecently eager to talk of spending money, obeyed Tamsin's stricture of silence. Immediately afterward, the courier appeared in the doorway with the object the young sorceress had requested.

''Here it is, young ma'am—a witching wand fresh-cut from good green ash.''

The rod was of the age-old, traditional kind: a crotched stick, slant-cut cleanly at each of its three ends. Taking the two angling limbs into her fair young hands in a curious overhanded grip, with her doll hugged beneath her arm at one side, Tamsin poised the stem out straight before her.

"Come," she said, turning from the table and leading the way out the inn door.

Emerging into the town's main street, she strode forward resolutely, her body young and straight under her blue-flowered robe. It was unclear whether she followed the lead of her divining rod; her steps, in any case, led to the town's existing well, which lay broad and open, a stone-curbed trough under the noon sun. Looking into its bottom, observing the yellow-green deposits rimming stagnant puddles, and wrinkling her pert young nose at the rotten-egg stench, she made a declaration to the onlookers.

"This well is accursed. It is beyond saving."

With her wand projecting before her, she turned indecisively . . . and set out this time with tentative steps. Her way led down the main thoroughfare from inn and fountain, through the narrowing of the street at the archway, and off the apron of cobbles onto a dusty, rutted road. Behind her came the council of elders. A crowd of townspeople rapidly gathered, with children frolicking and scampering along after.

"She leads us downhill," one shopkeeper was heard to remark. "Unusual. The other diviners have always headed straight for the town heights."

Without comment, Tamsin led her entourage along the dusty lane. Once among the poorer, unfenced dwellings, she left the road to amble through cottage gardens, sooty fireplaces, and poultry yards. Following the apparently supernatural promptings of her stick, she hopped ditches and picked her way through bramble patches, even leading the mob into the reeking, hide-covered shed of a protesting tanner.

Finally, in the dry, dusty wallow of a hog pen on the fringe of town, she called for silence. At the burgomaster's order, the townsfolk pressed back from her, kicking and cuffing aside the snuffling swine. In rapt seriousness, the young witch roamed the enclosure, moving in ever-tightening circles, till at last she settled on a spot near the corner of an adjacent stone dwelling. There the protruding end of the ash wand bent straight down to earth in her firm grasp, curving with such force as to make the bark crack and split.

"What ho, here is the place!" Some of the villagers who had brought along picks and iron-bladed shovels immediately set to work.

It became a long, sweaty business in the midday heat. The soil just below the surface was hard-crusted. The men took turns digging, making the hole large enough for two diggers to wield spades or one to swing a pick, while the women raked aside the broken earth with hoes and brooms. The elders of Phalander looked on patiently, as if they had been through this a number of times before.

"My house . . . do not undermine it too much!" the anxious owner cried repeatedly. "You have already chased away my pigs!"

"Here are roots," a voice announced from the hole, once it was dug man-deep. The sound of heavy chopping-strokes commenced.

"They must run from yonder hedges," one onlooker said, pointing to a dusky-green thicket that stood nearby.

"Aye." Another man bent and picked up fragments of

roots as they were cast out of the hole. "They are thick and tough—but moist, see?"

"Here is gravel," a voice from below called. "And damp sand—no, water! The hole begins to fill!"

Moments later, bright silver droplets glinted high in the sunlight, dashed up out of the pit by joyous hands. Village folk around the well began to laugh and frolic, crowding up close to splatter one another and taste the droplets. At length the diggers emerged, their robes sodden to the waist.

"Wonderful," the cottage owner exulted. "My well is brimming over! I will make it open to all, for hardly any fee!"

"The witch Tamsin has succeeded where the others failed!" a villager cried. "She must indeed be blest of Amalias!"

"Nay, she is a sorceress of great power," others said, "greater even than the priests, who could not help us at all."

"Tamsin, may I commend our deepest thanks to you, and to your idol," the burgomaster proclaimed with a courtly smile and a flourish, though he refrained from embracing the maid and her peculiar doll. "May I offer you both the very gracious hospitality of my own villa. Come, stay with us tonight, Tamsin, I beg you! Then in a day or so, assuming this well maintains its excellent flow and purity, we will reward you richly in gold drachms and grain." He paused, with a quick glance to his fellow councillors that presaged bargaining. "The amount we had settled on was, ah, fifty drachms, I believe, and a thousand bushels of groats."

"Nay, burgomaster," Tamsin replied. "We do not wish your gold and grain."

"Oh, no?" The elder spoke cautiously, with another glance to his fellows. "You do not have to accept the grain, of course. But we are not wealthy here in Phalander, not any longer, and so we had determined to pay you mainly in barter."

"That is very good," the girl declared, "for Ninga and I wish to deal in barter too . . . in a way. Do we not, Ninga?" She addressed her doll in a girlish, confiding fashion, pausing as if waiting for an answer; then she looked back to the councillors. "In return for finding this well, we ask only your loyalty."

"Loyalty?" To the old politician, the word was evidently suspect. "What exactly do you mean?"

"In payment for this fountain, for as long as it shall flow, you must put aside the worship of Amalias and declare homage to a new patron-god of Phalander."

"A new god?" the elder said in genuine, baffled surprise. "What are you suggesting? Yourself, you mean?"

"No." Clutching her doll, Tamsin held it up before her. "Ninga shall be worshiped as Phalander-town's supreme goddess."

"What? You mean that doll?" The burgomaster halted in consternation, amid the muttering of the elders and others who had overheard. "Can you possibly be serious? But no, of course not."

"And why not?" Tamsin asked directly and reasonably. "Amalias and his priests failed you, but I, calling on Ninga, succeeded. Why should you continue to worship a spent god who lacks power?"

"Amalias is still a great lord," the elder said nervously. "More important, he has a powerful priesthood, one that stands closely allied with King Typhas and his earthly armies."

"Aye, my child," the fat old shire-reeve said, coming to his burgomaster's assistance. "Even if the High God cannot strike us from his unseen heaven, that does not make it wise to blaspheme against the church establishment."

"In truth, we might be judged apostate," the town treasurer added, shaking his balding head. "Why, it could cause us no end of trouble!"

"And what of the water Ninga and I found for you?" Tamsin asked. She gestured to the well that was now overflowing, making a small marsh of the neighboring pasture, where adults stooped to draw water in buckets and children splashed and played. "Does a well not spare you no end of trouble?"

"Surely you cannot, would not, take it away from us, would you?" The burgomaster hovered over Tamsin uneasily. "Look here, my girl, let us be reasonable! I can see that your doll—Ninga, is that her name?—likes necklaces and pretty things. Let her accept this medallion, my official emblem of rank, as a token of our town's good faith." He lifted the ribbon from over his head, shortened it by knotting it in the middle, and looped the disk of golden metal onto the doll. "This way she will understand that even if we cannot exalt her as a goddess, we respect her greatly. Is that all right, my child?"

Accepting the gift without acknowledgment, Tamsin

turned to the shire-reeve. "And you, Sheriff, what think you of the fountain?"

"Well, of course it is very fine," the fat man assured her, smiling nervously. "We all thank you most sincerely for it."

Tamsin turned once again where she stood. "And you, Treasurer?"

"Why, it is wonderful . . . pure and plentiful, as far as I can see. Of course—" he then added, plainly not wanting to seem too beholden "—if the well sprang from higher up the hill, the water could be channeled straight to our homes. Drawing water from the foot of the town will involve much carrying, quite an expense of vessels and servants, to be sure. And there may be problems in keeping the source clean, here among the hovels." He glanced at the pigpen and the surrounding cottages, wrinkling his nose. "But then, even a miracle-worker cannot accomplish everything, I suppose—" Looking into Tamsin's face, he broke off, suddenly uneasy. "I . . . I certainly did not mean to complain, or to question your doll's power as a god."

The young maid glared around at the three town elders and at the surprised villagers who stood watching.

"How many wells will you have, then?"

Taking up the divining-stick from where she had tucked it into her sash, she held it out once again—yet this time she managed things differently, holding her doll Ninga out before her, with the effigy's small, sewn mittens pressed onto the shanks of the stick beneath her own hands. Turning and striding then, as if both of them were drawn forward by the urgent, irresistible force of the wand, she started back through the hovels. Word spread quickly among the villagers, who hastened to follow.

Back along the dusty road she led them, uphill to the paved roadway, passing between huddled tenements and shop stalls. She did not pause when she came to the archway and the dying fountain, but hastened on farther, proceeding between the blank stone walls and trellised thresholds of the town gentry. As she strode onward, the rabble capered around her, and the councillors strove to keep up, carrying on a whispered debate as to whether they should offer the witch some token homage as a demigoddess, or find some other way to buy her off if she found them more water.

Soon the pavement ended, giving way to the rocky earth of the hillside; still Tamsin strode on. At last she stood at the top of an open, rocky yard that served as a cart turnaround, lying between the walled, stone-faced edifices of the burgomaster's palatial home and the shire-reeve's. Above them lay only the dark basalt ridge of the hilltop; below stretched a panorama of town and parched, grassless valley. Tamsin, drawn by the mystic power of the witchingwand, with her doll-fetish propped between her wrists, began wandering in circles as before. Meanwhile, the rich old burghers beamed at one another, rubbing their hands in anticipation.

This time, without preamble, the divining rod touched stony earth at the base of a half-buried boulder, one that looked even redder and darker than the witch-girl's auburn tresses. Bending, she dug at the soil with the pointed end of the stick, then arose and kicked at it with the toe of her sandal. From one side, a peasant with a mattock came running, eager to commence the digging. The tool point, swung high over his head, struck the earth one ringing blow. At that, its wielder gave a low outcry, and others crowded around to look.

Where the pick dug in, the boulder had chipped away, and from a tiny fissure beneath it, there hissed a draft of hot and sulfurous-smelling gas. As the villagers bent near, rock dust and cinders were blown out of the hole, stinging the eyes of the curious.

Then, with a deeper, fracturing noise, the embedded stone split open. The whistling gust of vapor became an outpouring, a hot, dizzying exhalation that sent the towns-people staggering back from the crevice. Barefoot children began to yelp and dance, leaping to escape the sudden heat they felt in the ground beneath them.

Then came a faint tremor underfoot, and the broken segment of the boulder fell aside, opening the cleft wider. Before it there began to form a lip of ash and stony soot, blown up out of some dreadfully hot place in the earth's innards.

"What is it?" the townsfolk cried. "Urlauf," they demanded of the peasant, "what hast thou struck thy pick into?"

"That is no water-well, but a gaping mouth of hell!"

"Witch Tamsin, do something, please!" the burgomaster entreated. "We meant you no disrespect!"

But the girl had turned from them and did not look back. Her divining rod, which she had thrown down by the new well-mouth, now curled and wilted in the heat blasting from the earth. By the time the forked stick burst into brief, lambent flame, she was gone.

Striding off downhill, proud Tamsin gave no sign of hearing, even as behind her, with a series of sullen roars, the vent exploded, bowling over townsfolk as they tried to flee and sending pillars of smoke and soot billowing heavenward. Amid the stentorian bellow of the escaping gases—more than loud enough to drown out the thin, faint screams of villagers—chunks of flaming stone shot high in the air and struck the nearby dwellings, setting ablaze the homes and orchards of the wealthy.

In later days—so the half-mad survivors said—nothing remained on the heights of Phalander but a jagged cone of scorching-hot cinders, raised up around a seething hell-pit that belched forth fire and poison, while Tamsin, the enchantress known to have caused it all, traveled home to her village to brew more spells.

SIX

Stalkers of the Hills

The gazelle raised its pronged head, ears a-prick for danger, and surveyed the dewy meadow. On all sides spread wild flowers, grass tufts, a few solitary clumps of shrub and weed. There was no motion or change, except for the occasional flicker of birds and insects, and the slow amble of other animals grazing in the middle distance. Resolutely, the deer lowered its head and resumed cropping grass.

As it did so, one of the low, motionless clumps changed shape and glided forward. It was a man, sun-bronzed, with fern fronds tied about his brow to obscure his crouching shape. His motion was noiseless, as smooth and minimal as the shiver of an airy draft over the soft grass. Yet it brought him near his unwary prey and left him poised, a crude spear braced level in his muscle-corded arm.

The animal must have sensed something—the glint of sunlight perhaps, on a facet of the chipped-stone spearpoint—for it raised its slim, tapering head in alarm. Its ears flexed as it gathered to spring. At that instant, a similar tautness coiled in the limbs of the hunter, and the make-shift hood of foliage fell away from his slate-black mane.

The motions of man and deer were one. As the gazelle catapulted into the air, the stalker's body lashed mightily, launching his spear to intercept the flying form. Aloft, the two missiles met, combining their momentum into a flail-ing, tumbling roll across the meadow grass. Before the thrashing animal regained its feet, the man darted forward; snatching a heavy tomahawk from the girdle of skins about his waist, he struck with it once, twice, savagely, until the prey lay motionless before him.

Bending warily, Conan tugged his spear out of the ani-mal's vitals. The weapon was undamaged. Both spear and ax must wait to be washed clean at the nearest stream; for the moment, the blood was left to congeal in their crudely shaped, hide-lashed crevices. Reaching to his waist, he drew forth the long obsidian shard that would serve as a gutting knife. His awkwardly tied girdle of rabbit skins enabled him to carry weapons at least, and to keep his hands free, though it scarcely afforded him the luxury of modesty. He should be able to do better with the hide of this good-sized animal, not to mention the valuable horn, bones, and savory meat thus provided.

He gutted the kill quickly and cleanly, without troubling to bury the blood and offal. He would have eaten the liver for a quick snack had he not feared worms or, worse, ill dreams from the dead doe's lingering spirit. The carcass was small enough to be carried; it made far more sense to bear it away to his lair than to skin it here and risk interruption by meddlesome and dangerous scavengers.

With a thrill of superstitious dread, he thought of the unseen thing that had stolen his first and more formidable quarry some days before. He was now better prepared to face any animal, large or small. Even so, there was no sense in squandering his strength or taking needless risks, not when his survival was at issue.

That first buck had been too large for him, a target of rash desperation. He would scarce have been able to lift its whole skin and antlers, or to consume an entire haunch of its meat before it spoiled. The gazelle, by contrast, hefted comfortably across his shoulders. It rode there solidly as he retraced his course—by an alternate route so as not to confront any predators stalking his upward trail—back toward the river.

His present camp was conveniently located and fairly well protected. It lay on a narrow islet, reachable in this season by a brisk wade through twining, waist-deep river currents. Rocks of all kinds were plentiful in the river's bed and banks, as were both driftwood and standing wood, and his now-dreary staple breakfast, trout. At the forest island's upstream end a stony outcrop rose into a sort of bastion, one that promised him a safe retreat once he had explored and fitted it out properly.

For now, his lair was in the lowest cleft of the rock castle, at the head of a sun-pierced grove from whence he could view anything that might approach from either flank of the islet. Returning in late morning, wet from having bathed himself and his gory kill in the river, he hung the gazelle over the lowest limb of an oak and bound it there with stiff cords of rabbit skin.

Kneeling then in a natural fireplace near the base of an overhanging rock where his tinder and kindling were stored, he set about making fire. Laying out a long, crudely shaped plank with a notched indentation at one edge, he knelt on it and bunched soft tinder under the notch. He took up his drill—a shaved, pointed stick of finger-thick wood—and the fire-bow, a long, pliant stick bent taut by a length of rawhide. This cord he tightened further by looping it twice around the shaft of the drill. Inserting the drill point into the notched hole in the plank, he used a fourth piece—a smooth, shallowly indented stone—as a socket with which to steady the butt end of the drill and force its point into the notch. With steady sawing motions of the bow, well-practiced in recent days, he made the drill twirl rapidly in the board, its point digging into the notched hole.

In a short time, smoke began to curl from the hole; he could feel the stone socket heating in his palm from the friction of his efforts. After some moments, a glowing stream of sawdust began to sprinkle through the notch into the nest of tinder. When smoke rose abundantly, Conan laid aside the socket and bow. Cupping his hands around the smoldering heap, he blew on it ever so gently. Once a clear flame sprang into existence, he was ready with dry twigs and shavings to nurture it into a healthy, hungry fire.

Banking the blaze with hard, dry, broken limbs, he turned back to his kill. He worked at the carcass with a keen shard of rock glass. Difficult though it was to grip the tool in blood-slimed fingers, he gradually stripped away the tough skin and laid it aside. Then he set to work dismembering the game, cutting apart its flesh and bones with his various-shaped stone blades and choppers. One whole haunch he roasted over the fire. Spitting its length on a supple green stick raised between two forked poles, he tried to remember to turn it frequently over the blaze, which gradually burned down to glowing, low-flaming chunks.

The rest of the meat he cut into long strips and set out on stones and wooden racks—either close beside the fire to dry and smoke rapidly, or on the rocks above to cure more gradually in the bright sunlight. This food would be his hedge against famine. It might in the coming days enable him to rove farther afield and explore his surroundings without having to worry about day-to-day sustenance.

This land, to be sure, was bountiful, with plenteous and varied animal life as well as countless other sources of food and material. A man alone could live richly here, more so than in the sparse, craggy highlands of northern Cimmeria. Yet inevitably these pristine valleys, for their very richness, must also hold danger. Whether it was in the form of mere animal predators, or mayhap human foragers, like the wild Picts of the Western Sea—or some supernatural influence, which Conan had already half-sensed in the breathy stillnesses of dusk and midnight—he thought it best to broaden his knowledge and be prepared for any threat.

Also, if he was going to make his way here, there was the question of long-term survival. Though lush now in early summer, the country might grow barren later. Just how fiercely snow or drought could smite these rugged lands was hard to guess, since he had no fixed notion of his whereabouts. From experience, he knew that a seeming abundance of wild game and food could vanish practically overnight. Whether he ought to build and provision a winter lodge in which to sit out the snows, or mayhap follow the game downstream to some milder pasture, remained an issue. It would require sound thought and intuition, now that he was on the way to lording it comfortably over the wilderness.

Of one thing he felt certain. However prosperous he became—well-armed, well-provisioned, and free to explore the limits of the land—he would never feel obliged to skulk back to the haunts and hovels of civilized Hyborians. Their power and grandeur, as often as not, he had found a hateful thing: a compact of mutual slavery, glorying in insatiable excesses, and exalting the ruthless few over the nameless many.

He was born a savage, after all. He had been taught the code of a wild hill tribesman, along with the skills that served him now; and, while dragged or hounded through half a hundred great cities, he had clung to those native values as his steadfast virtues. Now, returned here to a feral paradise by the will of Crom—and granted the boon of ignorance as a defense against any feeble claims his past might lay on him—he resolved to yearn no more for the gleam of decadent capitals, or for the perfume of soft, sybaritic pleasure. He could take civilization or leave it, he swore; given his way, he would never tread its paved, soiled byways again.

Once he had finished butchering, he turned his attention to the joint of venison, now scorched crisp on the outside but moist and succulent at the center. Wolfing the meat greedily from the bone, chewing and smacking with gusto, he dined; then he rounded out the repast with roasted roots and swamp greens out of the ashes, and deep draughts of cold water from a vessel he had made of river clay baked hard around tight-woven basketry.

After drinking, he laid the basin on the bed of coals to boil the remaining water. Into it he scraped those brains that remained in the antelope's cloven skull, along with as much of the spinal cord as he could pluck from the vertebrae. He had already peeled tendons from the animal's legs and back, to save as valuable bindings; the bones and skull he stacked beside the fire to dry. At length, taking up the gazelle's hide and a digging stick, he walked down to the river.

The skin was far too fresh to be processed, but delving into the muddy sand near the eddying currents, he unearthed the roebuck hide that had lain there for several days. It was adequately decomposed, the hairy outer skin beginning to slip away from the tough inner hide. Wrinkling his nose at the stench, he dragged it out of the hole and buried the fresher skin in its place.

A few paces downwind of his camp, he stretched the hide over a stream-worn nubbin of pine log. Using a deer rib as a draw-knife, he carefully scraped away the hair and loose skin, a slow process that took him well into the afternoon. When he had finished and disposed of the scrapings, he bore the limp hide back to the fire.

The deer brains had long since boiled and now waited in a steaming broth into which he lowered the hide, stirring it through the slurry with a stick. He removed the vessel from the fire and set it aside, knowing that the salty brains would bleach and preserve the skin overnight. In the morning, if he wished, he could rub and stretch it dry, then smoke it over smoldering willow wood to cure it further and stain it a deep brown hue.

From such prepared skins, he knew how to make strong garments: buskins, blouse, and breeches that would protect him against night chills, sharp foliage, and insect stings. More important, he now possessed tough thong for binding his weapons strongly and for fashioning game traps. He even had fabric for sacks and canopies.

As his wealth increased, he would be able to live more comfortably, he foresaw, but there would always be one limit: he must either be able to carry his belongings with him, or else provide for their safety in his absence. Caches of food and skins would ever be prey to roaming predators and scavengers unless he could secure them in some safe, inaccessible shelter or lair.

Having gorged himself at midday, he did not feel like eating a heavy supper. He contented himself with munching tree nuts and small, tart fruits he had gathered up in his makeshift basketry. The smoked and partially dried meats from the afternoon he wrapped in leaves and buried under heavy rocks as sunset approached. The twilight hour he spent in front of the fire, splitting and grinding one of the gazelle's tough ankle bones into a well-shaped awl. Then he retired to bed.

His sleeping place lay along an arching rock face that rose near enough the fire to catch some of the heat and reflect it downward. The camp was well above the water, escaping the worst of the river's cold and damp; and Conan's blanket of woven rabbit skins gave him more protection as it grew longer day by day. Even so, he kept a large supply of firewood within reach and awakened periodically to feed the fire when its flames would die and the night's chill begin to close in. This he did as much for the protection the fire offered against night-stalkers, both animal and supernatural, as for the warmth of the flames.

It was in deepest night that the sojourner's dimmest and most formless fears would begin to take shape. Alone in darkness, with only the flickering outlines of stones and bones near at hand—and beyond, the ghosts of looming trees—lying chill against hard, uneven earth, Conan would wonder about the reality of it all. This timeless, soulless wilderness, this sudden and total break with his past, did it bear any true relation to the world of toil and human vainglories he had left? Did it really lie on any map of the Hyborian kingdoms?

Or had he, once he abandoned himself to the down-rushing currents of the underground river, passed much farther out of human ken, into some land beyond earthly borders and time? Had he fallen back into the primal days of the world's youth? Or had he in fact died, and been swept off to some underworld or celestial paradise?—an afterlife that tight-lipped Crom, the god of his Cimmerian fathers, had given his worshipers no inkling of? Was he now expected to correct or atone for sins and infelicities of his earthly days before facing the stern judgment of the gods? Or must he contemplate each mistake of his past in a sort of feral, endless purgatory? If this life, or illusion, stretched on to infinity, what could he accomplish during its span? Would he be able to endure it long—alone—without slipping into madness?

Here lay the gateway to vast, mystic recesses of the soul.

Some men, and some women too, might carry such musings very far indeed, using them to conjure up whole cosmogonies of spirits and demons, giving their fears tenuous but terrifying substance. Yet Conan's natural reaction when faced with such imponderable questions was to cling to the familiar, to anything vivid to the senses, to anything tangible and known. And so, as on many previous nights, it was with fond thoughts of the past—memories of pliant Zamoran dancing-maids and of pungent Aquilonian ale—that he slipped off to sleep.

By sunrise, he was stiff and chilled, dull and groggy, yet eager to start his limbs working and generate internal heat. The fire had not quite died, so he warmed himself with the task of fanning and stoking it back to a lively flame.

Then he went to check his fish trap. The funnel-mouthed corral of poles he had driven into the sandbar at the foot of the isle had snared one trout—a medium-sized fish, too large to wriggle out through the fence and too young to leap over its top. It was enough for breakfast. Conan, not inclined toward a frigid morning dip, did not bother to tickle up any more fish. This one, spitted and toasted over hearty flames, was as satisfying as any two of its predecessors eaten raw and cold.

With meat and other foodstuffs in ample supply, Conan decided to use the morning to complete the exploration of his islet. His recent hasty survey, made by climbing to the highest point of the stone outcrop, had revealed a granite dome well above tree level, with stone hummocks falling away steeply to the pools and rapids of the river below. Thick underbrush filled the hollows and crevices where trees could not grow, and so he had left several likely spots for a later and more leisurely visit. His current site at the base of the rock, though comfortably close to wood and water, was too openly accessible for his liking.

Girding his rabbit-skin clout about his waist—and taking up knife, hatchet, and spear, since one could never be too well-armed—he started up the mound behind his camp. The way was easy, treading along bare rock shoulders and leaping from outcrop to outcrop. That was one thing he liked about the place: a man could make his way from the crown of the island down to the waterside, day upon day if he so wished, without leaving any visible sign or track. So it was with fire-smoke, too—Conan's experience had taught him that smoke kindled on such an airy height would soon dissipate and be far less visible than any that rose up out of the windless well of the valley floor. He had as yet seen no sign of human presence, but if man was here, he wanted to know so before being found.

Partway up the mound lay a couple of likely spots: shallow clefts that might conceal a camp. He saw where, if brush was carefully cleared, access could be restricted. Snares and deadfalls might be installed to further discourage surprise by prowling marauders, or at least to give warning. The views of valley and hills the sites afforded were splendid and commanding. Even so, Conan decided that both clefts were still too exposed.

Very soon he neared the summit, without finding what he sought. The whole island was, after all, only a hundred strides across, so its possibilities were limited. He would be better off shifting camp frequently about the countryside, traveling light . . . but then, for the first time, he noticed a sloping, brushy terrace on the steeper streamward side of the mound.

The place had its advantages. For one thing, the sharp drop-offs immediately above and below made it highly defensible. Angling his way down across sloping granite, Conan found the shelf deeper than it first appeared, receding under an overhang of black, lichen-stained rock. The outer court was a mass of shrubs rooted in gravel, tough and harshly weathered; a series of jagged rock ledges along the cliff led him deeper into a more sheltered platform—and further yet to a dry, sandy gallery that would surely be safe from rain and winter snowdrifts. The place narrowed almost into a cave . . . especially just there, where a massive roof slab had tumbled down in some past eon, creating a dark, triangular niche in the cleft's dimmest recess.

Too late Conan saw his mistake. His glance came to rest on white wreckage strewn before the opening—a ghastly litter of cracked, crushed bones—but by then, a maddened, thunderous roar already hammered at his ears. The cavebear came tumbling forth out of the impossibly narrow crevice, forcing before it a wave of its own musky stench.

It was an incredible creature, swelling as large as a small cottage, its bristling fur shading from blood-caked brown to hoary silver, its face a flaring, slavering mask of hungry ferocity. The beast roared again, exposing handsbreadths of dripping yellow fang; this time the noise in the enclosed space was so dreadful that it stabbed Conan's ears and shook the stone underfoot, threatening to bring more of the low roof crashing down.

A few backward steps gained Conan nothing; the bear

only lumbered forward and reared up taller, as high as the rock ceiling permitted. The monster was frenzied, outraged at finding an intruder so near its lair. Doubtless, as the sustained, echoing pandemonium of snarls and squeals in the cavern now told, it was protecting a sow and new cubs in the cavern behind it.

The place was a trap for fools, Conan saw. Clearly, everything that had drawn him here, the bear also found attractive. He should have foreseen this. In his readiness to foil predators, he had walked straight into the fangs of one of the largest and most fearsome ones he had yet seen.

He must not give ground too easily; to do so only allowed the beast freer movement. Conan dismissed the notion of turning and fleeing across the steep, precarious granite. Over open ground, no earthly creature could outrun one of these agile, muscle-slabbed behemoths; but here in the uneven cleft, Conan's smaller size was a temporary advantage. Darting forward with spear raised, he stabbed the creature in the back of one forepaw.

The bear's wrath at this was terrible to see. The outpouring of noise and foul carrion-breath smote Conan in the face, and a swipe of the beast's sickle-shaped claws pelted and stung the warrior with broken bits of a woody shrub that grew in close on one hand. The snarling face surged forward—but then, darting angrily after a wave of Conan's spearpoint, the snout swung aside and scuffed up hard against a ridge of unyielding granite. As if stunned, the beast planted its feet and shook its head—just once—before lumbering forward in renewed attack.

Conan jabbed with his spear, once narrowly missing the creature's face, once striking its shoulder, to little effect.

He avoided the batting paws, which would splinter his crude weapon to matchwood . . . and the jaws, that could easily bite through wood and stone alike. The shaft's fighting-reach was scarcely longer than the bear's massive arm, so he had to leap in and dodge back to protect his own skin. Seeing an opening at last, he lunged at the monster's hairy flank . . . and felt his sharp stone point jab into heavy hide. The raging beast boiled after him like a hairy avalanche, forcing him to scurry backward for life.

Though pricked, the animal was anything but cowed by Conan's resistance. It reared taller now and swept its paws in broader swaths, pressing forward in an ambling gait that might at any moment become an unopposable charge. Conan feinted at the monster's belly and snout, trying to teach it to fear his darting point.

Instead, the bear lost patience and lashed out to take off his head. Ducking under its extended forepaw, whose coarse bristles scoured the skin of his naked back, he drove his spear into the animal's flank. Once embedded, the blade caught in the leathery hide and broke free of the shaft. An instant later, on the backswing, the flailing paw splintered the pole in two. Conan barely rolled free, dragging his ax from his belt and raising it to defend himself.

Yet the bear, vexed by pain, no longer recognized any obstacle. It swarmed straight at Conan, driving him out onto the down-curving granite slope. A deft stroke to his adversary's hairy brain pan did not even slow the beast; it only loosened the head of the stone ax in its crude binding.

Meanwhile, writhing to escape the monster's killing hug, Conan was struck a light, glancing blow by its forepaw. Chisel-claws shredded flesh from his thigh, ripped the flimsy fur clout from his groin, and battered into the frail cage of his ribs, sending him sprawling across the granite like a broken stick-doll.

Rolling and scrabbling to escape, unsure whether the brute was charging or merely tumbling forward onto him, Conan felt himself pressed flat. He took the bear's whole tremendous weight on his back, its thrashing bulk, its pelt like an armor of steel bristles; its musty, choking stench crushed him down against hard granite. As it rolled over him, the burden abated, but a pitchfork claw raked him up off the rock, and he felt himself clutched in a murderous embrace.

The pressure then grew even greater, stifling his breath, purpling his vision, cracking his bones aloud in their sockets. Desperately Conan lashed out, smiting, writhing to break free.

Then came a series of heavy blows, a loosening, a rushing blast of air. Conan's vision flickered on madly alternating earth and sky, and he understood why the beast could not hold him—it was rolling down the cliffside. He, too, was falling, hurtling off the stone overhang past any hope of escape. Below was the river, a blue-black pond lathering and swirling amid fanged rocks. Kicking free of the snorting, flailing bear, Conan gathered himself for the impact.

Numb and chilled, he crouched by the waterside, probing his bruised, torn flesh and testing his aching bones. He must have blacked out. Again, as before, he could have been swept any distance downstream. This part of the river was unfamiliar; his island was nowhere in sight. As to the bear's fate, he could make no guess.

It mattered nothing. Here he was again, devoid of food and belongings, and lacking the strength to try to regain them. What he needed now was a warm, sheltered nook in which to sleep off these wounds and the fever that would likely follow. He could worry about food, clothing, and weapons later.

The trees here rose tall enough to shade both banks of the river, making its waters pool and swirl sedately down a broad channel. Where Conan stood, a tributary stream joined the main flow, cutting through the steep, root-knit bank. Thankful for the pathway, he followed the stream's course, trudging along its shallow margin where it flowed down from the forest. Though sore and murky-brained, he was aware that by following this course, he left no track. He also knew that wherever he chose to hole up and recuperate, he must stay within easy reach of water.

The tree trunks on either hand stood as broad and stately as the columns of some great palace or temple. Even in his depleted state, and perhaps more so because of it, Conan sensed the awe and mystery of the age-old forest. Down through its canopy pierced occasional sunbeams, slanting a-sparkle with insects and dust motes, softened and scattered in their fall to earth by lattices of foliage overhead. Along the stream, lily and fern sprouted, though not thickly enough to bar Conan's way. And just ahead, through looming curtains of greenery, he could hear the rush of water as from a small cataract. It was a welcome noise, since he wanted to climb some way above the river before sinking down to rest.

Pushing stiffly through the screen of shrubs and vines, he looked out on a shallow, partly shaded pond. At its further end, where sprays of water pattered down from overhanging rocks, his eyes encountered a searing, paralyzing vision. There beneath the waterfall—with back turned to him, and with shapely arms and petal-like hands raised briefly overhead to catch the gushing torrent—was a woman.

As innocent of garments as she was of his presence, she stood bathing in the ankle-deep pool. The sight, in the echoing gallery of rocks and greenery, was one of unutterable beauty. Her delicate contours and full, lush curvatures shimmered palely radiant in sunlight reflected up from the water's dappled surface. As Conan looked on, she lowered her arms and, cupping her hands full of water against her throat, laved herself generously with the foamy torrent. She spread it across her shoulders, breasts, and thighs, and wrung it down through the dark rope of hair that lashed and clung as far as the delicate hollow of her back. Bending forward, she bathed supple legs and tapering feet, lifting and bracing them in turn against a stone outcrop to do so. Without warning, she turned and stepped out of the flow. Her gaze, sweeping the far side of the pond, settled at once on Conan.

The outlander did and said nothing. So thunderstruck was he by the discovery and the splendid female charms revealed to him that no other thought came into his mind. He forgot his perilous situation, his wounds, and the fact that he stood as naked as the woman; instead, he remained frozen in the timeless instant.

The woman, for her part, reacted similarly. She did not

cry out, nor did her hands dart in false civilized modesty
to cover particular parts of her body. In attitude she somewhat resembled a fawn surprised while feeding—glancing
up, alert and expressionless, to determine whether the noise
that had roused her represented any threat. Her dark eyes
took in everything, clearly: Conan's impressive physique
and his unfamiliar, probably foreign-looking face. Then
her gaze dropped to his midsection, unable to ignore the
ragged, four-clawed wound furrowed from ribs to upper
thigh. The look on her face remained one of cool appraisal,
without fear or plea.

What broke their silence, it was hard to say. It might
have been the sound of a branch cracking in the forest,
which could signal the presence of other humans, or it may
have been the unfolding of inevitable thoughts and doubts
between the two. For whatever reason, Conan stepped forward out of the hanging poolside foliage, resettling his
weight on the slimy pebbles of the streambed. The woman
moved similarly, stepping clear of the random spray from
the cataract. Then abruptly she was running across the
pond, her legs raising lacy cascades as they bore her off
with deerlike swiftness.

Conan's pursuit, as he lunged across the pool to intercept
the woman, was instinctive. This rare prize—this creature
of soul-wrenching beauty, a longed-for and long-dreaded
link with others of his kind—could not be let go. He
bounded after her—staggered into a deep channel, floun-
dered, then waded clear—in pursuit of the strong, lithe
flanks and delicate heels flying before him in the forest
shade. His pain and fatigue were forgotten, so rich and
heady were the blood-humors that coursed through his

veins. He felt an exuberant, reckless energy, greater than hunt or battle could bring. She fled swiftly, on feet well-toughened to the barbs and chafes of the forest floor, yet such was Conan's impulsive, feverish strength that he knew he would overtake her.

It was later—as the woman's flashing soles grew dirt-stained, leading him up a loamy forest embankment—that reasons and justifications crept into his awareness, reasons vague and unformed, but imperative even so. The woman must have kin, after all, or a tribe or a nation; he must learn of them before they came seeking him . . . to slay, torment, or possibly devour him, as was the way of Picts and other wild folk he had known. He must catch and restrain her, somehow dissuade her from giving alarm to her kinfolk. The fact that she ran in silence now was favorable, if it meant no others were in earshot.

How he might prevent her—what, precisely, he would do once his grasping fingertips closed on the lush flanks and velvet skin that raced and rebounded before him . . . once he dragged her to earth—those thoughts never took definite shape, but swirled and receded into a red, dim haze that began to drift before his eyes.

He was drawing close now. Once, where her foot slipped in the crook of a root just before him as she scaled a stony embankment, he reached out and touched the deft, firm curve of her ankle, which barely slid free of his fingers. At the top, as he labored up after her with earth sliding loose under his bare soles, she turned and cast a wide-eyed look back at him. She was winded, gasping heavily with soft, reedy overtones to each breath, her full breasts heaving and undulating, her flesh dirt-streaked and sweat-sheened. Her face he found appealing; it was large-featured, a blend of northerly shape and dusky southern coloring. Amazingly, he saw in it no trace of fear.

Finding footholds, he swarmed up the embankment with an agility that must have surprised her. As she turned away, weaving through the low-hanging branches of a stand of oak, he followed close behind. At last he caught her scent; its musky fragrance wafted to him on the forest breeze, maddening him. With a raw surge of vitality, he bolted forward, lunging straight after her—and suddenly found himself staggering, his vision swimming, stunned as he was by a collision with the oaken elbow of a massive, leaf-screened tree limb.

The blow to his head smarted sharply, intensely, sending a trickle of blood to mingle with the tears blurring his eyes. Worse, the shock drained away his strength. Staggering forward half-blind, he stumbled on a knotted root and fell to his knees.

Before him, the woman—a pale, shapely blur in the forest dimness—stood gazing down where he knelt. She stepped nearer, raising one graceful foot from the carpet of dead leaves. Her kick swept high, smiting him on the jaw, and he passed from consciousness.

SEVEN
The Healer

The gateway to the baronial keep of Urbander arched tall and jagged against mottled gray skies. Its dark-weathered heights were in the process of being topped with new, loftier bastions of lighter-hued stone. In spite of winter's chill and the hard crust of snow that lay in the roof gutters and cobbled angles of the outer bailey, work was yet underway. From the battlements could be heard the shouts of foremen, the creak of frozen tackle, and the patient tap of chisels as stones were dressed and fitted into place.

Young witch Tamsin had never before been summoned to a provincial capital. Urbander, one of the northernmost cities of the Brythunian Empire, was strongly fortified against attack by the unruly warlords of the Border Kingdoms; it also flourished with trade and raiding spoils from those same exotic lands. Command of such a remote and vital outpost required a firm hand indeed. Along with it, as all Brythunians knew, came considerable autonomy and freedom from the supreme ruler, King Typhas in Sargossa.

"The baron will receive us at once, I do not doubt," the armored officer said as he alighted from the mud-spattered travel wain. Turning to the door of the low-slung coach, he offered his hand to help the young woman down. " 'Tis close upon noon. His Lordliness will likely have arisen from slumber following his nightly, ah, revel. This is the hour of day when he is usually most desirous of a healer's care."

"Yes, Sir Isembard." Ignoring the gray-mustached officer's hand, Tamsin alighted from the chariot in a single, girlish hop. As ever, she carried her conjuring-doll cradled in one arm. It rattled, and its many bright ornaments flashed and jingled with her swift movements. "Ninga will be most pleased to meet Baron Einholtz, as I shall be."

"He is in grave need of your ministrations," Isembard assured her with an earnest nod. "His Lordliness has been . . . unfit for some time." The lieutenant turned briskly to his duty. "Sergeant, assemble the baronial staff, and assign a few guards to keep this rabble clear of the doors." His curt wave took in a crowd of peasants and city idlers who pressed in at the gate with considerable interest. They had gathered on the track of the mud-encrusted chariot that was rumored to have carried the famed enchantress so many leagues across the broad empire.

Isembard, having issued his orders, turned smartly toward the keep. His young guest, flanked by a pair of palace guards who fell in at the rear, followed him up the broad steps and through the arched portal.

Inside, the place was grand and impressive to one of Tamsin's humble origins. Its broad, low-vaulted cavern displayed intricate stonework crafted by skilled slaves brought up from the southern conquests. The decor was sternly masculine, fitted out with racks of pikes and stands of shields, adorned about the walls with heads of boar, moose, ram, and bear, and crowded with trestle tables well-hacked and battered by roistering and weapons-play. In spite of this provincial roughness, the carved stone pillars, fretted arches, and soaring balustrades bespoke elegant possibilities; they loomed spectral in the yellow beams flickering from the broad, blazing hearth.

Before this central fire, in a large armchair surrounded by a half-dozen servants, presided a figure of truly aristocratic shagginess and girth. He was craggy-faced and ruddy-colored, with whitely tufted eyebrows and white hair spiked and tangled in an unruly hedge around his balding, liver-spotted head. The noble lord, though burly chested and resplendent in his silken blouse, sash, and pantaloons, slumped where he sat in a manner indicating some profound bodily unease. The thrust of his gray-bristled face at the approach of the brisk lieutenant hinted at a dyspeptic's early-morning ill humor.

"Milord Baron," Isembard formally began, "at your bidding, I have sent throughout the kingdom for a healer to secure Milord's ease and relief. This morning I bring a witch who is unequaled at diseases of the mortal frame . . . as well as being mistress of numerous other conjurations and divinations." Half-turning in his place with a stiff nod, he indicated the girl beside him. "The seeress Tamsin, from the neighborhood of faraway Yervash, awaits your pleasure."

"My pleasure, eh?" Craning his neck further, the old baron keenly appraised the young woman who waited in her long, flower-painted robe next to Isembard. "If that is what she wants, she may have a very long wait indeed . . . until tomorrow evening at least, unless she is a most able healer!"

The jest, spoken in coarse eastern accents and followed by a bilious, ill-humored stare around the company, drew polite, cautious laughs from the lieutenant and one or two other high-ranking servants.

"But come, child, move over here into the firelight where I can see you without cracking my battle-weary old neck. Ho-ho," he exclaimed as the young woman silently complied with his wish, "you really are but a child! Isembard knows my tastes well, as I would expect him to, having procured so many young lovelies for my bed and bolster over the years."

"Milord Baron," the lieutenant ventured stiffly, "I remind you that this maid is no mere mattress-trull. She is a famed physician, and a conjuress of unequaled renown—"

"Yes, yes, I know!" The baron spoke impatiently, raising one puffy-looking hand to wave aside Isembard's protest. "Tamsin, is it? I have heard tell of your fame even in this wild outpost—" he fixed the girl with a leer of his grizzled, somewhat bloated and red-seamed countenance "—even though I place no stock in such overblown tales." The old warrior harrumphed. "Mayhap as my need for such things grows, so will my credulity. In any event, the local healers have accomplished nothing. And the gods know, praying to haughty Lord Amalias and to my native Nemedian war-sprites has availed me little enough. Nay, child, if you can offer me hope, then Isembard has done wisely to fetch you here."

"Our thanks, Baron Einholtz." Tamsin, in spite of her

tall, erect bearing and the jingling burden underneath her arm, gave a pretty half-curtsy. "Ninga and I are most eager to serve you."

"Ninga? Ah yes, now I remember the gossip. This is the wench who plays with dolls!" Flicking a dropsical hand at Tamsin's spangled fetish, his slack body quivering with hoarse, half-choking laughter, Baron Einholtz shifted in his chair. "She bedizens the village buffoons with her mannikin's spells and jinxes, and even pretends to be something of a walking religion." Rocking in his seat, he stifled and sputtered. "See, Isembard, the lass has done me good already, ho-ho, lifting my spirits at this raw hour of the morning!"

Wheezing heavily, the old baron settled back into his place. "Tell me, girl, what do you and your tiny friend Ninga propose to do for me—but say, Isembard, what is the meaning of this interruption?" Einholtz's attention was suddenly diverted by a number of nobles and household guards who filed in through archways at the back of the chamber, taking up positions at either side of the fire. "Are the peasants up in revolt again? Has the alarm been struck? What in Ulfgar's name is at issue now?"

"Nay, nothing, Milord Baron," Isembard said calmly, forestalling his commander's wrath. " 'Tis no mischance or emergency. I have merely summoned your most loyal retainers here to your side to witness young Tamsin's cure. For know you, the girl is a miracle-worker of fabled power. Whatever passes here may be spoken of for years to come. 'Twere best, I thought, if some few dozen watchful eyes were present to observe and affirm . . . or elsewise refute any false tales that could arise later."

"Aye . . . most wise, Isembard." The baron smiled

cannily to his lieutenant. "Better to have witnesses and ready hands, if only for safety's sake." His red-rimmed eyes shot a moist glance at Tamsin. "For when I think on it, I have heard tell how this maiden's soothing magics sometimes have a rough edge to them. Idle stories, to be sure, but daunting enough if one were to believe them. For instance—" he flashed his droll, fish-eyed gaze about the watching company "—are you not renowned to have reared up a mountain in the midst of some southern market-town and set it ablaze with brimstone and pitch, because the townsfolk would not pay your fee?"

"Baron, you need not fear such a fate at our hands." Tamsin's answer was plain-spoken, if not wholly direct. "Ninga and I would not use our powers to harm your fine city, or do anything Sir Isembard has not bidden us to do. Is that not true, Ninga?" The young woman looked down at the doll, reaching to primp its wiry-looking hair with charming, childish innocence. "As for our payment, you need not worry, since we shall not ask you for any. To render service to a nobleman as famous as yourself, Baron, is reward enough for us."

What seemed so girlish and ingenuous in the young woman's manner must have struck the old aristocrat as impertinent or subtly threatening, since his response was chill. "You wish no payment?" he rumbled at her. "Very well, then, you will be given none . . . if you succeed in your cure, that is. If you fail . . . well, Seeress, if I were you, I should be wary of what payment will then be forthcoming!" With a subtle move, surprisingly quick for one so decayed, the warlord whipped forth a long, gleaming saber from beneath his waist sash.

"Know you, whatever arcane arts you and your little dollikin may command, I am far more adept at the play of steel. What else do you think has made all these warriors loyal to me?" His wave, encompassing the entire hall, was met without quarrel. "Steel, as you may learn, is the bane of sorcery! Enchantments wither in its shadow like petals beneath an early frost. My edge has the keenness, when I wish it—" a quick thrust and slash of the baron's blade traced a wicked yellow gleam in the firelight "—to cut through devious skeins of treachery, and even webs and mazes of sorcerous illusion. Be warned, Seeress!"

"Yes, Baron Einholtz," Tamsin answered her employer with a humble nod. "Ninga and I have heard much of your skill at weapons and command. Your prowess as a captain of Nemedian mercenaries is still celebrated from past times, before the king in Sargossa made you baron of this province. We have heard of your victories in those days as being many and total . . . have we not, Ninga?"

Einholtz looked askance at her byplay with the doll. Yet he seemed to accept her praise guardedly, putting his blade back in his sash. "Indeed, child, there is no gainsaying it. When old King Typhas created me Lord of Urbander, he was not merely thanking me for my aid in the southern wars . . . for my swift arrival, with troops fierce and ruthless enough to press his campaign through to a victory. No indeed."

The old warrior seemed suddenly inclined to seize on this opportunity for a speech before his retainers. "The King was also protecting himself and his royal borders, for in his shrewd kingliness, old Typhas sensed in me the hard, ruthless mettle that would be needed to hold down an outpost on his northern frontier. He judged rightly that I, Einholtz, could sustain the Order of Barony—'' with puffy, dropsical fingers he tugged at the heavy gold medallion pinned to his sagging chest ''—not just against raiders and hillmen on the border, but against upstart squires and treacherous serfs brewing rebellion in my own domain.'' He paused for a moment, cocking an ear toward the main entryway.

''And say, speaking of rebels, what is that hubbub outside in the alley? Are the village clods up in arms again? Bridling at their winter tax assessments, perhaps, or at our latest levy of young recruits and virgins? If so, then crush them, fellows, as we have always done before!'' Einholtz was half out of his chair again, waving his saber on high. ''The will of the baron is unopposable, never to be challenged by common peasants—''

''Nay, Sire,'' Lieutenant Isembard intervened, hurrying to calm his lord and prevent any of the company from rushing outside. '' 'Tis nothing to bestir yourself over. A handful of townsfolk have merely gathered to mark the arrival of the noted witch-woman, here. Doubtless they hope to celebrate the occasion of Milord's miraculous recovery. There is no threat of civil disorder. I have assigned guards to keep them back from the palace, so Milord Baron need not vex himself over it.''

''What of the bailey-gate, then? Lock them out securely—or aye, drop the cullis down on their gawking necks! That should hold them back.''

''Milord, during construction, as you know, the gates have been kept open. They are frozen in place by sleet storms, and it would be inconvenient just now to chop them free.'' Isembard leaned closer to entreat his master, prevailing on him to put away his sword. ''Truly, Sire, we should see this as a chance to cozen the goodwill of the townspeople. I pray Milord, let them have their revel. Later on, once your cure is accomplished, we can celebrate by sending down a cask of ale to be broached in the town square.''

"Humm . . . all right, Isembard, whatever you say.'' The baron, suddenly weak from his tirade and his fitful illness, let the matter go without further haggling. He turned back to Tamsin.

"Well, then, witch-maid, unpack your magic spells. How do you propose to heal my miserable frame?''

"First, as to the nature of your ailments.'' Tamsin regarded him critically, holding up Ninga as if to afford the doll an equal view. "You seem to be afflicted with a creeping palsy of the extremities.''

"Yes,'' the baron declared. "It is most troublesome when I am at rest,'' he added with a defiant glance around the assembled courtiers, "and in the early mornings before I have fortified myself with ale.'' After a moment's hesitation, he raised his mottled old hand from the chair's wooden arm so that his infirmity could be seen. It was readily apparent: a vague, aimless fluttering of the fingertips, matched by random twitchings of muscles and tendons beneath the splotchy, papery skin of wrist and arm.

"An advanced case indeed,'' the young witch observed in a somber tone. "Never doubt that it will grow far worse if not treated. Such may be the result of the lush foreign wines and liquors Milord has quaffed in excess, and of too many nightlong revels amid the captive spoils of fallen palaces and manor homes.'' She murmured something almost inaudible to her doll; then she listened in silence for a moment, as if receiving the valued counsel of a senior physician, before continuing. "Tell me, Baron Einholtz, do you also suffer from gout?"

"Gout? Aye, yes, to be sure," the baron volubly admitted, "though it is not among my ills at this present moment. But there are times, especially during autumn harvest and midwinter festival, that it has given me damnable swelling and tenderness, so painful that I can scarce move." He held up one foot, which looked, through its shiny silken sock, to be somewhat puffy and dropsical even if not currently disabled.

"Quite so, as we can see," Tamsin affirmed. "Such is a hazard in these temperate climes, especially in seasons when the festive meats come plentiful and richly spiced—not for all the country's inhabitants, of course," she reminded him, "but for those like yourself, whose fare is the best and fattest, as befits the lords and possessors of all. It is a price that nobles pay—a sacrifice, some would say—for the health of the state." The young woman gazed around at the listeners without any visible irony in her look. "And, Baron, what of the state of your bones?"

"Oh aye, my bones!" Baron Einholtz was by now enlivened to the subject, quite willing to discuss his ills before the assembled court without fear of seeming weak or infirm. "The rheumy pains I suffer, on late evenings and in the hours near dawn, are quite a plague to me. Even a hot brazier, a cup of mulled brandy, and the laying-in of two or three village lasses in my sleeping-closet cannot avail much against the chilly ague that creeps to my marrow. If you can do anything to banish that, young witch . . . and this other malady . . ." his aged hand brushed vaguely across his face ". . . why then I might reconsider the pledge I made to pay you no reward."

"Yes, Baron Einholtz, we can see your plight." Pensive for a moment, with her doll still clutched by her side in an attitude of alertness, Tamsin examined the old lord's reddish, waxy physiognomy: his furrowed, scar-cratered, sunsplotched bald pate and brow; the puffy, bloodshot eyes; the lips liverish and slack from relentless indulgence; his nebulous jawline bristled white with a carelessly cropped beard—and amidst it all, the bulbous, purple-veined nose, with one nostril deeply eroded and eaten by some creeping blight that left but a thin, runny scab in lieu of the once full-blossoming organ.

"We see, Baron, only too well." Tamsin listened for a moment to her doll, then resumed: "The worm that gnaws you, sadly, is not one that admits of an easy cure. It is a ravaging blood-sprite, a creeping malaise that haunts its victims and depletes them over a score of years. Worse, the damage it shows to an untrained eye is as nothing to the havoc it wreaks within, invisibly, to the victim's mind and substance. It results from unconsidered matings . . . couplings with brute beasts, or with low commoners who are nowise better. As an affliction of such duration and subtlety, it can, alas, accompany a great man from his years of modest or uncertain station to the fullness of his power and rank."

"What are you saying, Seeress?" Einholtz demanded, seeming both impatient and frightened. "That you cannot cure me after all? Or that you wish to raise your price? And what is that disturbance outside, curse those peasants!" He glanced up at the chamber's high, flat-arched windows of stained glass, against which objects were striking and rattling, most likely stones or ice chunks flung up by the crowd.

"Your affliction, O Baron—the chancrous rot of your nose and, perhaps, other organs we cannot see—resists any cure because it is one with your being, a natural consequence of your youthful exploits and tastes. Your bone-ague, likewise, is but the result of harsh, violent struggles against man and nature—the effects of the fighting and philandery, the horsemanship and swift marches, the riot and rapine that carried you to this lofty seat. And your gout and palsy, are but mere adjuncts to aristocratic vice and privilege—attested to by your love of strong wines and highly tainted victuals—and your righteous seizure of the country's wealth. How can Ninga and I, though gifted with godlike power and understanding, hope to correct the ills that are so much a part of the man, without changing the man himself out of all recognition?"

"What outrageous treason is this, you insolent witch?" The warlord at last jerked upright in his seat. "You allege that I, Baron Einholtz, am one with my ills?—that I am a walking pestilence, a spouting pustule of disease? That I conjoin with beasts, and taint myself with impure things? Such infamous talk cannot be borne, witch! It must be stopped, even if that means severing your pale young throat with sharp, bright steel— Ah, aieee, no!"

With his words, Baron Einholtz had again produced the heavy saber and, with surprising quickness, sprung out of his seat to wield it. As he extended the weapon before him, however, it glinted in the firelight, flashing with such an intense, lingering brightness that it seemed as if a star or a fragment of sun had come to rest in the dim hall. The fire's blaze was yellow and faint, yet the steel's blinding glare lingered and grew, forcing the courtly onlookers to avert their eyes. Einholtz, closest to the source, had his face illumined and even scorched by the light, his gawping, bulbous-eyed expression burned vividly into every watcher's memory. An instant later, he fell to his knees, shrieking and clasping both hands to his eye sockets, with the saber spinning away unnoticed across the floor.

"Aiaah, I am blind!" the baron moaned and wailed piteously, while the unearthly light receded and the onlookers' vision recovered. "My eyes sear like hot coals in my head!" When Einholtz removed his hands and blinked about the chamber's vaultings, vainly seeking some ray of vision, those present caught a ghastly glimpse of his two orbs, pale all over like poached-egg whites.

"Guards!" the unhappy baron shrieked meanwhile, "kill that damnable witch, I command you! Throw her carcass onto the fire, to roast unto perdition and—" the decrepit man groped pitifully on the flagstones around him for his weapon "—lead me back to my chair!"

As the blinded one must have sensed from the ensuing silence, none made the smallest move to obey. Instead, a moment or two later, Tamsin's unruffled voice resumed lecturing him where he groveled on the floor.

"Your physical infirmities, as we have told you, are part and parcel of your mental and mortal history and sins. They are beyond cure, and yet the least Ninga and I can offer, in view of your earnest summons and our agreement, is to protect you from their most extreme consequence. It is possible to grant you the blessing of perpetual, unending life. Ninga, do so, I pray you!" With these words, the young enchantress bent forward and brushed the shoulder of the kneeling baron with the doll's crudely stitched hands, almost as if the puppet had reached down to confer a blessing with its swift touch. At the motion, Einholtz started. He cowered there, groping in the air and clutching himself all over, as if invaded by some alien force.

"Now, Baron," Tamsin spoke on, "rest assured that however harsh the effect of your wasting diseases—however they may pain you, eat away at your mortal frame and dissolve your will—you cannot die, but will linger on inviolate for all eternity. Henceforth it is impossible for you to be slain, even by such a blow as this . . . Isembard!"

At the seeress's firm, precocious word and gesture, the baron's lieutenant stepped forward. Unsheathing his long rapier with a flourish, he stooped and drove it into Einholtz's cringing body. The thrust went straight and true through the old barrel chest, unarguably deadly. On the sword's long, silver shank, the old baron writhed for a moment like a spitted fish, moaning and drooling blood from his distorted lips.

And yet, when Isembard jerked the blade free and stood upright, Baron Einholtz, after a shriek of pain at the removal, continued to stir and breathe, his fingers sifting feebly at the air, with only a thin stain of red dampening his shirt where the wound was made.

"And so you see," Tamsin was saying, "Ninga's magic has made you proof against death! 'Tis the best miracle our powers can accomplish, and we hope you enjoy the boon of immortality. In recognition of our gift, we desire but a small, nominal token . . . .this." Leaning forward over the baron, avoiding his blind, vainly groping hands, Tamsin bent and deftly snatched from Einholtz's chest his badge of baronial rank.

"You have small need of it anyway, since your ailments seem to have worsened so." As she spoke, she hooked the brass pin of the bloodstained medal into the richly decorated blouse of her doll, adding one more bangle to Ninga's emblazonments. "You should retire someplace quiet, to convalesce. Lieutenant Isembard has consented to fill your throne for the nonce—an event that is sure to be met with rejoicing by all present."

When Tamsin's speech was complete, the hall stirred with shouts and cheers, an acclaim that echoed moments later from the throats of the mob outside. The courtiers gave a brave show of approval as Sir Isembard assumed the baron's raised seat. Shortly afterward, at the new baron's command, the outer doors were flung open and a half-dozen of the town rioters admitted. These handpicked ruffians knelt dutifully before the new baron and, at a gesture from him, laid hold of the old one, who still fumbled and pleaded in his agony and confusion. They dragged him out into the bailey-yard, where his screaming soon recommenced in earnest.

"There now, the people's will is served," Tamsin declared. "Your former captain may be hanged, or quartered, or torn to pieces for that matter, but Ninga and I will warrant, by all her godly powers and mine, that he shall never die. Good Isembard, having pledged himself a better lord than Einholtz was, rules under my magical protection. Further, in return for his promise of faith to the supreme goddess, Ninga shall ensure that he enjoy the obedience of the common herd through all the years of his reign.

"A glorious day," Tamsin continued, "the naming-rite of a new goddess, her name drawn large in noble blood! To complete the covenant, there remains but one thing: your contribution, a tithe of sacrifice." She turned slowly, raking the circle of courtiers with her green-eyed stare. "I have sworn, with Ninga's lenience, to condemn only three. Let this be a test of your loyalty to the new baron. Let none falter in obedience to him."

Isembard, following the girl's gesture, arose from his chair. "Stand forth," he declared to the circled watchers.

Slowly, with an uneven movement that rippled hesitantly around the circle, all rebel officers took one step forward toward the center.

"Well enough, then." Bemusedly now, Tamsin went to those standing nearest her and began peering into their faces. "First, for my sergeants-at-arms, you . . . and you."

Obediently, if a little hesitantly, the two helmeted warriors she indicated stepped out of the circle and fell in behind her.

"Now then, to find a face . . . after so many years, 'tis most difficult." Musing aloud to the doll cradled in her arm, she moved around the circle, looking critically at her new worshipers. The women, linen-wrapped and fur-caped, she passed over easily; the men, peering nervously at her from behind mustaches and brushed or braided beards, she examined more closely. She also propped her doll up to a position where it could seem to review the faces. One after another, the lords of Urbander passed beneath its flatly disconcerting stare.

"Your memory is keen, O Ninga," she murmured. "Aid me if you can, to find those who were seen only from afar

127

. . . so fleetingly, so long ago. If you can point to one who has given you offense . . . Ah, there he stands. Seize him!'' The doll gave a flip . . . whether it was some divine omen or merely a twitch of Tamsin's enfolding arm, none could say; but the pigtailed soldier, a high-ranking baronial knight, was instantly locked in the grip of the two burly sergeants and marched away, to be chained to one of the heavy andirons of the broad fireplace.

The pair of marshals soon returned, and Tamsin resumed her search. ''Look carefully, Ninga. Einholtz's henchmen were faithful and steady in the old days. Many of these present must have marched and ravaged with him through the forests near our home. Aye, Ninga, mark well those looks of doubt . . .'' In a moment, with a strangled cry, another victim was chosen to be dragged scuffing and struggling to the fire.

''Aye, Ninga, now the little foxes are penned. There remains only the wolf. The end of the circle draws near. Look sharp, old friend, for one whose heart is corrupted by guilt.''

As Tamsin neared the starting point in her circuit of the hall, one of the officers—a high lieutenant, Bohemund by name, who had been field commander of the two men already seized—forsook his stern composure and sprang forth out of the circle.

''This is a wizardly farce!'' he shouted angrily. ''Are we expected to yield up our lives to a prating monstress and her puppet?'' As he spoke, he yanked his curved sword from its scabbard.

Exiting its metal sheath, the rapier-blade rang with a rasping note . . . which sound, instead of dying out naturally, continued to grow and chime until it drowned the warrior's angry shouts and became an ear-wrenching din. Many of those in the hall cowered back from the noise, or covered their ears, while Bohemund himself, casting down his blade and thereby only redoubling the cacophony, sank to his knees with both hands ·clasping his bleeding ears, and agonized, muted howls issuing from his mouth.

As suddenly as it had begun, the supernatural clangor subsided. In its wake, Tamsin was heard to murmur to her doll, "Good, my Ninga. So much for the power of steel against sorcery!" The courtiers reassembled, eying the witch-girl in leery awe. The three male sacrifices—including deaf, maddened Bohemund—were duly taken, stripped of their armor, shackled hand and foot, and given to the ravening and ever-growing mob outside the hall.

When at length the new chorus of screaming had dwindled away outside, the seeress went up onto the balcony to address the crowd, above whose gaping masses one of four severed heads, raised high on bloody stakes, still mouthed and gaped in soundless agony. Tamsin's speech was brief and to the point.

"You have taken vengeance on the rascal Einholtz, whose numberless crimes were but a small part of the misrule of King Typhas in distant Sargossa. Your new leader, Baron Isembard—" here she led forth the pretender, to furious acclaim "—has declared himself a faithful follower of the goddess Ninga, and an ally in her crusade against the tyranny of the old king and the old church. Thus begins a new age in the life of our land. Your rebellion is completed, but Brythunia's has only begun! All hail Ninga!"

EIGHT

Ax of Justice

Death, as so often before, took a passionate fancy to Conan. The grim, faceless specter, during the hours and days following his encounter with the cave-bear, wooed and coaxed him like an eager lover. It overhung him as closely and heavily as the night-black petals of a breath-stealing jungle lotus, even as it spread out beneath his reclining form like a pool of soft, thirsty quicksand. Death whispered soothingly in his ear, too, tempting him with its dark delights. As time fled past, the Cimmerian felt himself almost yielding to its restful languor.

What prevented him from doing so was some unknown, torturous power. Each time he felt ready to lapse into blissful peace, rough hands would seize him and tug him back to semi-wakefulness, back to the shuddering chills and parching fevers that racked his earthly hours. Light would pierce his eyes, and cold water would be dashed into his face . . . or poured down his throat, making him choke and gag, lacking breath even to curse decently. Then hard, insistent hands would pound and pummel his back—or worse, poke and pry at the raw, burning wounds in his side. His nostrils were violated by the sharp, acrid odors of unguents and potions, while his ears filled up with the rattle of charms and the guttural rasping of rough, foreign spells. These torments, this meaningless round of semi-oblivion and brusque, insistent handling, seemed endless to the sufferer's crippled, brutish awareness. It stretched on eternally, ceaselessly.

Even so, there came a day when Conan, feeling harsh light falling across his face, was able to crack his eyes and let the rays flood in. The effort of doing so was vast, each eyelid seeming to weigh more than a talent of silver. He doubted he would have the strength to close them again soon.

Above him, he saw the vast dome of heaven—a web of curving, converging lines with a bright, blazing disk at its center. The light was exquisitely painful, and his vision blurred with tears into which swam, at that instant, a face and form of such loveliness as to sear right through the haze.

Conan felt convulsions travel the length of his body, leaving behind a weary, fever-spent weakness. The concentric universe overhead resolved itself into the woven, translucent peak of a pole-framed hut; a smoke hole was left open at its center, through which a column of blazing-bright sky streamed in. The impossibly lovely form was that of a woman, brown-haired and tan-skinned. She seemed somehow familiar to him, though her features resembled no race he had ever known.

There was little in her garb to strike him as foreign, especially since the maid's outfit was so laughably sparse. It consisted of several objects woven into her hair, most of them bird-shapes cut from light tan wood; an array of three necklaces across her bare chest, adorned with carefully polished bits of tooth, bone, and soapstone; and around her waist an artfully fringed and braided thong that supported a somewhat larger and more elaborate pendant just below her navel.

The healthy, nubile body set off by these objects was enchanting enough, endowed with full, sun-browned breasts and softly rounded hips, belly, and thighs. Her face bore planes and hollows that gave it an equally captivating interest, especially as she knelt breathlessly close to his paralyzed body. Her aspect combined the sturdy, firm-jawed look of northern maids with the dusky skin, dark brown hair, and hazel eyes of southern Hyborian beauties—and a further trace of the fine, sinuous shaping of more easterly faces.

This combination made her countenance—demure and expressionless as she gazed down on him in the hazy light—an endlessly fascinating puzzlebox of small surprises. She leaned further over him, and her various adornments, both handmade and naturally bestowed, dangled tantalizingly near his nerveless face and hands. He caught her scent, and again some faint memory whispered to him, as before in a half-remembered forest. A white heat kindled in his forehead, and a new tremor passed through his fever-ravaged body.

His exquisite agony was interrupted as the woman seized hold of his cheeks, pinched his mouth open, and forced something wet and bitter between his jaws. He jerked and struggled, mustering a feeble effort that barely dislodged her stubborn grip. Nevertheless, he managed to spit out whatever it was.

The woman recoiled, her face a kaleidoscope of foreign emotions. "Juwala!" she cried angrily.

Conan, in his fog of weakness, waited resignedly for some hulking male of that name to come charging through the hut's open doorway. Instead, the woman turned impatiently and rummaged in a basket near the door. She produced a handful of limp, uprooted weeds and, turning back to her patient, shook their gray-green foliage in his face. "Juwala! Juwala!" she repeated insistently.

The plant, he vaguely recognized, was a flowering ditch-weed of a kind he had heard was useful as medicine. Its leaves, macerated and moistened, apparently were the stuff she had been putting into his mouth; it was nothing poisonous, just a folk remedy of dubious value. This time, when she picked up the damp ball out of the dust and shoved it between his lips, he chewed weakly and disconsolately, then did his best to swallow. His efforts were helped along by a choking draught of water the woman ladled into his mouth with a gourd spoon.

So he came to trust Songa's good intentions—for such was her name, as he learned during the hours she spent overseeing his recovery. She was pleasant-natured, entirely matter-of-fact about his physical incapacity and his grisly, suppurating wounds, and amazingly tolerant of the little pats and prods he would venture as she bent over him and ministered to his needs. It was only when, in the flush of his rapidly returning strength and agility, he sought to catch and clasp her to him that she would rebuff him, with a deftly planted knee or elbow, or by dousing him with cold water from a nearby vessel, or perhaps by thumping him with the container itself.

Even this she managed good-naturedly. Songa seemed, on the whole, to enjoy her labors and trials, as proven by the long afternoons she spent sitting just outside Conan's reach, resting on her shapely folded legs and haunches, patiently teaching him the correct names of everyday objects.

She respected his wounds, too, recognizing them as the work of a fearsome animal. In return, with a mixture of pensiveness and pride, she showed him the white parallel scars on her ankle and thigh that had been made by a mountain cat.

The others of her family or tribe seemed wholly tolerant of her efforts. Occasionally a tall, muscular, dark-limbed man—his face similar to Songa's, if heavier and less benevolent-looking—would stoop down before the hut's doorway and peer inside, but he never interrupted the two of them or did any more than grunt. From the inquiry Conan contrived to make, he gathered that the man's name was Aklak.

There were others as well, a score of them at least, as Conan guessed from the occasional babble of voices and the varied sounds of chopping, chipping, scraping, and chanting that went on outside the hut in the course of a day. When he tried to ask how many, sketching stick-figures in the dust beside his pallet, Songa would obligingly rattle off an endless list of semi-pronounceable names—Orpa, Emda, Urga, Ekdus, Amawak, Piliwak, Fnan—but she seemed vague about numbers amounting to more than five.

It may have been deliberate, Conan knew, arising from a wish not to reveal too much about her kinsmen. When she had tried to question him about his own tribe, he must have seemed less than forthcoming; there was nothing he could do but wave his hands overhead to indicate someplace far, far away, beyond forests and mountains. He tried to explain further by making rushing, roaring sounds through his teeth and flowing motions with his hands.

"*Targokan*," Songa understood, repeating her word for river. That became Conan's second name to all her people: *Targoka*, river-man.

The language she taught him had no parallel in his experience. It was unlike the common eastern Hyborian dialects, and for that matter, the Turanian and Hyrkanian tongues, so it gave Conan no clue as to his whereabouts. Instead—and to his surprise, he found this gratifying— Songa's speech seemed to prove that her tribe and her broader people, if any, lacked significant contact with the great world of his experience. As far as he could tell, these valley dwellers had no name for themselves other than *Atupan*, "people." Songa herself showed little interest in the foreign words Conan tried to teach her, or even in his own birth-name. She may have assumed that no real human language existed other than Atupan, and that before learning her primitive tongue, Conan possessed only the vague gestures and grunts he resorted to in her presence.

If so, the misconception did not trouble Conan; he had no wish to carry the scourge of civilization to these untrammeled innocents. Their way of life, from what he could gather of the sounds and activities going on outside the hut—and from the variety of mashed, boiled, and roasted foods that were brought to him, and from the array of proud male and giggling female faces that peered in at the door—their life seemed easy and congenial to him, almost like coming home to the Cimmerian camps and strongholds of his boyhood.

Having mastered the fundamental challenges to survival—as Conan himself thought he had been doing splendidly before his encounter with the cave-bear—these people lived a relatively comfortable life, in a relaxed harmony with nature that was only occasionally lethal. Their prosperity, primarily due to the lush, varied landscape around them, was even greater than that legended to the Cimmerian by his hill-grandsires in the age before the arrival of land-stealing southerners and steel weaponry set the Cimmerian race on a permanent course of war and destruction.

These notions, during the dim, lazy period of Conan's convalescence, came to him not so much as thoughts and resolutions, but rather as feelings, smells, images. Following Songa's example, he became less reflective of civilized ways, falling back to a more basic level of awareness. His senses were again renewed, particularly those of smell and fine hearing, which he had deliberately learned to repress in the raucous, reeking hive of the city. What he desired now was plain: the trenchers of honeyed, steaming pine-nut gruel brought in by his buxom nursemaid, the clumps of berries, pots of stewed greens, and hanks of smoked venison that he eventually mustered up adequate strength and spittle to masticate and swallow.

Once those immediate needs were satisfied, his next goals were already in sight: the soft contours and mystic recesses of Songa's splendid body, accented rather than concealed by the flimsy trinkets, capes of soft animal fur, and drooping flower garlands that she adopted in lieu of clothing. The meaning of these natural promptings of his, their advisability in some abstract system or their ultimate consequences, Conan never paused to consider; he merely followed his urges as his returning strength allowed.

Unfortunately, his ability to secure this higher goal was hindered—first by abject weakness and the pain of his gaping wounds, and later by the subtle wiles and precautions of his intended prey. Songa, through some natural instinct of her own, continued to withhold the lushness of her charms from her admirer's touch, if not from his vision. Conan's strength returned rapidly; and at its best, his physical power was unequaled. Yet even so, it was not in his nature to feign weakness or to lie in wait for a woman as if he were some stalking flesh-eater. His amorous cravings demanded assurances of female readiness or complicity, which Songa always contrived to deny him—even after fervent preliminary nuzzlings and caresses—but without permanently closing off hope of agreement. In this tricky course, she seemed more adept than any civilized girl Conan had known.

"Songa," he called to her across the hut as soon as his language skills permitted, "come and rest." He patted the coarse reed mat beneath him. "You come by me and lie down, Songa. We rest and make happy-happy."

"No, Targoka," she told him absently, flicking a hand horizontally in the Atupan gesture of firm denial. She pronounced the words slowly and distinctly through habit, as if speaking to a child. "No lie down, no make happy-happy. Targoka too sick."

"Targoka not sick," Conan insisted, half-arising from his pallet. "Targoka strong." He gestured at his side, which had finally scabbed over into a thick crust with very few open, runny crevices. He tried to formulate the concept that he would be sick if he didn't make happy-happy soon, but gave up for lack of words. "Songa come rest with Conan," he finished lamely.

"No come, no lie down," Songa repeated. "Targoka too sick, no go out of hut." She gestured to the doorway, which was now shadowed with early dusk. "Targoka no go out, Aklak no kill." She pantomimed striking someone with an ax. "Later, Targoka not sick. Targoka go out of hut, Aklak kill. Then make happy-happy."

"Uh?" Conan asked, feeling hairs stir at the back of his neck. He tried to fathom the various possibilities. "Aklak kill Conan . . . Targoka?" he clarified.

"Yes, Aklak kill Conan." The forest girl shrugged, as if the result was of little consequence. "Conan kill Aklak, then be happy-happy."

Conan temporarily dismissed the problem of how he could make happy-happy with her once he was killed. Instead, he asked, "Songa make happy-happy with Aklak?"

"No!" The forest girl had been mashing ground nuts in a calabash with a heavy wooden pestle. Now, straightening without warning, she flung the pestle at Conan, striking him smartly on the shoulder. "No make happy-happy with *oonka*! Targoka no say bad-bad!"

"What is *oonka*?" Conan asked, wary. Even so, he left

the pestle lying on the mat, hoping Songa would come to retrieve it and let him snare her in his embrace.

"*Oonka—oonka!*" Songa said impatiently. Leaning forward, she sketched four stick-figures in the dirt beside the fire, two large and two small. Then, to clarify further, she pantomimed removing an infant from her loins and holding it to her breast. Then she removed another shadow-infant and held it to the other breast. "*Oonka,*" she said, wiggling a finger to denote the gender of the second baby.

"Oh, *oonka,* brother!" Conan interpreted aloud in his native Cimmerian, which was the most rudimentary tongue he knew. "Aklak is *oonka.* No make happy-happy with Songa." Nodding heartily to signify agreement with the fundamental taboo, he remembered to flap his hand up and down at chin level in the Atupan fashion. But the main issue still troubled him. "*Oonka* kill Conan?"

"Yes, kill." Songa made snatching and grappling gestures between her hands in the air before her.

Relaxing somewhat, Conan eased back on his mat. From Songa's performance, he guessed that the word he interpreted as "kill" might only mean "fight." There was no difficulty there; the prospect even sounded appealing.

"Aklak kill Targoka," Songa was continuing. "Get rid of bad-bad. Targoka make steal Songa." She now affected a righteous, wronged look. "Targoka look Songa naked, too much bad-bad," she finished, primly straightening the charm that dangled across her bare belly.

Conan lacked the strength just then to pursue such intricacies, but their meaning became clear over the next few days of language lessons. Evidently the Atupan tribes relied heavily on the practice of woman-stealing—a virtual necessity, given the small size of their tribe and their firm prohibition against incest. Conan heartily approved. Having seen countless clans and villages living in remote places, he sensed that the Atupans could never produce individuals as sturdy and splendid as Aklak and Songa if they resorted to inbreeding. Woman-raiding had been an honored Cimmerian custom, he was told, though in his early days, a good part of the raiding and ravishing had involved the sleek, perfumed females of the southern invaders.

In any case, the theft of women among the several Atupan tribes that roved these forests and meadowlands was openly accepted. Marriageable girls would be left unguarded by the men during long ritual baths—preferably in groups, Conan gathered, since they preferred to be abducted along with friends so as to ease the pangs of separation from their families. The rapine was mutual among neighboring tribes, and usually limited to girls as yet unmated, so that it seldom resulted in war or violent retaliation. Since harems and slavery were unknown among these primitives, the other obvious abuses did not occur.

Songa's case, Conan learned, was somewhat singular; she lacked any age-mates as mature as herself, and she was also reluctant to be carried off because of her attachment to Aklak and to her aging mother, Nuna. Her father Tubuhan, a distinguished man of the tribe, had perished years before in a bison stampede, making the old woman dependent on her offspring.

Songa, at the time of her encounter with Conan, had not been expecting a strange male to burst out of the forest and carry her away—certainly not an outlandish one who looked half-dead with grisly wounds. Their current encampment lay far from any known tribe's territory, but her male kinsmen were in easy reach and had helped her carry the foreigner's bulky, senseless body to the hut. Part of the mirth of the young women who now peered in on him, he realized, was at the notion of him—a strapping hunter of some foreign tribe—having been abducted by Songa.

One further aspect of their meeting that served to complicate matters was the issue of Songa's nakedness at the time. Ritual nudity, he understood; it was a distinction that would scarcely have mattered between a tribesman and his properly stolen mate. Rather, it seemed here to be some odd elaboration of the Atupans' incest taboo.

And a ludicrous one at that. The notion that some dangling copper gewgaw, along with a few jiggling strands of buckskin thong, could make Songa's lush, ripe nakedness any less pure or prurient was a comical one. Conan would have laughed long and deep if it had not threatened to burst open the partly knit wound in his side. But Songa's complaint though, so to speak, transparent—nevertheless served as a barrier. Beside giving her one more reason to fend off his advances, it raised the prospect of a duel of vengeance, driven by what seemed like mere jealousy and perverse brotherly pride on Aklak's part.

The young tribesman's attitude had grown more provocative of late. Sometimes of an evening, while Conan awaited Songa's appearance with his dinner bowls, he could hear Aklak's sharp voice assail her with grudging remarks about the quantity and distribution of the food. Occasionally, when he thought that his sister lingered overlong with Conan, he would toss angry comments in through the door;

and once during a language lesson at fire-lit dusk, he thrust his pockmarked face straight into the fringed opening and said, as nearly as Conan could translate, "Teach him well the trick of speech, sister. Then he can beg and plead for mercy when I pound him into fish-paste and hurl him back into the river!"

That, for Conan, was enough. Wounds healed or not, he sprang up from his pallet and lunged for the door, only to find Songa crouching there, blocking his way and commanding him to lie back down again. She was a fierce nursemaid; furthermore, Conan thought it would be unseemly to rout her along with her carping kinsman.

So he turned aside and, not troubling with the doorway, burst straight through the wall of the hut. The bent poles were tough, but several pulled free of the ground and parted before his lunge.

There, just before him, gaping at the outcome of the argument, stood Aklak. The burly, tan-skinned savage wore only beads, bison-hide sandals, and the jeweled metal gewgaw that served as a tribal insignia.

It was not in Conan's nature to delay or call out a formal challenge. Anyway, he preferred to fight Aklak without weapons and so lessen the chance of murdering his beloved's brother. Accordingly, he drove straight at his target, bunching one fist like a mallet to strike the man down.

He ran up hard against him, but his fist swung harmless above his adversary's crouching, twisting form. It was an agile enough dodge, and bore a further surprise, for as Aklak spun away, his hard-sandaled foot slammed into Conan's side opposite the place where the bear's claw had laid him open.

142

A wall of pain shimmered in Conan's vision like a blazing curtain, momentarily stopping him. Through it came an exultant victory cry as Aklak whirled back to the attack.

The Atupan used his coarse-shod feet with the same dexterity his sister had shown with her bare ones. Even so, he must have thought the Cimmerian stupid; his new assault came in the form of a straight kick at the crotch, an unmanly blow more suited to sporting games—as one of Conan's countrymen might have launched the grisly trophy in a game of "kick-the-Vanir's-head." Effortlessly, Conan stepped away from the kick. With his ready hand, he caught at the flying ankle, preparing to wrench it upward and send the tribesman crashing onto his neck.

But the devious Aklak, whirling in mid-stride, extended his leg half an ell further. His hard heel drove a mule kick straight into Conan's gut-basket—once, and then again, ruthlessly.

The fighter danced away triumphant, to the cheers of tribe members who had begun to gather 'round. Conan stood stock-still for a moment, battling nothing more tangible than nausea, breathlessness, and a pain that gnawed his vitals like a clawed, fanged dragon-pup striving to be born. When Aklak came spinning back, Conan dodged one darting foot successfully, only to take sharp buffets in the groin and neck from a knee and a hard-heeled hand. In return, he managed to elbow his assailant in the chest, lending extra force and speed to his departure.

The Atupan took longer to spring back this time, and Conan was ready for him. As the lean, wiry leg flew up, aiming once again at Conan's weak side, the Cimmerian's own bare foot lashed up underneath in a kick that, if it had struck the tribesman's crotch cleanly, would have ended the fight, and possibly the family line. Instead, due to Aklak's twisting agility, it glanced off hard tendon and muscle. His balance upset, the Atupan staggered backward toward the broad, blazing fire.

Conan pressed after, his big hands darting before him to rend and pummel. One ham-fisted blow connected with Aklak's temple; while the Atupan reeled from it, Conan laid hold of his neck and shoulder and drew him close, thinking to stifle him into good fellowship. But the tribesman's resources were not expended. As Conan dragged Aklak into the circle of his fullest strength, a sharp, vicious butt of the shorter man's skull smote him on the chin. The blow made him bite his tongue, caused stars to swim in his vision, and loosened his grasp momentarily, almost allowing his wily opponent to break away.

Yet by now, pain was a devalued coin in Conan's inner economy. Instead of grunting or gasping from the smart of his riven tongue, he roared in wrath and, tasting coppery blood, picked his opponent up bodily. Clutching the Atupan by neck and thigh, he hove him, not into the fire but over it, to crash into a mess of pole racks set out for smoke-curing meat and hides on the far side. As he did so, amidst the hubbub of the excited onlookers, some few of whom were scattered by the toss, Conan heard behind him one exuberant cry—a breathy, involuntary cheer that rang forth in the unmistakable voice of Songa.

Aklak, cursing in phrases Conan had never yet heard, rummaged through the mess of poles, meats, hides, and crockery he was flung into. From it he produced something noteworthy: a long, thick-hafted, stone-headed ax suitable for felling and butchering a boar or an ox. This tool he brandished high with an exultant howl of his own. Whirling it dextrously overhead, he advanced around the fire toward Conan.

The Cimmerian, in the fire-lit dusk, found nothing within reach to defend himself with except firewood chunks burned half through, as useless as twigs against Aklak's heavy implement. None of the tribesmen around him came to his defense, but he was certainly not minded to turn and run. So he stood empty-handed, waiting for Aklak, knowing he must rely on quickness alone to counter the massive weapon. He started forward, but was restrained by a tight female grip on his shoulder. Songa's? Had she decided to aid her brother after all, and treacherously?

Meanwhile, the Atupan, stalking to within several paces of Conan, altered the flashing arc of his tomahawk and hurled it—straight aside, into the largest chunk of wood laid in the fireplace. It struck with a red flare, lodging fast and sending a shower of sparks heavenward. A sudden cheer rose as Aklak, his snarl converted to a broad, fixed grin, led others of his tribe forward to hug and pummel Conan in a display that, in spite of its ferocity, the Cimmerian had to assume was congratulatory and friendly.

"Aklak has burned the ax!" he heard voices crying out. "The river-man is forgiven! Now he can go free!"

The villagers were enthusiastic in their rejoicing. Indeed, the occasion seemed to satisfy some pent-up need for revelry. In mere moments, all manner of foodstuffs were produced, a pot of aromatic bark tea was set to brewing, and straw mats were dragged out of the huts to form a convivial space before the fire. While women did most

ot the work, men and children cavorted around the com-
batants, retelling various parts of the fight and pantomim-
ing it, to widespread laughter.

Conan stood amid the jubilant strangers, concealing the
pain and weakness his struggle had brought back to him.
In time, even these faded—so welcome was the exhilaration
of the crowd—with the growing assurance that he had not
been fattened so long for a cook pot, or for sacrifice to
some tribal god.

Songa, now modest and bashful-looking, was brought
before Conan. Aklak and a wizened woman accompanied
her like proud parents. When Songa looked closely at the
sticky blood seeping from Conan's reopened wounds, she
shot him a reproachful look, then turned to Aklak. She angrily denounced her brother, striking at him with a hard
fist where he had kicked and battered her patient. Catching
her wrist to restrain her, Aklak turned and addressed Conan
directly for the first time.

"Songa is a rough, proud woman," he observed gravely.
"She lacks proper respect for a huntsman. She has pro-
voked you and used you badly." He frowned in pious dis-
approval. "You should strike her and teach her her place."

At his words, the tribe around them drew breath and fell
silent. Songa looked up at him with bright, watchful eyes.
Conan paused, aware that his response would have weight,
yet unsure what was expected of him. At last he spoke.

"Songa has done nothing for days but nurse me and tutor
me," he announced. "If she were less proud and strong-
willed, I would not be here. I cannot rebuke her."

"Nonsense," Aklak insisted. "She is a tree-cat! She
spurned you with her foot the day she found you, before

she summoned the men of the tribe to have you dragged here! She told everyone that.''

Sullenly, Conan shook his black mane over his massive shoulders. ''Even so, I would not strike her. I owe her my life.''

Aklak sneered. ''River-men, I suppose, live in fear of their women.'' He looked around to the watchers, who began to snicker.

''Oh, yes,'' Songa joined in suddenly with a spiteful look. ''Targoka's brothers let women abuse them! Men of his tribe never speak their will. See here, I'll show you!'' Pulling free of Aklak's grip, she turned on Conan, smiting him on the breast with doubled fists. ''See, he fears me!'' Reaching up, she clawed his cheek with a sharp-nailed hand.

Lightning-quick, Conan cuffed her on the side of the head. Though slight, the blow stopped her; she clutched at him for balance, then lay her face submissively against his chest.

Word spread swiftly through the crowd. ''He struck her, now they are wedded,'' the men affirmed.

''He loves her,'' the women cried more emotionally. ''Before all the spirits, 'tis proven!''

Aklak, now beaming, embraced both Conan and the woman who clung unashamedly to him. ''Welcome, brother!'' he exclaimed.

The tribe began celebrating in earnest. Dancers fanned out before the fire, stamping and prancing with arms linked, or alternating front-to-back. Hot meats and viands were passed around in gourds and basket-dishes, with Conan and Songa being made to scorch their fingertips on the first handfuls of each. Later came the singing of legends that Conan could only dimly understand, telling of how animal spirits had fashioned the heavens and the earth. This was not entirely strange to him, though in Cimmeria the worship of dour Crom had relegated these older legends to the rank of children's tales.

The food and universal goodwill lulled him, as did the warm tea, though it did not confound him as fermented spirits would. Through it all, Songa clung meekly to his side with no further outburst of vixenish temper.

Yet later in the evening, when the fire burned low and the couples dragged their mats back into their huts, she proved as worthy an adversary as her brother—every bit as strong and demanding, nearly as careless of his wounds, and with an even greater determination to carry the contest through to its finish.

NINE

Mountains of Fire,
Torrents of Blood

Like a flood-maddened river, the crowd poured into the streets of the capital. No mere deluge of water, this—rather, a seething torrent of molten stone, like the river of holy fire that had at the goddess Ninga's command cleansed and consumed the erring southern city of Phalander. This flood, like that other cataclysm, left devastation in its wake: ravening flame and ruin and the seared, writhing bodies of the unrepentant. It coursed through the city's dark-roofed labyrinth under gray, overcast skies, its way marked by pillars of smoke and yellow flames surging heavenward. The seething human cataract poured over heaps of rubble and broken bodies, leaving behind quiet eddies that puddled red with blood.

Swifter than fire, the holy torrent of rebellion had spread from Urbander to Tamsin's home valley and a hundred other disaffected rural districts and small cities. Inevitably the fires converged on Sargossa—the vast metropolis of Brythunia, home to the gilt-trimmed Temple of Amalias and the lofty Imperial Palace. Fanned by winds of unrest and heresy against the old gods, the greedy blaze now threatened to scorch the fabled Gryphon Throne itself and unseat its royal denizen, King Typhas the Sly.

Fiercely now, the mob surged through plaza and boulevard, carrying destruction to every shrine of Amalias and every doubter of the bloody new faith. With fierce abandon, Ninga's adherents pillaged and rampaged, repaying the wrongs of half a lifetime's tyranny. Yet such was their discipline and devotion, in the midst of chaos, that a slender young woman and her pampered doll, riding in a chariot at the middle of the press, could go unmolested—screened, to be sure, by a double row of drilled pikemen, and flanked by mounted guards from the revolutionary high command.

The moving perimeter was carefully maintained amid the throng, not only by horse and foot guards, but by the zealous horde itself. For this was none other than Tamsin, High Priestess and Oracle, clad in a loose green, flower-embroidered robe that set off her piercing eyes . . . and riding with her, nestled under her solicitous arm, the new goddess Ninga herself. Love and devotion made everyone respect the divine presence, as did the deepest, devoutest fear rising from the mystic powers of these two. For was it not whispered that far to the north, in the now-holy city of Urbander—deep in the crypt of Ninga's bright, new-built temple—there abode a living witness to the goddess's power? No talkative witness this, but an eloquent one nonetheless: a severed, breathless, bloodless head that mouthed and gaped in endless agony, giving silent testimony to the casual, terrible power of the High Goddess and her High Priestess . . . and never, ever dying.

So it was that the human flood, with the chariot borne in its midst like a royal barge, entered Sargossa's main temple square. Here the lavender marble columns of the Temple of Amalias reared tall under the great dome, the last and mightiest bastion of the Imperial church. And here the High Priest Epiminophas, newly raised to leadership, had vowed to turn back the rising tide of heresy . . . if necessary, by a new confrontation with the witch-priestess herself.

Here, too, King Typhas, with deft economy, had positioned his elite troops for the defense of the capital. ''If the mob would run riot, why, let them do so,'' he remarked to his generals on the eve of Tamsin's arrival. ''In their own neighborhood, that is! Let them level their wretched tenements, battle and burn and rape one another, and be scattered and diminished in drunkenness and pillage! With Imperial regiments cordoning the borders of the respectable districts, I can easily contain them. And by sweeping the central square, where all streets conjoin, we shall crush them.''

Yet the king's forces did not immediately march forth to battle out of the palace gardens, the noble tomb-yards, and the low-walled estates where they waited with grounded halberds. King Typhas stood in command from the loftiest tower of his palace, accompanied by a pair of signal officers with semaphore fans, which remained motionless. In his frugal way, Typhas hesitated to commit an army where a single man might do the job.

Instead, striding out onto one of the gilt-carpeted marble promontories that flanked the massive temple steps came white-bearded Epiminophas to confront the rioters. The High Priest had changed greatly in the few years since he first saw Tamsin; his square-trimmed beard had grown out hoar-white, his figure had slimmed, and his face was less sleek and pudgy, chiseled instead with priestly dignity. His bearing was altered from a complacent waddle to the light, direct step of purposefulness. In place of the rich, fur-trimmed gown of his former district priesthood, he now wore plain gray robes lacking ornament.

Epiminophas did not surrender himself to the mob but kept to the terrace above it, with a row of sword-belted acolytes taking its place behind. This, it seemed likely, would be adequate to protect his retreat if the mob should begin to swarm up the temple steps—which, to signify the greatness of Amalias and to humble the pilgrims, were hewn each half as tall as a man, and so had to be clambered up using arms and legs together. Epiminophas's gold-fringed perch loomed as high as ten of these steps, standing forth sheerly above the broad plaza. Thus it was that the priest could survey the crowd, safe at least momentarily from its smoldering discontent.

To any who could gaze out over that square, the sight was an intimidating one: a bobbing sea of heads, a forest of waving fists with makeshift weapons and standards raised aloft at crazy angles. Moving toward the front of the mob were several long, painted banners, each one affixed to a series of poles held vertical by a score or more individuals. As these billowed and snaked nearer through the crowd, the temple's defenders could see all too clearly what they portrayed. The long, colorful paintings depicted the destruction of Phalander-town by fire-belching volcanoes, famous massacres by Ninga's holy zealots of priests faithful to Amalias, and other grim triumphs of the rebellion. Yet the paintings, though lurid, did not seem exotic against the backdrop of pillaged streets and flaming buildings that ringed the square under dark-clouded skies.

Far back in the crowd trundled the humble chariot carrying Tamsin and her god-puppet. Without waiting for the conveyance to halt or even to draw near the priest's bastion, Epiminophas commenced.

"Children of Amalias." His voice tolled forth over the angry roar of the crowd, echoing from the facades of distant buildings. "Errant sons and daughters, I welcome you to the home of your father and his servants."

The crowd, surprised by the priest's welcoming tone, diminished its chantings and mutterings to hear him; except for horselaughs and skeptical cries, and the scuff of still-moving feet, quiet reigned. Thus Epiminophas achieved his greatest victory, that of merely being heard.

"I know that some of you refute your Great Father's holy power, as the child will mock and defy the parent. Some of you would even level this holy house of his to shards and dust if you could. Many more have allowed doubt and heresy into their hearts, in place of righteousness and pious teachings." He paused with one arm extended and swept the crowd with a stately gesture, signifying that he addressed everyone. Ignoring the hoots and hisses, he continued, "That is why it is well that you come here."

"Ninga is the One God!" a zealot near the front screamed.

By not contesting the assertion, Epiminophas was able to defuse the crowd's anger, and he went on, "I say your presence here is good, because Great Father Amalias means to heal all doubters and embrace all heretics. For troubled souls like yours, his temple is a haven of peace and healing. None knows that better than I . . . because, until recently, I was one of you! My sin, too, was heresy; my guilt was doubt."

At this, even the hecklers and japers were silenced—for who in the hostile crowd would disagree with self-denunciation by the High Priest? He availed himself well of the silence.

"Know, fellow Brythunians, that far, far greater is my sin and guilt than yours—because even as I inwardly repudiated our Father Amalias, I stooped at his holy altars and donned the sacred robes as his servant. All the while, I lacked faith—yet I made no open, honest show of my disbelief, but concealed it under priestly vestments and pious manners. In my hypocrisy, I mocked the High God's commands and made my false obedience a reason for amassing wealth, comforts, and tyrannous power."

"Scoundrel!" an onlooker exclaimed. "You still do it. Why bother to pretend otherwise?"

"The state priests all steal from the people," another voice chimed in. "Every one of them shall be burned!"

"My teachings were hollow," Epiminophas cried. "My aims were corrupt, I admit it!" His frenzy again headed off the mob's turmoil. "My dishonesty may have helped to plant the seeds of heresy in all your breasts. For that, I am truly sorry!"

"Ninga is God," a group of fanatics had begun chanting. Epiminophas was forced to resume his speech above their clamor.

"How have I changed? Hear me, please. On seeing the strength and belief of the Lord Amalias's enemies, I had to question my own lack of faith, and to doubt the power of doubt itself! I asked myself then, Brythunians, and I ask you now: is this great temple, the grandest in any of the Hyborian kingdoms, built on hollow untruth?" His arm, in a theatric gesture, indicated the massy pile above him. "Have all the vast multitudes of our Great Lord's faithful, who were, and are, and shall be yet again—have they all been deluded by guile and greed?"

Over cries of "Yes, yes!" he insisted: "No! And I shall furnish you proof! But first I ask you, are all the elaborations of our Amalian teachings—the Laws, the Prophecies, the Divine Revelations of our great race's origin, and the names and histories of the lesser gods—are those things all foolish lies? Those great truths we teach our children from earliest speech?" Too wise to pause for an answer, the priest pressed on, "No, it cannot be! If there is any such thing as divinity in this world, why, it has not spurned and made a mock of our great empire! Nay, if gods exist at all, then Lord Amalias exists, and is the greatest of them!" Waving both arms, by sheer force of emphasis, he held the watchers' attention.

"Brythunians, I have ventured down into the forbidden catacombs! I have read the ancient petroglyphs and pored through parchments so old they crumbled with the weight of my gaze! I have delved at the very roots of our ancient faith, and I am here to tell you, and to show you, that Amalias lives!"

"All lies, all nonsense!" the zealots jeered. "Enough of this priestly prattle!"

"It was our Ninga who restored your faith, Epiminophas," another accused, "not your old dead god!"

"In truth," Epiminophas said, answering his tormentors directly for the first time, "I owe a debt to the witch Tamsin and her sorcerous doll, who have reaffirmed to me the power of magic. We all owe them thanks for awakening us—"

"Mark him well, O faithful!" a listener cried. "This is the priest who first gave Ninga her name in the sacred scrolls at the Abbas Dolmium. Mark him for a coward!"

Above a scattering of laughter, Epiminophas continued, "Aye, mark me! For I now understand that all this strife, all this turmoil—" he gestured out over the crowd "—that all this is part of our Great Lord's plan to renew and purify our devotion to him, once he demonstrates his true, awesome power. Then Ninga, then all other gods, will shrink and quail before his strength. Know you, citizens, that you are not meant to abandon Lord Amalias and follow this new pretender—" his finger pointed at Tamsin's chariot, which was finally drawing up opposite his perch "—for I ask you, is a great god but a dust-broom, to be used only so long, then cast into the fire and replaced with a new one? Nay, Brythunians, give somber thought to what glory you would be losing, and to what foul burden you might be taking on, by toiling under this grubby, gourd-headed witch-doll that has sprung up from the most backward and ignorant corner of our empire, like some vile, spotted toadstool from a rural dung heap!"

At this remark, the mob's outrage and frenzy burst forth instantaneously. Objects were hurled, most of them falling short of the speaker's lofty perch; chants were set up, to swell like waves through the human sea; spasmodically the whole mass surged forward, trampling and crushing some of its comrades while hurling others up like wavelets onto the high temple steps—where they scurried immediately forward and mounted higher toward the row of sword-bearing guards.

"He profanes the goddess!" the fanatics near Tamsin's chariot cried. "Slay the blasphemer!"

Epiminophas, however, paid scant attention; already he had fallen to his gray-robed knees. Alternately bowing low and supplicating above his head with both arms, he began his prayers and expostulations to Great Amalias.

"O Lord of all gods! O terrible Ancient One," he called out to the storm clouds overhead. "Thy humble servant Epiminophas invokes thee! If thou hearest, Great Lord of the Rivers, pray grant thy patient worshipers some sign."

"Kill him! Silence the devil!" The cry passed from tongue to tongue. "He prays to a dead, corrupt god whose name is infamy!"

At that moment, however, as if in direct answer to the priest's sonorous prayers, thunder murmured faintly overhead. The sound rumbled vague and distant, like a door grating open somewhere in the heavens. Moments later, tentative, scattered raindrops began to fall.

The large, warm spatters drove deep into the dust of roofs and alleyways, giving rise to the charged, musty smell that heralds a thunderstorm. It mingled with the ripe, sweaty stench rising off the angry mob, thereby creating an air of dread anticipation.

"Priestly fool," the zealots cried, "your prayers accomplish nothing! Ninga brings this rain! She mocks you and your old, weak god!''

"Huzzah, give thanks!" Epiminophas nevertheless exulted. "A thousand humble obeisances, Great Lord, for your all-knowing attention! We have called upon Amalias Pluvias, our High God in his role as rain-bringer," the priest declared to the crowd, "and he answers us! Heaven praise this glorious day! I now beseech Amalias Feroher, Master of Thunders . . . Terrible One, your faithful servants invoke thee! Pray, bring forth the lightnings!"

"This rain comes late for last year's drought in the south," a skeptic was proclaiming, but his words were drowned out by new tollings of thunder, heavier and more distinct. As the crowd looked around, lightning strokes etched themselves above the horizon, and the raindrops fell thicker and faster.

"Aiaa," Epiminophas screamed unto heaven, "Lord Amalias, I pray you, persuade the doubters—and smite down the blasphemers!"

The mob was hardly slowed by the display. If anything, their righteous frenzy increased. The insurgents on the temple steps came up against the swords of the acolytes, and the coppery stench and spatter of blood was added to that of the rain.

"Fraud, hypocrite!" the fanatics cried. "Why does your feeble god Amalias trouble to scratch the sky with lightnings, when Ninga swallows whole cities in flame?"

The rebels took further heart as the broad parade banners, now nearing the front of the crowd, were suddenly lowered and furled. Their function became clear, as behind them were revealed neat ranks of armored horse-soldiers:

carefully drilled cavalry, Nemedian-trained and equipped, the sort proven so grimly effective in the northern province rebellions. A new standard was raised above them, drooping from a steel-pointed lance: the emblem of Isembard, the rebellious Baron of Urbander.

"Huzzah the cavalry!" the mob cried. "For Ninga, unto death!"

"Ho-ho, the dying god sends rain to rust the armor of our Nemedian allies!"—though even as the cry went up, the rain stopped.

"Great Amalias, now is the moment—ugh-uhrk!"

From among the horsemen grouped near Isembard, an ugly, blunt-nosed crossbow was raised. Its twanging snap sent an arrowshaft whirring over the heads of the crowd— straight into the heart of Epiminophas. The priest, with his next prayer transfixed in his chest, toppled and died.

"Rejoice, the false prophet is dead!"

"Ninga is triumphant!" As if in confirmation, the sullen rumblings of thunder had ceased.

Sharp-eyed observers stood with King Typhas atop his lofty tower. When they reported the death of the High Priest, the storming of the temple, and the uncloaking of the rebel cavalry, an order was conveyed by swiftly flashing semaphore fans. Moments later, Imperial household troops and mounted guards moved forth through broad gateways and over low walls to confront the armored vanguard of the mob.

Who might prevail in such a battle? The outcome was difficult to judge. The Imperials, well-fed, well-mounted, splendidly trained and armored as they were, with crack morale and ample experience at the ruthless craft of city fighting—even these elite warriors, facing off against hard-eyed northern campaigners in equally tight and heavy armor, with the many-handed, fanatical mob pressing at their back to pull down and tear apart whatever enemy the horsemen had bowled over—even these staunch defenders could promise no easy victory.

It would be a vicious fight, spilling over into the gardens and stable-yards of aristocratic dwellings, the courts and porticoes of temples, and the villas of the empire's richest merchants. It would have brought greater devastation to Sargossa—if King Typhas had not called a truce

Yet he did so, sending his First Steward Basifer hurrying down from the castle to strike a conditional peace with Tamsin and Isembard. Thus it was that the young witch's chariot, and by her side the baron astride his battle-charger set out for the castle. With Tamsin on the chariot's platform stood stepbrother and fellow-priest Arl. Flanked by three other highborn, clanking equestrians, they followed a phalanx of Imperial knights.

The crowd left behind in the temple plaza roared in mingled triumph, disappointment, suspicion, and apprehension. The summer rainstorm conjured by slain Epiminophas—or merely taken advantage of, some few guessed, by shrewd timing on his part—had all but dissipated. Only occasional distant lightnings etched the southern horizon and a few volleys of rain spattered the crowd. Most of the teeming rioters were secretly grateful that Ninga had relied on a crossbow rather than her dreaded magic, and that the apocalyptic battle foreseen between the old god and the new had not come to pass. Yet other, more rabid believers felt vaguely dissatisfied, cheated of the supernatural spectacle and the fierce, bloody strife that had seemed imminent.

Most of these zealots were satisfied for the moment with looting and defiling the Temple of Amalias—pulling down ornate tapestries, toppling idols, and hounding forth the last few acolytes and vestal maidens who cowered within. Soon there would be holy torments, public burnings and quarterings, to occupy the mob. Yet in spite of the temporary peace, there remained the prospect that a battle with King Typhas's forces would be unleashed. The Urbander cavalry waited ready, its steeds champing and pawing a scant dozen paces from the iron-masked muzzles of the enemy horse troops.

One worrisome prospect, a cause for vigilance, was that the priestess Tamsin and her small retinue, even traveling under the goddess Ninga's powerful protection, might be slain or taken prisoner by wily King Typhas. Or worse, they might unwittingly sell themselves and their loyal followers into some unwise bargain with the reigning tyrant. Yet surely, the worshipers told themselves, great Ninga would not permit such an injustice . . . ?

Goddess, priestess, step-priest, and knights were led into the palace. They passed through an elaborate defensive maze of cullised gates, narrow courtyards, and barred vestibules, into the main audience chamber. King Typhas had retired for this meeting to his seat of honor, the legendary Gryphon Throne of Brythunia. At the head of the long, intricately vaulted hall it stood, beneath the multicolored arabesques of a wondrous octagonal window, formed of ten thousand transparent gems set in delicate metal webwork high overhead. By its light the monarch slouched on the vast ebony chair, a single chunk of black stone carved in the shape of a crouching mythical beast.

The king sat on a cushion in the lap of the animal, whose foreclaws rested on its bent knees, with lion and bird talons picked out alike in keen points of purest emerald. Above the king—aggrandizing, yet somewhat diminishing, his mortal form—hung the gold-beaked, vulpine head with eyes carved of gloating rubies. Arching up behind were the half-open wings, resplendent in plumage carved of platinum and mother-of-pearl.

Typhas himself, lounging in a simple doublet of gold-trimmed purple, with gold sword-chain about his waist and a fine, narrow gold circlet crowning his balding brow, was less whelming in appearance than his massive throne. His warriorly muscles had long since collapsed to the paunchy slack of middle age, his campaigner's bronze skin had washed out tallow-pale, and his conqueror's erect bearing now stooped to the more clerkly posture suitable for sign-ing numberless writs and sitting through obscure, inter-minable counsel. Yet there was about him a remnant of restless energy, signaled by his darting gaze and his con-tinual shifting in the high seat. These things suggested an active, penetrating mind.

The legation approached the raised end of the throne room, where it was cordoned off by a velvet cable. As they did so, a plumed herald's voice rang forth. "Your Majesty, the First Chancellor begs to approach the throne. In his company: the rebel knight Isembard, pretended Baron of Urbander; the proscribed seeress Tamsin; the warlock Arl; and three proscribed gentlemen-at-arms."

"Approach." At a gesture from the king, Tamsin, Isembard, and the chancellor were conducted forward toward the throne. Arl and the three rebel knights, meanwhile, were kept back behind the cable with the small throng of courtiers and military officers who waited on the king. Coming to the fringed end of the plush carpet before the dais, the chancellor knelt on one knee, then bowed so deeply as to touch his forehead to his other, half-bent knee—an obeisance pointedly omitted by the rebels.

"We should reprimand our court herald," the king amiably began "—have him burned in oil, as seems so much the fashion these days—for failing to proclaim the presence of a goddess among us, alongside these stiff-necked mortal rebels! Therefore let us correct the omission: hail Ninga, soul and spirit of an uprising so strident that it merits even our Imperial attention."

Whether King Typhas spoke satirically, or whether he might be embarking in a roundabout manner on one of his famous stratagems, it was difficult to say. The herald, from his sudden, sweatily pale and grim-faced look, obviously gave weight to his monarch's words; Sir Isembard, ever alert for an offense, looked uncertain whether to take umbrage.

But Tamsin, innocent-seeming as ever, appeared to accept the king's homage as genuine. "Thank you, Typhas," she boldly began, meanwhile propping up her doll to face the ebon throne, "for being the first in your royal peerage to acknowledge what your subjects have long understood."

The king blinked, impressed, then leaned forward on one elbow to answer. "Often we mighty, secure in our high castles, are slow to attend to stirrings and upheavals in the farm fields and city gutters. 'Tis hard to know how broad and portentous they may become."

"Even so," Baron Isembard declared, obviously wanting to press the king and have his voice heard, "when miracles are sung and celebrated throughout the land, when ancient prophecies unfold, and when the old kings and gods are cast out of their thrones, it hardly serves as a fit excuse for a king to vouchsafe ignorance."

"Sir Knight, some respect, I must insist—" the black-browed first steward set out to rebuke Isembard. But the king waved him quiet; Typhas betrayed neither outrage nor fear at the rebel knight's harsh impetuousness. He answered patiently.

"Where miracles and prophecies are proclaimed by the rabble, anyone with a viewpoint as elevated as our own is bound to have considerable skepticism. After all, we have gulled the commoners often enough ourselves to know how easily it can be done." He smiled. "As to topplings from thrones, be assured, my ersatz baron, that you will never unseat our reign. This interview does not concern our Imperial survival, but our convenience and enhanced power . . . possibly yours as well, Isembard, if you go carefully."

"The king recognizes the new goddess Ninga," Tamsin spoke up, "yet doubts the miracles she has performed. Know, Typhas," she said with a cautionary glance at the doll nestled in the crook of her elbow, "that our sacred mistress does not smile upon doubters."

"Come, now, young priestess," the king cozened good-naturedly. "Do not try to persuade us that supernatural dooms, demonic conjurings, and summary damnations play so large a part in your religion as the popular myth would have it! If we believed so, we would scarcely be talking so cozily with you, and you would hardly need to be here.

But know that we, in our kingly tenure, have dealt over so many years with priests and prophets of the formerly dreaded Amalias that we have gained, after all, a fairly clear notion of how this god-business plays out. Knowing this, I—we—would guess that there is room here for an understanding.''

"If you mean to say," Isembard broke in again, "that our sacred Ninga is the same sort of lax, feckless god as weak old Amalias, it would be a slander to our faith."

"Nay, nay, of course not," the king soothed the impetuous knight. He switched his position on the taloned arms of his throne, yet kept the force of his looks and arguments directed at the female. "Nay indeed, young Tamsin, the mob that surges from the temple steps clear up to the postern wall outside—" he gestured to the ornate, vaulted end of the chamber "—is enough to apprise us that your Ninga is no weak, common slackard of a goddess! That, indeed, is what we find most likeable about her.

"Yet on the other hand," Typhas continued, "you must confess that your goddess acted with admirable circumspection during the recent dispute with High Priest Epiminophas. She did not unleash her apocalyptic talents on him when she had a chance; she did not engulf the citadel, or even the temple, in burning slag, nor did she upheave the earth and rend apart our much-despised palace, stone from stone. Instead, she relied on no miracle greater than a crack Nemedian crossbowman to achieve her purpose. Admirable economy, we must say!

"That is why, faced with the incontrovertible evidence, we are ready to see reason and acknowledge a change in the tides of our empire." Typhas spoke magnanimously from his place on the throne. "We propose, therefore, to bring the full force of our kingship to bear in your behalf; to repudiate once and for all the old god Amalias, and to embrace your Ninga as the new state divinity, performing public devotions to her in our own royal personage—while maintaining our Imperial dignity, of course—and assisting you to apprehend and punish any dissenters with the full weight of government power."

All those present in the throne room heard the king's words with muted reactions: the guards frozen-faced, the courtiers watchful, some officers barely able to conceal their surprise, the herald and first steward wide-eyed with astonishment. Isembard's response seemed to veer in a moment's time from outrage to equally repressed but gloating anticipation. Only Tamsin showed no inner flurry, her pretty young face looking almost as demure and unsurprised as that of the effigy clasped at her side.

"So you propose, King Typhas," she questioned, "that instead of a new and pious rulership—instead of relief from a thousand grievances, and holy vengeance against their Imperial oppressors—Ninga's followers should be content with their goddess's installation in the same place foul Amalias formerly held, in the same corrupt order, under your odious rule?"

The courtiers' collective gasp at Tamsin's insult was mirrored only slightly in their king, by a faint darkening of his waxy-pale countenance. "Your words are strong ones, Priestess . . . no less than I would expect from one who uses them, along with myth and priestly sleight-of-hand, to inflame a mighty rabble to rebellion." He shook his head, frowning. "Even so, I will ignore them and continue to essay reason, for a while longer at least. For I remind you that one of your small age and experience cannot possibly know what is involved in the governance of a vast empire— the trials and responsibilities, with complications enough to madden a general or confound even a middling king.''

By this time, King Typhas, the consummate negotiator, had managed a return to his former amiable smile. ''You may crave power, my child . . . and in truth have shown yourself entitled to it. More power, indeed, than a woman ever had in Brythunia. But believe me, you would not want my throne.'' He thumped the black stone arm beside him with the heel of one hand. ''It is a hard seat, weighted o'er with cares and tribulations of office—'' he gestured to the looming gargoyle face above his head ''—hounded and haunted by a thousand dilemmas and crises, of which you and your conquering goddess are not the least, nor either the greatest. Nay, my girl, it is not for such a fresh, pretty young lass as you to take on such a burden—''

''No, you are right,'' Tamsin agreed suddenly with the king. ''Your throne is ugly, too dark and garish for this bright chamber—do you not think so, Ninga?'' she queried the goddess at her side. ''Ill-favored too, with such a menacing look about it. Do you not agree?''

As the seeress spoke, others in the room could not but turn their eyes to the throne, so eerie was her manner. And surely enough, a change was occurring. Before their gaze, the bright ruby eyes of the carved gryphon flickered to sinister life, animated by a dark, shadowy interior flame. Stiffly, ponderously, the throne's ebony limbs began to move, flexing and straining to enfold the one seated in its gargantuan lap.

"Nay, it is a monstrosity," Tamsin declared. "I wish it were gone from here—and you with it, Typhas!"

The king, with a sudden, quavering cry of astonishment, tensed to spring up from his place—but too late, for the ebon arms were already closing across his chest. As the bird talons clutched tighter to arrest his writhing struggles, their emerald tips pierced his flesh, and a scream of agony lanced from his convulsing throat.

On either side of the dais, guards sprang forward and attacked the gryphon, but to no avail; their halberds and swords bent and shattered on its hard stone flanks. Meanwhile, the beast reared up, its feline hinder-claws gouging into the ornamental tiles underfoot. The long lion tail swung like a mace, knocking over one guard, then another, with grunts and clankings of armor.

"No, Tamsin," the king screamed, "have mercy, please! Great Goddess, I meant you no disrespect! Release me, please, Ninga! All praise to Ninga—ah, ah, aieee!"

With King Typhas struggling and shrieking in its grip, the monster spread its vast gem-laden wings and gave them a preliminary shake. Then ponderously, impossibly, the stone gryphon rose upward from the dais, its pennons gusting and flashing in the multicolored glare of the overhead window. It spiraled high above the watchers, carrying the trapped king in its embrace even as the maid Tamsin carried her beloved doll. With a buffet of wind and a great noise that drowned out the screaming chorus below, it drove straight out through the many-colored octagonal window, smashing it to a million shards as it vanished from view.

Outside the palace, the rebels thronging the temple square were visited with a truly apocalyptic sight: from the main keep that loomed over the palace wall, out through the ornate window overlooking the square, a giant black demon came with a crash, showering those nearby with jewels of precious beauty and gem-bright droplets of blood. The flying monster wore the shape of Brythunia's Imperial symbol; it bore in its talons the flailing, purple-robed figure of King Typhas himself. As the crowd watched in mingled fear and exultation, the gryphon clawed at its prey like a wild eagle. It tore their monarch's flesh with its talons and plucked at his eyes with its golden beak, even as it bore him off screaming under thudding dark wings, far, far away into the cloud-darkened east.

Meanwhile, inside the throne room, guards and courtiers quailed back in horror at the monstrous event, fearful that Tamsin's sanguine power might be further displayed. For there was no doubt that the miracle was of her making—or rather, that of the dire goddess Ninga couched at her side.

Of the three standing nearest the now-vacant dais, the first steward blinked after his disappearing king, then fell to one knee in immediate obeisance. Baron Isembard, with an expression of mingled triumph and uncertainty, eyed King Typhas's golden circlet where it had fallen from the monarch's head during his struggles; but then, turning to Tamsin, the knight knelt to her in imitation of the steward.

Tamsin, for her part, addressed the goddess at her side. "Oh my, what a pretty crown . . . is it not, Ninga?" With girlish grace, she strode forward and stepped up onto the dais. Stooping there gracefully, she picked up the gemmed diadem and placed it, not upon her doll's wizened brow, but upon her own fair, youthful one.

TEN

The Eater of Trees

Living among the Atupans, Conan soon forgot that he had known any other existence. He had always been footloose, a wanderer. So were these people, moving from site to site as dictated by season and the strayings of the game herds. Seldom had Conan lingered in any civilized country or outpost long enough to feel drawn back by homesickness. But now, making his way among the quirky, congenial personalities of Songa's tribe, he felt that he *was* home again, once more enjoying the closeness of his youthful clan fellowships.

He was brought before the lodge fire of the Elder Council. That fire, a bed of glowing embers laid in the middle of a longhouse, was stoked with heady, aromatic herbs to enhance the council's wisdom. Around it sat the elder hunters and storytellers of the tribe, who were regarded as wise.

Among them was Songa's mother Nuna, who had been a famed huntress in her youth.

These wise folk viewed Conan's fitness and his scars with nods and grunts of approval. But when they questioned him, their laughter at his floundering answers was uproarious. He flushed at their ridicule, yet somehow bore it, perhaps because his Cimmerian fathers would have treated a stranger no better—or perhaps because Songa was there, laying pliant hands on his shoulders to calm him. He bore the interrogation stoically, agreeing to learn more about the Atupans' sacred sky-demons, and of the animal spirits who had created the forest and earth.

Conan was drawn with his mate into other areas of the tribe's life as well: the pranks and teasing rhymes of young camp girls not yet mated, who viewed Songa as a sister and who doted over her muscular man-catch with half-feigned covetousness and half-concealed fear; the pesterings of the small children, who swarmed through the camp in shrill terror raids or, alternately, sat rapt and silent around some wizened oldster who droned a legend; the patient labor of mothers and aged men over flintwork, hides, baskets, and pottery; and the continual weapon trials and roughhousing games of the young hunters, both male and female, including some new wives recently stolen from neighboring tribes.

The Atupans, in return, good-naturedly tolerated Conan's foreign looks and his doting, proprietary interest in Songa. They watched the pair's cuddlings and skirmishings about the camp with frank interest—though Conan, perhaps accustomed to sturdier and more discreet Cimmerian timber lodges, or else spoiled by his years among civilized men, felt somewhat constrained against venting the full energy of his passion before a dozen prying eyes. Fortunately, his new kinfolk were tolerant; they smiled, uncomplaining, when he took his mate off on long hunting treks in the forest. From such trips they would return at dusk, weathered and weary but happy-looking, with only a few small fish or a brace of squirrels to show for their daylong exertions.

In each of the tribe's interlinking worlds, Conan was able to win grudging acceptance, even respect. His native strength and keenness of perception allowed him to catch on quickly at most activities and discussions. In the course of it, he gained vital knowledge of local stones, earths, herbs, and animal varieties. In daylong hunts and wanderings about the countryside, the canny tribefolk showed him how and where to obtain salt, flint, pot-clay, pigments, hardwoods, barks, fibers, scores of game species, and hundreds of edible or medicinal plants. He learned new and ingenious snares, birdcalls, hut- and fire-building techniques, and tactics useful in hunting and tracking. The more he learned, the more he was impressed by the richness and diversity of the Atupans' life.

Just once, aware of a gap in his instruction, he asked about something that had troubled him now and again. What animal or demon was it, he wanted to know, that could snatch away a full-grown forest antelope, frenzied and alert in the heat of pursuit, without leaving behind spoor, carcass, or even the slightest track or sign?

Aklak, who led their small hunting band, grunted deeply where he sat cradling his spear in the shade of a split boulder, but made no answer. The others present, Songa and a pair of lean-limbed youngsters, Glubal and Jad, deferred to their hunt-leader with uneasy looks. Arising, Aklak turned and carefully scanned the broken forest fringe around them, meanwhile flaring his nostrils to sniff the air. At length he spoke.

"What you ask is forbidden." His voice had in it a gruff edge of resignation. "To speak of it, or to try to name it, would only bring down the doom itself, swift and final. Nothing can be done. So say no more."

Conan, having adapted to a simple existence among these straightforward people, had relearned the habit of simple obedience. So he shrugged and followed the others as they threaded their way, more cautiously now, among the rocks and trees of the rugged slope.

Their goal this morning, as his companions had hinted to him, was a special one. In the course of their walk so far, they had paused to take game birds and squirrels that could be slung from their belts. But they had bypassed larger antelope that, if slain, would have to be manhandled immediately back to camp and prepared as food, lest the carcass spoil or be stolen by scavengers. With the wealth of game in the valley, such chances for kills were hardly rare; even so, for a hunting band to let one pass meant that the other business at hand must be serious indeed.

Their route angled through shallow ravines and across low ridges that crouched as foothills to the taller, steeper crests rising to eastward. The forest was dense in places, mainly along the ridges and valley bottoms; in other places, jutting rocks and loose shale hindered the growth of trees. But in all parts, the way was rugged; the forests were choked with fallen limbs, trunks, and underbrush, while the stony outcrops rose abrupt and jagged. Fortunately, a faint but definite trace left by game and by previous human parties lay unobstructed in most places.

Maintaining the habitual silence and physical economy of trackers, the band proceeded at a swift, steady pace. In time, they found themselves skirting the edge of a broad talus slope that rose eastward toward the craggy palisades of a beetling cliff face—which evidently tended to crumble away and slather downhill, forming the shaley rubble at their feet. The debris lay in blocky, regular-shaped sections, heavy enough to scar or flatten those few trees rooted near it. To Conan's eye, the six-sided basalt pieces looked suspiciously uniform, as if shaped by human tools . . . or by unhuman ones, considering the size and hardness of the chunks. He glanced up periodically at the darkly etched cliff face, half-expecting to discover in it the ports and battlements of a mountain fortress reared high by gods or devils.

Then, as the party rounded the rotting stump of a great tree that must have given way before some avalanche, Conan spied a monument that he knew could never have been hewn by raw nature.

It was the jagged cylinder of a tower—a narrow, windowless spire jutting tall out of the thicket near the base of the slope. It appeared to be fashioned of a paler, softer stone than the dark cliff, and banded with carvings of some kind; their patterns were visible under cables and sprays of flowering vines, which used the tower's height to drag themselves beyond the forest shadows and overlook the sunny treetops.

"Crom!" On spying the structure, Conan murmured the

foreign oath. An instant later, recognizing the thing as a hoary ruin most likely unrelated to the eerie geometry of the cliff, he felt less at peril. Looking to his companions, he found them unimpressed; they already knew of the tower's presence, obviously, and were mainly interested in his reaction.

"Look and marvel, river-man!" Aklak said with a proprietary smile to his brother-in-law. "It is the great Stone Tree," he explained further, "made by the squirrel-spirit Chukchee to store the nuts he stole from Twik the badger. In revenge, Twik burrowed underneath and dug out all the nuts. He made the cliffs tumble, too, and ordered Chukchee to live in the treetops forever. But he left the nut-tree standing as a reminder. And there are other things here, too. Come along, come closer."

Wending their way through the damp, tangled logs and undergrowth, following a trail faint enough to prove that few men or animals ever visited the place, they approached the spire, which rose well above the treetops. The cliff rubble, overgrown by weedy tussocks, forest mold, and the knotted roots of bush and tree, covered any other ruins that might exist nearby. Indeed, Conan realized, it was difficult to tell how high the tower might truly stand, since one or more levels of its original height could easily lie underground, heaped over with rubble. Most likely the entrance, if it ever had one, was buried, since the rubble-choked, vine-knotted base did not reveal any means of ingress.

"Do you see this wall?" Aklak demanded as they came up to the base, gaining an almost clear view of the massive spire. "A hunter can scale it—any true, daring hunter of the Atupans."

Looking up the monument's side, Conan merely grunted. Though its height was impressive, he did not doubt his clanmate's words. The seams and carved recesses in the stone, as well as the woody robustness of the vines, should make the task somewhat easier than climbing a tree of comparable height.

"Every hunter of the Atupan race has done so," Aklak went on. "It is our test of fitness before the great animal-lords, who will decide if the candidate lives or dies."

Conan looked from his stepbrother to the two younger braves. Then he turned to Songa, who nodded and chin-waved to him in the affirmative. "I have done it," she assured him. "My mother, too," she gratuitously added.

Aklak resumed, "You must scale the tower, climb down inside, and bring out something you find there as proof. We will wait for you and carry home your bones if you fall."

This time Conan did not even grunt. Laying down spear and ax and kicking off his sandals, he stepped forward across the stony forest litter to tug at one of the vines, testing its strength. For the ascent, he trusted his expert, mountain-honed climbing skills to stand him in good stead. Yet at the same time, he did not doubt that his companions had completed this test when they were mere children, as light and nimble as monkeys. His own full-grown warrior's weight could only increase the risk of a vine pulling loose, or a ledge of rotten stone breaking away. Nevertheless, he set his foot on one of the sculptured reliefs and started upward.

Climbing briskly, stretching and groping for ledges and footholds, he felt no great worry about the tower itself toppling under him. If the weight of centuries and the mallet-blows of temperate seasons had not yet leveled it, his puny mortal bulk certainly would not. The stones felt massive and skillfully hewn under his grasp, their weathered joints resisting even the intrusion of his tensed fingertips; formed of some hard, pale rock, they clearly predated the basalt tumbled down from the cliffs. In some places, the carved surface—even to his tentative, sweat-damp touch—retained its original smooth-streaked polish; yet this did not deceive him into believing it was not old. Something in the tower's obdurate stubbornness—jutting up here between forest and cliff as it did, with no apparent relation to the present-day landscape or its inhabitants, except for the fanciful, childish tale Aklak had recounted—told him that the obelisk must be very old indeed.

Further, the style of its carvings brought to mind no Hyborian kingdom, current or ancient, that he had encountered in his civilized wanderings. At least not as far as he could discern eyeball-close, through screening lichen and vine fronds, with his face drawn back a couple of handspans at most from the carved surface.

The subject matter of the sculpture, even so, was surprisingly standard. The tower was evidently a victory monument, the panels near the bottom depicting massed armies and navies, flaming forts, and city walls under attack by rams and siege machines, much as might be seen engraved in the main gate or palace wall of any modern Hyborian capital. The images now seemed oddly discordant and even repellent to Conan, who had been living so recently and so intensely in the raw world of nature.

He wondered what his fellow Atupans might think of the carvings, if indeed their unschooled eyes could distinguish them at all. It might be that in all this civilized panoply of power and destruction, no single image would be recognizable to an innocent savage; the straight and sharp-angled lines of battlements and troop formations would lack any basis for recognition, certainly. The ships, engines, and contrivances of mass death would look hopelessly complex and purposeless, and the plumed, heavily armored and often mounted warriors would seem like blind insects or monsters. Indeed, it was hard for Conan himself to tell surely from the carvings whether their subjects were men and horses, or what other, older faces might lie behind the cruel-slitted helms and ribbed carapaces of both soldier and steed.

As he climbed higher, far from the view of any ground-level spectators, the carvings changed to coarse abstractions. Coincidentally, as the vine ropes spread and thinned, Conan regarded the designs less critically as artworks and more so as handgrips and toeholds. The shouts of encouragement from his friends below grew thinner and fainter; he tried to glance down only with the merest edge of his vision to avert dizziness. Lit now by bright sunlight, and stirred by sky-breezes, the vine's leaves and blossoms flapped in his face, bathing him in a wash of heady perfume.

Edging his way upward into a vertical pasture of yellow trumpet-flowers, he realized that he was surrounded by droning, hovering bees. Drunk on pollen, they did not seem prone to attack, though his bare skin jumped and crawled with anticipation of their stings. He continued, trying not to think of the prospect of climbing down later.

The view over forest tree-spires opened out, revealing no other ruins nearby; and not long afterward, the broken, angling rim of the tower lay in Conan's reach. Establishing a triple purchase first, with two feet and one hand braced against outcrops, Conan raised his free hand up to the edge, then clapped on the other hand and pulled, preparing to haul himself up. But stone scraped dryly against stone, making a sickening noise as it began to pull loose.

So it was, then; the fabric of the wall was thin and delicate near the top. With a sideward lunge, his legs swinging free, Conan avoided the loose stone as it tipped and fell. Rather than carrying him over with it, it only scraped one thigh. His hands, meanwhile, slid to the next lower stone, which grated in its place but held. Using arms and toes to raise himself without levering outward against the wall, he threw a leg up and straddled the narrow rim of masonry.

The fallen stone shattered on the rocky earth below, to yelps of glee from Songa and the others. Looking down and ascertaining that they were unhurt, Conan waved to them but made no outcry. He was wary now of what might be roused out of the tower's shadowy inner well: frightened birds, bats, swarming spiders, or blood-supping ghosts. The central cavity was obscured, bushed over with a blazing bright nest of yellow-flowered vines and happily abuzz with bees. Though he could see nothing beneath the glare, his foot, which hung down inside the leafy canopy, found a toehold of some kind. Therefore, assuming from his friends' words that there was some means of descent, he lowered himself into the unseen depths.

After some moments of clinging to the inner curvature of the wall, waiting for his eyes to adapt to the gloom, he discerned the internal structure of the tower. It had formerly supported a spiral stair running down through part of its height at least, with stone steps protruding inward from the outer wall. When the tower had fallen in, due to mighty Twik's burrowings or some less personal cataclysm, the steps must have been snapped off by collapsing rubble. Enough of their level surface—a handsbreadth in places, more in others—remained to be traversed, if the user was careful—and if Conan had dared to trust his weight any farther out along the cantilevered stone.

Half-clinging to the smooth wall, squinting in sunshot darkness and pausing to brush cobwebs from his eyes, he inched his way downward. There were gaps in the spiral path—landings perhaps, or former laddered galleries— where he had to lower himself vertically, dropping so far at times that he wondered how he would make his way back up. Then a sloping pile of rubble, with a broken arch at its bottom, led him into a deeper, ramped chasm. Was he below ground level yet? He cursed himself for not bringing along a fire-rubbing kit. As the light filtering from overhead dimmed, his eyes compensated as best they could, but now it was nigh impossible to make out even the shadowy loom of stone walls and archways.

Then at last he gained the feeling of a floor underfoot, level, if littered with rocks and debris. But an eerie yellow glow rose up before him, glistening on bright droplets or rime-flakes scattered about the chamber. And, suddenly, hunched shadows moved in the wavering torchlight; there came low moans, building swiftly to a chorus of blood-curdling howls. Conan, pivoting wildly with his obsidian blade clutched in one hand, discovered his mate Songa and her fellow huntsmen around him, their groans dissolving into peals of echoing laughter.

He waited resolutely while they staggered and rolled on the floor, howling with mirth. Patiently he stood; having willed his heart to slow its gallop, he now fought down, more fiercely than any creeping terror, a murderous urge to crack their childish Atupan heads together. If these fools knew anything of war or sorcery, or could have guessed what horrors he had faced in places such as this . . .

Gruffly he let out a sigh. Unclenching his fist from the stone dagger, he slid the weapon resolutely back into its sheath at his hip. These were savage innocents, after all. Somehow, he felt no desire to educate them.

"You are a good hunter, Conan," Aklak assured him, still gasping with laughter. "You did not let your fears master you. And so I do not have to fight you and take away your knife." He smote his hunt-brother a solid buffet on the shoulder. "As a reward, you will wear the token of a hunter." He gestured around the chamber. "Go ahead, choose any ornament you want."

Songa went to her mate's side now and clung to him with one arm, though still laughing with apologetic hic-coughs. In the light of the torch she held on high, Conan could see that the sparkles strewn about the place came from some sort of crystals, or rather crafted gems. He could also see a narrow strip of sunlight, falling through some hidden entrance at the far side of the chamber that the tricksters must have used. Motioning Songa to follow him with her torch, Conan walked over and knelt by a pile of the glittering objects.

They were precious or semiprecious ornaments—charms, amulets, neck chains, and pendants—scattered from broken stone jars and bowls that must once have been arranged around the stone walls of the circular room. The pieces were strange, and somewhat crude in manufacture. They were not the faceted crystal rubies, emeralds, and sapphires that Conan had most often dealt in, but were comprised of muddy or smoky-colored oval and teardrop stones set in coarse whorls and flowerlets of soft gray or red metal, appended to ringlets and coarse-linked chains of the same alloys. Conan recognized their workmanship as being similar to the opal pendant that Songa sported so tantalizingly below her navel. The style was like no other he had seen, in all his years as a careful appraiser of other people's wealth. He noted that the armlets and finger-rings in the pile were outsized and markedly oblong-shaped, which made him again wonder about the physical aspect of the tower's builders—in point of fact, about their humanness.

"This is quite a hoard," Conan suspiciously observed, using the Atupan tongue as adequately as he could. "Why is it still here?"

Aklak, gazing down on him, made the flat-handed motion that passed among his people for a shrug. "Because the great spirits will it, I suppose. Why are the trees here, or the waters?"

"No, I mean . . ." The northerner found himself hampered, because as far as he knew, the tribe's language included no word for wealth. "Since it is so easy to get in here—" he gestured toward the dim-lit entry "—why has no one come and taken it?"

"But, river-man," Songa protested, "all of us have come and taken it. Look!" She waggled her hips suggestively before his face, making the opal gem dance gaily on its thong dangling down her supple belly. "Every hunter of our tribe has gone through the same ordeal as you, and has chosen an amulet in honor of their initiation."

"Yes," her brother affirmed. "Other tribes know this spot too, and revere it highly."

"You must mean . . ." Conan shook his head, groping for words ". . . there is a curse on this treasure, surely, one that limits each visitor to a single gem." He blinked up at his companions. "Otherwise, why would one hunter or one single tribe not empty the whole room and keep its contents for themselves?"

"A curse?" Glubal puzzled aloud. "What curse?"

"And what do you mean, one person take all?" Aklak demanded. "What would be the use of that?" He twisted a bent knuckle in one ear and squinted, the Atupan way of questioning another's sanity. "Would one hunter kill all the game in the forest, though most of it must rot before he could eat it? Or would a single tribe lay claim to the Glass Mountain, and have more obsidian than they could possibly use?" He laughed in outrage at the idea. "Why, there would be nothing left for anyone else!"

"Besides," young Jad pointed out, "who would want more than one gem? Two of them would rattle against each other and scare off the game. Anyway, they are of no real use. They cannot keep you warm, or fill up your belly!"

Conan slumped where he sat, all but overwhelmed by the childlike innocence of these primitives. "Believe me, there are men in the world who would take all there is in this room to themselves. And take a hundred times more, if they could find it—and kill the lot of us if such a deed enabled them to keep it."

Aklak grunted, impressed by his hunt-brother's earnest tone. "I do not pretend to know where such men can be found." He knuckled his ear again. "Surely they are mad."

For his initiation charm, Conan selected a girdle of linked circular plates, the largest ones inset with purple sardonyx-like gems of irregular shape. Songa polished and mended the amulet, using a thong, and with an air of solemn ritual, tied it about Conan's middle. Then, impulsively, she printed its shape against both their bellies with a quick, passionate embrace.

The others cheered, dealing out shoulder-slaps and rough hunters' embraces. Scarcely touching anything else in the ruined shrine, they departed through the hidden, half-buried portal in the base of the tower, which led them up a few paces to ground level.

On the way back, Aklak and the two youthful hunters resolved to stalk after meadow deer. Conan and Songa, by quiet agreement, took leave of the others and set out together along the rocky apron of the eastern ridge. The stream that watered the village, while pooling and cascading down from the upper valleys, passed through a broad, stony gorge that contained many sand beaches and deep, sapphire-blue ponds. The bare granite had, by mid-afternoon, stored up the balmy heat of the day's sun; furthermore, the canyon was relatively treeless and exposed, making it easy to watch for the approach of enemies or predatory beasts across the surrounding slopes.

In this desolate paradise Conan and Songa took their ease, swimming and idling, rolling and chasing across the sand. Having knocked down a pair of plump pigeons with slung stones, they roasted them over a driftwood fire and ate them ravenously, crouching together in the sand and wiping greasy fingers on sun-bronzed thighs. This main course they filled out with crisp swamp-grass tubers and a dessert of berries plucked from a thorny hedge among the rocks.

Watching Songa's tongue dart hungrily to her berry-stained lips, Conan felt his passion stir. He reached out to tousle the sun-lightened strands of brown hair lying across the supple bare shoulders—but she, with the alertness of a huntress and the coy instincts of a much-sought prey, sprang up and danced out of his reach, laughing at him. He lunged after, following her out onto a shelf of rock alongside the stream, where she, turning suddenly and clutching him against her, bore him over into the deep, clear chill of the pond. The shock was total, smothering all their senses at once; he watched her body twist pale in the greenish light, trailing silken hair and bubbles, luring him deeper as she teased and stroked him in the cold caress of the current. Moments later they crawled out onto the bank, gasping and clinging. Finding precarious comfort between the chill wetness of their bare skin and the sand's scorching heat, they rolled and grappled together.

"The tribe will laugh, and our hunt-brothers will think us poor stalkers," Conan observed later, brushing sand from his nether limbs. "Today I wear the emblem of a hunter, but we return empty-handed."

"Do not worry," Songa reassured him, going to the pond to rinse sand from herself. "You have stalked your prey tirelessly, I can witness. And slain it most nobly," she added, looking back at him with a smile of contentment.

"Yes, but will I return home bearing a fat, succulent hind to share with the rest of the tribe? I do not think so."

"It does not matter." After wading thigh-deep in the stream, she came ashore and tied on her scant garments. "You have caught a swift and wily prey, one that many others have sought after without success, and they will envy you." Going over barefoot to his side, she twined her arms about his neck and hugged him close. "I, too, have snared and netted well today."

Conan held her quietly for a while in the rays of the late, sinking sun. At last they relinquished one another; they must leave soon if they wished to avoid groping and blundering through the forest by night.

"Your fame as a hunter is already established," Conan told his mate. "But I . . . I had better make some noted kill soon, lest your tribe-brothers doubt my fitness."

"The chance will come," Songa assured him, lacing on her doeskin slippers. "For both of us, for I too would wish greater fame. I want to become as great a huntress as my mother."

Conan grunted. "I doubt not you can, Fisherwoman." He used the nickname the tribe had bestowed on her for finding him by the river. "But your mother's reputation came mainly after your father's death, did it not, when you were half-grown?''

"Yes." She tossed her head, her hair now dry and loose across her shoulders. "That is why I remember it so well."

"But what will happen when you join the circle of mothers, who sit around the fire before the women's longhut?" Conan's brow was furrowed in frank puzzlement. "Will you hunt with your belly swollen, or with babes suckling at your breasts?"

"Oh, Conan!" Songa laughed, her voice soft in the coloring twilight. "What strange land do you come from, that you know so little the ways of women, and of the world?" She laid a hand on his shoulder. "Has no one taught you the simplest fact of life—that little babes come from the moon, from the owl-spirit? If a woman does not lie with a man under the full moon, no babies will come." Her touch on his shoulder was patient, her laughter gentle. "Why, if a woman did not know that, she would end up fat with children all her life, and the forest would swarm with babies!"

"I see." Conan's voice rumbled with profound uncertainty. "You're sure it works?"

"Of course it does," she rebuked him. "Our tribe has always observed the will of the owl-spirit! That is why there is a longhut for the mated women, and why so many of us stay there at month's end." She glanced up at the plump, gibbous moon in the deepening blue overhead. "It will be just a few days now—" she paused, anxious "—and I would go there, Conan. I do not want babes yet. I want to hunt, to win fame, and someday be a respected elder of the tribe." She reached over to where he sat close beside her and embraced him. "At your side, if you wish it."

"If you wish it, Songa, I do too." Conan met her embrace warmly and firmly. "But come," he told her, arising. "Let us go, before night stalks us and catches us in the tangled wood."

Over the next cycle of the moon, life proceeded much as usual among the Atupans. Game remained plentiful into high summer, so the tribe did not pick up and move to a new village site. Some girls were lost; three young kinswomen of Songa's, bathing ritually in a rocky pool far from camp, were set upon by hunters of a neighboring tribe and carried off kicking and screaming, to be ravished. So, at least, the story was indignantly told around the huntsmen's fire at the lower end of camp, though later it was rumored that one of the maids had been in secret contact with a likely foreign male and had induced her two friends to join her in desertion.

Even so, a revenge raid was planned and swiftly carried out. Five young bucks, barely able to conceal their righteous enthusiasm, daubed their cheeks and chests with the customary red clay and set forth on a mating hunt. They returned several days later—four of them, including Jad and Glubal, trailing comely maidens behind them. The women did not seem overly terrified; indeed, they carried neat bundles of possessions and soon joined in the daily routine around the women's fire.

This event, to Conan's surprise, tied him yet more closely into the life of the tribe. For with the arrival of the young brides, love was in the air of the camp. He and Songa thereafter were less likely to slip off into the forest for their intimacies than to lie in the red glow of the dying central fire at evening, snuggling in warm furs, caught up with the other new couples in a shared interlude of murmurs, laughter, and caresses.

Then one day a tremor of excitement went through the camp. Something called "Yugwubwa" had been sighted in the hills. At first it was unclear whether this was supposed to cause rejoicing or fear, but then Conan learned of a great hunt being organized. It seemed to be regarded as a rare opportunity for valor, and for laying in a large stock of food for winter. He was quick to volunteer with Songa, although she was unable to convey to him exactly what Yugwubwa might be.

Most of the tribe's able hunters were recruited to go, as well as a number of youngsters who could be of use in beating the bushes. Aklak, as usual, was appointed huntmaster. The project called for every heavy spear in the village, since all the full-fledged hunters bore two, one of them tied with a loose hide banner meant for signaling and for turning back the prey.

The whole party, amounting to a score of men and a handful of women, set forth at dawn. A pair of trackers ran ahead unburdened to scout the way, which led southward along the first and lowest set of hills, toward a rolling plateau of mingled leaf-forest and grassland. Departing at a swift pace, they took no rest until mid-morning, when they arrived at an area of blind chasms and gravelly ravines that demarcated the plateau. It was not far from this place, evidently, that the prey had first been sighted.

Aklak took a handful of senior hunters aside and conferred with them. Then he ordered the band divided in two. The party that he took charge of included none of the more seasoned hands. Instead, he chose Conan, Songa, and several youngsters eager to make a reputation, including Jad, Glubal, and two of the new females: lean, wiry-looking young women who already moved with a hunter's swagger.

Striking out across the plateau, skirting the tangled thickets, Aklak kept his group silent and watchful. Then, intercepted by one of the scouts, they turned to follow him across a stream. In time they arrived at the edge of a copse where the grass was flattened by a broad, furrowed heap of fresh dung.

"What kind of monster laid that?" Conan exclaimed, shouldering to the fore. "By Crom, the beast must be huge!"

"Looks like Yugwubwa," the scout grunted solemnly. Kneeling beside the pile, he laid a palm against it to test for warmth. Then, pinching up a sample of the brown stuff between thumb and forefinger, he crushed it before his nostrils. "Smells like Yugwubwa."

"Aye, indeed," some of the watchers concurred, wrinkling their noses.

The guide dabbed the excrement onto his tongue and savored it critically against his palate. "Tastes like Yugwubwa. Must be Yugwubwa," he proclaimed at last.

"Are you really sure?" Conan's remark, meant as a joke, was cut off as the scout, from his kneeling posture, scooped up a generous handful of dung and slung it at Conan, spattering him on the neck and chin.

"What? Why, you—" Conan started forward, his hands clenched for murder, but was kept from it as others in the group rushed forward. Laying hold of the offal, they began hurling it wildly at one another, laughing and grunting in a momentary lapse of hunt discipline.

"What in Sheol?" Conan snarled. Then at once he understood: the hunters smeared each other with dung to cover their human scent, so that they might approach their prey more stealthily. It was the one odor that would arouse the least suspicion, a hunter's age-old ritual, indulged in by these folk as a lighthearted frolic.

Once Conan understood, he willingly submitted. He let Songa smear the parts of his body he could not reach, then graciously returned the favor. His companions, by that time equally brown-clotted and pungent, silently took up their weapons and resumed following the track.

Shortly afterward, the scout's stalking skills were rendered unnecessary by a tumult in one of the scattered groves ahead. Trees shivered in the green expanse, flashing the pale undersides of their leaves and giving off cracking and crunching sounds that suggested they were being dismembered as well, and eaten.

"Yugwubwa," the murmur went through the band as, despite a qualm of uncertainty, they proceeded toward the unearthly din. Aklak led them around the side of the glade to approach the tumult from behind, along a swath of split, toppled, denuded limbs and trunks.

The beast was gargantuan, taller than a Stygian elephant, though leaner and less bulky in its proportions. Its four massive legs, rough and furrowed like great jointed tree trunks, stamped and flexed beneath the weight of the wedge-shaped muscular body that loomed half screened by lashing branches. Its hide looked impenetrable—thick and seamed, with mats of coarse red hair distributed patchily and rubbed entirely away in places. The hind legs were shorter than the front pair, which bore curved, stubby claws that looked highly efficient for both digging and self-defense. Another use for them became apparent as the monster reared up yet farther out of sight. The slothlike talons hooked and gouged like anchors into the bark, enabling the unseen head to attack the tree's upper branches.

"It is a rogue, a lone beast in its prime," Aklak breathed to the others. "No family group, no easy kills . . . this will be a hunt to remember."

His whisper was drowned by a near-explosive wrenching and tearing of living wood as the tree-eater had its irresistible way; half of the trunk that it had been mauling split and twisted aside, buckling to earth amid billowing foliage. This brought Yugwubwa's forequarters back down into view: the bony, muscle-wedged torso, the nearly nonexistent neck, and the long, broad, ugly head. The latter appendage was armor-crested, with six irregularly shaped horns paired along its length from tufted, mule-like ears to wet, snorting nostrils.

Those horns, some sharply hooked and some blunt or mushroom-tipped, were undoubtedly useful for snapping and levering the limbs off trees. Their bases were flattened and joined into an ungainly, elongated plate from beneath which blinked the beast's small pig-eyes. Its broad lips formed a splay-toothed, thick-tongued muzzle that flexed greedily to fold in sheaves and bundles of foliage, twigs, branches, and strips of peeled, curling bark.

"Beware," Aklak murmured to Conan as they crept up behind. "Yugwubwa is easily angered."

Conan said nothing, concentrating on picking his way quietly through broken, scattered foliage. It might have been opportune to attack while the creature was occupied so high up in the ruined tree; now that its forelegs were back on the ground, it could turn and discover them the moment they moved too far from cover. It devoured the greenery ravenously, yet the continuous twitches of its short, tufted tail suggested wary irritability.

"Our best tactic is to wound it," Aklak continued, "then hunt it back toward the main party. For that, we need a pair of strong spear-casters at the fore." His hand rested briefly on Conan's muscular shoulder, indicating his choice. "May the badger-spirit watch over us."

While the others edged through foliage at either side of the broken path, Conan followed Aklak forward, ducking from shattered stump to sagging limb. The noise of the monster's feeding was truly cataclysmic; its stench would have seemed much worse had the stalkers not already been pasted with it. Dropping to all fours and advancing at a crawl, the two advanced within spear-cast of the brute's scraggly hindquarters.

Slowly and lithely, Aklak rose to a crouch. Conan waited for him to poise for a throw, or else make some commotion to turn the beast around. But the latter proved unnecessary, since a wild orbit of one of the monster's eyes caught their movement. With a braying snort and a swift, tumultuous thrashing of foliage, the creature half-turned to face the intruders, bracing its mighty legs and swinging its head for a charge.

The Atupan's spear-cast was swift and fluid, with Conan's weapon hurtling close behind. The Cimmerian aimed for the leathery expanse of throat that looked softest and most flexible, but his point stuck instead in the hairy musculature of the monster's breast. Aklak's spear, aimed fairly for the eye or snout, glanced off one of the foremost, smallest horns of the oscillating head, its stone point shattering on impact.

Whether the weapon's force was enough even to make its victim sneeze was doubtful. Conan's shaft was snapped off by an angry swipe of one foreclaw; yet the stub-end hanging in the creature's chest must have remained an irritant, as indicated by Yugwubwa's sudden, trumpeting bray and furious forward lunge.

"Conan, stay clear!" Songa's slightly panicky cry rang from the forest.

The two stalkers retained one spear each. Yet further throws were impossible as the monster lunged at them, kicking up log splinters and shattered limbs before it. The two men's weapons instead served them as balance poles to help them cross the littered ground, racing and scurrying to keep ahead of the enraged monster. Hearing more cries from either side, they glanced over their shoulders and saw spears hurled by their comrades—but without any visible effect on great Yugwubwa. The infuriated beast did not noticeably falter or turn aside; once its attention was fixed on them, it followed relentlessly on their track, its rhythmic snorts battering at their eardrums, its ponderous gait shaking the turf of the meadow under their feet.

"What of your plan?" Conan panted to his brother-in-law as they broke into open meadowland. "Is this what you call driving the beast into a trap?"

"It is well," Aklak gasped. "Just lead him back the way

we came. Yugwubwa is slow and lumbering, with his heavy horns and short hind legs. If he decides to give up the chase, jab him some more with your spear!''

The notion was laughable in view of the beast's furious, plunging pursuit, even across the open ground. Its charge was as fierce and reckless, to Conan's recollection, as that of an armored horn-nose of Kush—a shade slower perhaps, but also harder to dodge because of Yugwubwa's tree-grappling nimbleness. The two spearmen were given scant opportunity to pace themselves for a long run, much less to turn and fight the menace that slavered at their heels. In swift, backward glances, Conan saw his five companions, with the exception of Songa, fall progressively farther behind. It was understandable, he allowed—since their steps weren't hastened by the imminent prospect of being crushed or champed alive by Yugwubwa's straining horns and teeth.

Crossing the plain from an unfamiliar angle, with dung-tainted sweat smarting in his eyes and the friction of dry air scorching his throat, Conan could not determine exactly the way they had come. Aklak seemed to know the terrain, so Conan stayed near him. Before them spread a patchy expanse of brush—potentially a dangerous snare for the fugitives, though it was unlikely to trouble their giant pursuer. It might, at any rate, provide cover; against his best judgment, Conan paced Aklak as he ran in between the stands of shrub.

The bushes forced the two a little way apart. It was Conan whom the monster followed, and as he feared, undergrowth soon hampered his steps. The chest-high foliage necessitated costly turns and leaps for Conan, while it only magnified the behemoth's progress with crashings and thunderings ever closer behind. Ahead, abruptly, there loomed a tangled hedge of flowering bushes Conan must either crash or slither through; holding his spear level, he ducked his head and dove into it—

—only to see the land fall away before him. Darting out an arm, he grabbed hold of a bush stem that promptly sagged downward, suspending him over the rim of a gully. Immediately overhead, the pursuing monster thundered, its speed carrying it far enough outward to miss Conan and strike the farther bank. Tumbling horn-over-hoof, it landed at the bottom with a bleat of stunned rage.

From nearby, Aklak uttered a triumphant howl, waving his bannered spear aloft to summon the others. Conan, meanwhile, clambered nimbly to escape Yugwubwa; his feet slid on loose earth as the beast hurled itself up the low embankment. By clawing at shrubbery, the huntsman dragged himself free even as chisel blows of the monster's horns and claws tore loose a small avalanche behind him.

The Atupans, it seemed, had planned for this outcome and had fanned out along the gullies bordering the plateau. Now they came hurrying along the rim of the ravine, bearing logs and stones to hurl down on their quarry, and fresh spears to harry it with.

"Conan, my mate! How I feared for you and Aklak!" Songa was at his side, embracing him as he regained his breath. "I put a spear into the monster's flank, but it did not even slow him!" Brandishing the stone-headed spear she still carried, she peered down through the broad gap in the brush whence snorting and pawing sounds issued.

"I will kill the devil yet, I swear it by all the nature-spirits!"

"We must slay it soon," Aklak affirmed, "before it finds its way out of the ravine. Stay near Yugwubwa," he called out to the others, "and spear him when he tries to climb up!"

The advice was easily given, yet it was no simple matter for one or two hunters, standing atop the shallow declivity, to drive back the frantic lunges of the trapped beast. The face it showed to its tormentors, for one thing, was a horrific one: slavering and splay-tusked, with curling snout, writhing purple tongue, and red, beady eyes gyrating beneath thick armor ridges. Surmounting it all, the bony crest of jagged horns could easily shatter spears; they might also hook a man and grind him to giblets if they caught him unwary. Luckily, the banks of the ravine were made of loose earth that crumbled away beneath the monster's massive weight, providing it with no solid footholds.

Fortunate it was, too, that Yugwubwa had a fierce temper, and hurled itself at the Atupans again and again in slavering rage. Otherwise, it might easily have followed the ravine out to the level plain, where the hunters would have been even less a match for it.

"Come, Yugwubwa! Try and bite me! I'll poke you in the eye!" Youths eager to earn fame goaded Yugwubwa, while the more seasoned hunters waited for the beast to turn aside and afford them a heart-thrust. Some few cast spears down into the pit; but even those weapons that struck the thick, jointed hide did not pierce it deeply. They were scraped off and forgotten because of the creature's restless, violent movements in the narrow space.

Glubal, trying to jab the hairy fiend in the neck, made

the mistake of standing too close to the gully's crumbling edge. He tumbled in with the monster, his fighting-yell changing to a terrified shriek; moments later he was tossed out by Yugwubwa's flailing horns. His limp body twisted high overhead, to land with a crash in a flower-bush and slide brokenly to earth.

"Demon! Man-killer! Come taste my spear, foul Yugwubwa!" Songa, having run some distance along the gully to a stone outcrop that gave her a vantage over the beast, now waved and gesticulated to attract it. Her sharp cries and frantic motions succeeded; as the monster snorted and turned, Conan ran along the rim to join her.

"Here, tree-eater! Come and try to crack my limbs! Peel my bark, you lumbering clump!" Kneeling on the stone overhang, Songa bent forward and jabbed with her spear, which clashed and scraped against the horned mantle of the lunging, straining creature. The beast blatted in rage; it tried to catch and crush the spearpoint between its nose-horns and the pale, chalky stone buttress. But the woman was too deft, driving her weapon instead at the creature's ear and starting a trickle of blood down Yugwubwa's dusty flank.

Most of the others, moving closer to the fight, raised a cheer at this. But Conan saw a danger that his mate could not: the prey-beast, ever wily and treacherous, was butting and clawing at the cliff side beneath the overhanging stone where its tormentress stood.

"Songa, be careful—"

Conan's warning came too late. As he watched, the pale stone ledge, really just an embedded rock slab, began to shift and settle toward the monster's raking, scrabbling clutch. Songa turned and sprang for level ground, vaulting across her spear-pole, but earth and stones slumping in the boulder's wake slipped loosely and bore her downward. Grasping and fighting for balance, silent and earnest, she disappeared into the dust cloud rising from beneath Yugwubwa's trundling feet.

"Aiaa!" Conan, in a reflex born of inarticulate rage, felt his shoulder spasm and his arm lash powerfully. His spear, its hide banner trailing, hurtled through air to strike the brute's back just behind the foreleg. It lodged there, loose in the muscle-slabbed flesh, giving rise to only a small, spreading bloodstain; the monster responded with a mere sidelong toss of its horns and a snort of irritation.

Conan, meanwhile, cast about frenziedly for another weapon. Sliding down the lip of the ravine, he seized hold of a pointed chunk of rock and dragged it loose from the earthen wall. Clutching it in two hands, he bounded out along the broken slope to a jagged fin of soil that protruded over the prey. Once there, careless of the spears flying down to strike the monster, he launched himself out into space and onto Yugwubwa's back.

He landed with a grunt across the knobby spine, near the place where a more graceful creature would have had a neck. Clinging tight with knees and elbows, using embedded Atupan spears as footholds, he worked himself astride the massive back. Then, wielding the pointed rock in both hands, he began battering at the plate of bony armor and the heavily corded muscles just behind Yugwubwa's eye-ridges and rearmost horns.

The beast's reaction was to lunge and toss, braying and snorting raucously while trying to dislodge the intruder from its back. Try as it might, it could not arch its mushroom-shaped horns around far enough to reach its own nape; instead, lurching sideways with scuffing steps, it rammed and scraped the gully wall in an effort to grind its attacker to pulp. But vainly, for the slope was not steep enough. Clinging tight with his knees, Conan continued to club and jab with his chisel-pointed weapon.

He strove desperately, clinging and pounding in frantic hatred while his skin dripped sweat and his nostrils sucked in the animal's dusty reek. Then, to his joy, he saw that Songa still lived, plying her spear agilely somewhere beyond Yugwubwa's flailing horns and foreclaws. Now other Atupans—reluctant, perhaps, to cast their spears down from long range and risk striking their hunt-mates—were clambering into the gully to harry the beast from its walls, or even from the level bottom. And the monster's reactions appeared different to Conan now. They were more scattered against the threats from all sides, with what sounded like a note of plaintive confusion in the thunderous bellows.

All at once, striking savagely with his stone bludgeon, Conan felt something give. Blinking amid stinging dust, he saw bright-purplish blood well up from a spot at the edge of Yugwubwa's bony head-plate. A sudden impulse seized him: abandoning the stone chunk, letting it slide away down the sloping back, he reached behind him to one of the spears that lolled in the monster's thick hide. A tug and a sharp twist were sufficient to dislodge it. Then, digging its point into the oozing wound, he gripped the shaft two-handed and bore down with all his strength. The effort, aided by an upward toss of Yugwubwa's convulsing back, was successful; the stone leaf-blade sank in a handsbreadth and more, meeting small resistance once it was past the tough hide and fractured horn.

That same instant, the monster's bleatings took on a choking, rasping tone. Looking down, Conan saw Songa clinging heroically to her bucking, tossing spearshaft—which must, he realized, be lodged deep in Yugwubwa's throat.

Whatever the cause, their quarry had stopped fighting; it reeled, its legs faltering beneath its vast weight. It lurched sideways, fetching up against the gully wall with a slapping thud. Then it slid to earth and lay motionless, surrendering without even enough violence to dislodge the enemy who clung to its back.

Beneath him, Conan felt deep tremors and a shuddering heave: massive heartbeats, he slowly understood, and the breath of Yugwubwa. As he crouched there listening, they gradually ceased.

About him in the gully bottom, there reigned a wary silence. Then, all at once, a plaintive cry sounded. The wailing, mournful voice promptly became a chorus.

"Yugwubwa is dead! Oh, pity! Alas!"

"Our great friend of the forest, the Eater of Trees, is no more!"

"We are sorry, dear friend, for your misfortune!" This last voice, Conan dimly grasped, was Songa's.

"How sad for us all—oh, sorrowful day!"

The moans and laments rained down on all sides now, from cliff top, slope, and canyon bottom. Conan, suddenly impatient, arose and jumped down from the hulking corpse. "What in Crom's name is all this blubbering for?" He made the demand of his mate, who stood near Yugwubwa's snout with her hands respectfully clasped together. "This stinking brute is finally murdered, and you're still alive—and a hero, to boot! Why must you mourn and carry on so?''

''But Conan, do you not see? It is a terrible loss, a tragedy! A cherished friend is gone this day, a great heart has been stilled—''

''River-man has a point, after all,'' Aklak spoke up abruptly. ''My sister is now a great hero, indeed. And none of us died in the hunt—not many, anyway. Our tribe will have a great feast, and food for the coming winter! It is a time for rejoicing!''

''Yes, rejoice!'' Now this cry was taken up along the cliff top and spread through the canyon.

''We have food. Yugwubwa is dead!''

''Songa is a hero!''

The mood of the hunters abruptly changed to what Conan would first have expected, with backslapping, frolicking, and excited pummeling of the huge carcass. Even Glubal appeared on the cliff top, grinning and waving excitedly—though from a prone position, having presumably dragged his broken nether limbs behind him.

With ritual celebration, a cup was brought forward and held to the spear wound in Yugwubwa's throat. The hunters, beginning with Songa, were allowed to drink the steaming blood of their slaughtered prey.

Then, to everyone's delight, more faces appeared on the cliff top. The rest of the tribe, moving far slower than the hunters and bringing with them appliances for food preparation, had followed on their track. They descended into the ravine, and the butchery of the fallen beast became a festival. The hide was stripped and cut into usable shapes, teeth and tusks were extracted, and long fillets of meat were removed and staked out in the noon sun to dry. Fires were built and carefully maintained, with choice parts of Yugwubwa set out roasting and smoking on an array of racks and spits. Water vessels, too, were filled from a nearby stream, with an ample supply made available for necessary washing and boiling. The hunters were even able, with the many hands present, to turn over the massive carcass so that the meat on the bottom side was not wasted.

As it happened, the tribe did not return to its former camp. The Elder Council decreed that it was time to move, so only a few small parties were sent back to strip the village of its remaining portables and put the place in order. Several nights were spent at the site of the kill. Then the tribe, burdened down with its fresh provisions, moved downriver to a new camp, a lower and more southerly one that promised good hunting and milder weather as leaf-fall approached. Conan and Songa shared the labor of carrying their belongings, bound up in a litter between two padded spear-poles they alternately rested on their shoulders or slung in their hands.

After three weary days' march, as the land leveled and began to seem boggy and mosquito-ridden, Conan grew gruff and openly dubious of the move. He himself, inured to colder climes, saw no reason why they could not have wintered where they were. But the others, who had seen the lower camp, were enthusiastic to go there. Some of the young hunters—including Glubal, who hobbled along on a splinted leg and crutches—acted jubilant or positively frenzied as landmarks told them the place was near.

At last they arrived, crossing a broad field of waving grass-groats to halt on the sandy shore of a blue, tree-lined lake. There lay the circles of last year's huts, the fire-pits, and, suspended from nearby trees, some canoes skillfully made of hide and boughs. But the hunters, heaving down their burdens, showed little interest in these things; instead, they flocked to a spot some distance from the lake shore.

Songa, holding Conan's hand, led him in their wake. "Follow me, and be careful where you step," she cautioned him.

Coming to an exposed, barren place where the young hunters clustered together, they stopped and waited uncertainly. Aklak knelt before them and pierced the hard clay soil with a digging-stick. Surprisingly, it gave easily. As Aklak lifted a chunk of clay carefully aside, a pungent but familiar smell wafted to Conan's nostrils. The men and women about him sighed appreciatively; he noticed for the first time that they and Songa carried gourd-flasks and dippers.

"It is ready . . . it is, ah, very fine!" Aklak called out, zestfully wrinkling his nose. "No, do not crowd, do not fall in! There will be plenty this year!" Dipping his arm into the hole, he ladled out a foamy substance and raised it to his lips.

"Come, Conan," Songa urged, prodding him forward with her gourd-spoon. "You will like it! Have you never had—" her lips formed a word he had thus far paid slight attention to, but that would now become a good deal more familiar to him "—no, you couldn't have, for it is our invention! How could you ever have tasted beer?"

ELEVEN
Queen and Goddess

Queen Tamsin's coronation was a discreet affair. Now that her popular uprising had achieved its victory, it was seen as unfitting to expose her royal personage—and the sacred fetish of the living goddess Ninga—to the prying eyes and coarse entreaties of the common mob. Rather, it was thought, an aura of distance and priestly mystery would help restore stability to the recently troubled empire; in this, Tamsin allowed her new court advisors to have their way.

Accordingly, the young queen's ordination was held before several dozen privileged members of her court, in the refurbished throne hall now made over as a shrine to Ninga—its vanished throne replaced by an altar, its gem-faceted window supplanted by a single disk of translucent black glass. Most of those present at the ceremony were old, familiar faces: a score or so of high nobles, officers, eunuchs, and other worthies who, on fervently renouncing their allegiance to dead King Typhas, had been allowed to retain their lives and estates under Tamsin's sway.

Outside in the temple square, the enthusiasm of the populace was satisfied with torments and executions—of the high chancellor and some few dozen knights, fugitive priests, and civil servants who were denounced as loyal to the old regime, or were at least deemed expendable to the new. These proceedings were carried out under the supervision of the new Marshall of War, Baron Isembard, and his crack troops.

Inside, the assembled court sat watching a program of newly devised Ningan Temple dances, which, though performed with stately dignity by gowned women and robed men, had much in them of rural Brythunian peasant reels and flings. This rustic innocence seemed to satisfy the girl-queen.

"Now you have seen, First Steward, the full penalty of misrule and kingly negligence." Tamsin, gowned in Imperial finery, with the diminutive goddess on her arm clothed in even costlier splendor, deigned to share a few wise words with her advisor during the dance. "There are some slights and abuses an empire will not bear, even from a clever, watchful monarch."

The eunuch Basifer, first steward of the Imperial household, was in appearance an unlikely tutor for the young queen; he was large and heavy-featured, displaying the hairlessness and excess flesh that so often accompanied his physical alteration. His hands, back, and head were welted and scarred by maltreatment during his boyhood in the palace service, and his coarse flesh had been stained a deeper tan by applications of fragrant nut-oil balm, as was the fashion among the castrated servants. Yet he, with his dispassionate wisdom and his leadership of his fellow civil officers and palace administrators, was the perfect one to carry over the smooth efficiency of the late king's regime into the new theocracy.

"Indeed, my Queen," Basifer responded in his measured tone, "Typhas was insensitive at times—headstrong too, and often willfully inclined to disregard my best counsel." He took care, as ever, to aggrandize his own role and yet disavow any fault during his former tenure. A little flattery too, he reminded himself, was never ill-spent. "How fortunate it is that one as far-seeing as Your Majesty—and of course, a goddess as all-powerful as our Ninga—arrived on the scene to set things right."

"Great wrongs will always be set aright, Basifer." The queen regarded him with her green-eyed, inscrutable . . . and now universally acknowledged as dangerous . . . gaze. "Do you even know, I wonder, why a supreme goddess ever saw fit to confront and vanquish Brythunia's former king, and trouble herself with the petty affairs of mortal rulers? It had to do with an event long past, Steward, the death of some who were favored of our goddess . . . and near to her. Very near indeed." Gazing down fondly at her bejeweled, resplendent doll, she seemed to have abandoned the thread of the narrative. "Enough to say that revenge is a powerful, implacable force. Once set loose, it may topple an empire, or even a mighty god."

"Aye, my Queen." Inwardly the steward wondered what bizarre springs and balances could possibly drive a puzzle-box like this, so charmingly and deceptively cast in the face

and form of an innocent girl. Also, what force might serve
to restrain and channel such a dire, prodigal energy? He
was less than straightforward himself in his mental work-
ings, so he sensed a deep inner kinship with the girl; luckily, she tolerated his counsel, so far.

And yet there might in fact be an even better means of
control, or at least of distraction. "Your Majesty, there is
one whose absence today I have sorely regretted." Basifer
shook his bald head, as if in mild embarrassment. "He
was summoned here for the ceremony. Yet his journey, I
fear, is a long one, all the way from the southern border.
And in view of the recent, umm, political changes here in
Sargossa, diplomatic questions have arisen most urgently
there of late. Some such matter may have delayed his departure."

"You speak of this disinherited prince, whatever-is-his-
name?"

"Indeed, Your Majesty," Basifer affirmed. "Prince
Clewyn. A most able statesman for his age—and quite a
dashing figure, really. His judgments are swift and keen,
yet entirely lacking in the headlong impetuousness of youth.
A handsome fellow too, cultured and regarded as . . . romantic, in his way."

"The late king's envoy to Corinthia, since the truce."
Queen Tamsin's voice revealed less than slight interest, as
she watched the slow and rather stiff temple dance unreel.
"Or was his duty more in the nature of a hostage? At any
rate, Typhas trusted him as far away as Corinthia, if not
here at court."

"What you say is true, my Queen." The first steward
unctuously nodded. "He was never in good favor here un-

der the old regime—how perceptive of Your Majesty! But as an envoy, Prince Clewyn has learned much of foreign mannerliness, while forming invaluable diplomatic connections.'' Basifer cleared his throat suggestively. ''Your Majesty understands, of course, that the prince is no blood relation to Typhas, who gained power through military channels these twenty years agone.''

''And lost it through religious ones.'' The young queen glanced upward toward the black glass window, through which faint cheers could be heard from the temple square outside. ''I should think that by now, Typhas has no living relatives.''

''Quite so,'' Basifer affirmed. ''While the king ruled, Prince Clewyn was denied any prospect of succession. And yet, by his ties to the former nobility, the hereditary kings and queens of Brythunia, the prince enjoys a place in the esteem of aristocrats and the populace that should not be discounted.'' The eunuch paused with exquisite delicacy. ''An understanding with such an eminent person as the prince could lend valuable underpinnings of tradition to a rulership that is already powerful in fact—''

''Enough, First Steward,'' the girl-queen finally overruled him. ''If you are implying that Ninga's holy dominion, and my own rule as queen and High Priestess, need to be legitimized by a tie with some declining royal family—or that, having seized an empire, I should now hand it away in marriage to some royal upstart, some handsome, ambitious boy . . .'' Her queenly indignation trailed off into a dangerous dearth of words.

''But nay, Queen Tamsin, I did not mean . . . forgive me.'' Basifer, an adept survivor, was swift and earnest in his self-abasement. "I only wanted to commend to Your Majesty's attention a personage whose acquaintance might prove congenial, one who could serve as a useful tool . . ."

"For you know, First Steward," Tamsin spoke on, paying scant heed to Basifer's protestations, "our eyes, Ninga's and mine, have never been set on the transient pleasures and temptations of life. Our gaze is on the spiritual world—" from the way the black-glazed daylight flashed in Tamsin's green orbs, Basifer could easily believe her words "—and on those things in this world that promote strength and permanence in the higher one." She shifted her slim body in her plain, straight-backed chair, causing the doll clutched beneath her arm to rattle its beadstrings and ornaments. "Our thoughts dwell on the constant, imperishable things, the tokens and repositories of power that continue to wax stronger, while mere mortal husks wither and die. If you wish to understand us better—" she rose from her seat "—come, Steward, and I will show you."

The temple dance had ended and the acolytes were filing out at the back of the hall. The guards and courtiers waited uncertainly for the next event of the hallowed day; yet the new queen gave no thought to them, instead beckoning her steward with a stern look toward the broad-arched main doors. However talented a priestess Tamsin might be, she was not steeped in the ways and duties of queenship; Basifer thanked all the stars that the palace household and civil administration, which had been carried over almost intact from Typhas's highly efficient kingship, retained charge of day-to-day affairs. He himself had no choice but to follow as his queen, carrying the goddess of all the empire under her arm, walked out of the vast hall, abandoning her own coronation festival. The rest of the courtiers, similarly, had no choice but to sit and watch respectfully—at least until she was out of earshot.

Under the eye of guards and attendants, Tamsin led her steward out through the grand vestibule, up the spiral staircase, and back through the royal apartment into her private chambers. One of the more protected sleeping-rooms, formerly fitted out as King Typhas's private armory, had been done over, as Basifer knew, by a flock of acolytes and artisans recruited wholesale to the Ningan Temple. Now, when Queen Tamsin unlocked the door to him, instead of the reek of hasp oil and the glare of polished steel, he encountered the scented warmth and soft shimmer of hooded lamps against dark velvet hangings, the burnished gleam of golden fixtures, and the rustle of plush carpets beneath his sandaled feet.

"In a lifetime of miracle-working," the young queen said, "I have found it useful to seek out the sources and conduits of spiritual potency." She moved to a tall wardrobe of dark wood at the back of the room. "Even an all-powerful goddess finds it useful to embody her will in tangible charms, amulets, and tokens for the understanding of her subjects." She opened the tall cabinet, revealing within it a sudden profusion of glitters and gleams. "Such objects as these can contain great power for good or ill through some enchantment that was conferred on them in the recent or more distant past. Once endowed, they retain such powers for eternity, but only for those who know how to draw them out."

After waving a hand to indicate the brooches, necklaces,

and other baubles that hung within the case, Tamsin selected one and carefully lifted it out, looped across her slender hand. ''Or they may have gained their power fortuitously through some grim or miraculous past event in which they played a part—and, so to speak, became haunted by it. It matters little, since both kinds of amulets have a place in my priestly art.''

The object she held out before Basifer was a bracelet, and a shabby one—a mere bangle of cheap Vilayet spiral-shells strung together on what looked like common thread.

''This,'' she told him, ''in spite of its looks, is an especially mighty token of my healing skill: the first object through which I ever channeled our goddess's power. It cured my stepmother of her wasting nervous affliction—that same pious woman who is now Chief Virgin of our temple vestals. It alone brought about her miraculous rejuvenation, all through the will of gracious Ninga, of course, and through my own loving attention.'' Bowing humbly, she rattled the holy doll with its blank, painted smile. ''You can appreciate that, in its way, this bracelet is the most precious token I possess. Would you like to experience its power?''

''My Queen, I . . .'' Helpless to resist the command implicit in his royal mistress's manner and gestures, Basifer had no choice but to comply. Dumbly he extended the hand the queen had indicated, palm up. Having witnessed her magic, he was unable to conceal a tremor of dread, but he also felt an eerie twining of hope as Tamsin positioned the slack circlet of shells not in his open hand, but across the exposed skin of his wrist.

There came an immediate tingling sensation. Gazing

down at the beaded loop in the room's lamplit dimness, he imagined it beginning to shimmer with a bluish glow. Its outline was suddenly wavy and indistinct, as if glimpsed through the swirling, salt-laden waters of an inland sea. The feeling where the circlet touched him was one of intense, prickling warmth. He watched, both fascinated and repelled, as the tiny shells once again sprouted their original, dead occupants: antennaed, tentacled sea-snails, shading from pink to saffron and chartreuse in eerily luminous hues, setting forth across his skin with a waving and coldly tickling progress.

Unamazingly to his dazzled eyes, it looked as if the sea creatures were not limited to the tether of their bead-string. Though still yoked together, they made their way outward—down his wrist, around both sides, and up his goose-prickling forearm, encompassing an ever greater area of his skin. Where they crawled, he experienced certain feelings . . .

"If we were to let the circle pass about your arm and over your whole body," Queen Tamsin said, "the result would be memorable indeed." Abruptly she reached forth and plucked the magic circlet from her steward's skin. "But now is not the time. Such deep transformations must be carried out gradually."

Trembling, Basifer turned his hand over—and saw that the scars on the back of his wrist were gone. His skin was supple and smooth, free of the binding tug of the old, ridged welts. The sensation of tingling change had ceased; yet the wrist itself felt younger, the very tendons more vital and resilient than those of the opposite whip-scarred hand, with which he now stroked his rejuvenated limb.

"Your Majesty . . ." With heart stuttering weakly, he looked to his queen. In he slim hand, the shell beads clicked dryly, as light and brittle once again as any cheap trade ornament, with no hint of the ghostly life that had possessed them mere instants before.

"Remember," Tamsin told him, "there is no part of you that cannot be healed, no wound so old or so deep that our mystic arts cannot in time soothe it and restore the sufferer to wholeness."

Her words, penetrating to him as through a fog, released an indescribable anguish in his breast—and at the same time, a rush of devotion coupled with a heartfelt loyalty at the implied promise.

"To be healed, the one thing that you must possess is total faith in Ninga as goddess." Returning the necklace to its hook, Tamsin gently primped the hair of her doll. "We are touched, Basifer, by your show of genuine fear, and by your new, stronger faith. If more of your elder generation felt it, fewer of them would have met the grisly fate of my own stepfather—inaptly called Arnulf the Good— who stubbornly refused to renounce his belief in old Amalias's cult.

"But times have changed," she continued airily. "That is largely behind us. We are now, Ninga and I, in a most fortuitous position as regards deepening and broadening our command of the invisible realm." She gestured to her cabinet of charms. "As empress of all Brythunia, I control the former Temple of Amalias and its entire magical dispensary; the royal treasury, within these very palace walls, whose extensive wealth of gems and artifacts has yet to be inventoried for items of supernatural efficacy; and, of course, vast natural treasures, including the convict mines in the far eastern mountains that are fabled to produce both gold and jewels in steady supply.

"This reliquary—" she gestured again to the tall cabinet with its dangling, glittering contents "—contains the few charms and tokens of arcane potency that have been unearthed previously, and in my short tenure here. From this day on, we may anticipate that our Ninga's magical arsenal—if you care to think of it so—will continue to grow, and with it, our powers of conjuration, and the worldly might of the Brythunian Empire. With more relics as ancient as this one, for instance . . ." Her hand settled on a pendant of dull silver metal. It was heavy and particularly foreign-seeming in design, with a coarsely polished gem of irregular shape set into its oval medallion. "This piece came out of the east, I am told, from unmapped territory near the border."

"Your Majesty, please," a voice interrupted. "Begging your pardon, and Milord's . . ." One of the unarmed attendants, two of whom had been stationed outside the open chamber door, made a sudden entry. He seemed apologetic—unsure, perhaps, of what protocols would be established by the new empress. "I have been instructed to inform Your Majesty of the arrival of a late guest, Prince Clewyn." The jerkined man glanced uneasily to the door. "He has been brought up, Your Majesty, and awaits your convenience in the antechamber."

"I see. That was done on the First Steward's suggestion, I take it?"

At the servant's timid half-nod, Tamsin turned to Basifer, who blinked, still unsettled by his recent experience and still absently stroking his wrist. "Yes, my Queen, I took the liberty—"

"Very well, then, bring him in." Tamsin ticked an impatient finger aside at the servant and spoke to her doll. "Let us see, Ninga, how winsome we truly find this dashing, courtly young lord." Her voice, as it penetrated to Basifer's ear, bore a note of ill temper. "Perhaps he too will taken an interest in our collection of baubles."

After a brief stir outside the reliquary chamber, a slim man in a feathered cap and short travel cape was admitted, striding in company with the attendant. The girl-queen did not at first turn to face him. Instead, she maintained a stylized attitude of conversation with silent, distracted Basifer; and when she did look around, her young face had in it an amazing degree of queenly coldness. Then at once it changed. On seeing the visitor, her gaze became inquisitive, following his actions with frank involuntary interest as he took two quick steps forward, bent slowly to one knee, plucked her half-raised hand from her side and kissed it.

"Your Majesty," the page announced, "Prince Clewyn of Brythunia."

The prince was thin and fragile-looking, a well-dressed but extremely elderly man. His aristocratic features were seamed and wizened with countless wrinkles, the whole framed by silver-gray hair and a white goatee. He had not evidently lost many teeth, for his face still had a square, noble look. His bow was gallant, his smile winning and confiding.

"Queen Tamsin," he said, rising to his feet, "Brythunia has never known a younger and lovelier ruler . . . not even recalling my own grand-aunt Queen Lyditha, now fifty summers gone!'' Again kissing the hand that he retained in his grip, Clewyn declared, ''Queen and Priestess, I swear my eternal love and devotion to you.'' Scarcely blinking, his sharp old eyes flicked to the doll resting under his empress's arm. ''And High Goddess Ninga—nay, the one god, the only true goddess.'' Knuckling his forehead devoutly, with a swift, half-smiling glance to Tamsin, he dropped again to his knee in obeisance to the puppet. ''Your Godliness, you are all that I expected and more.''

''Prince . . . Clewyn, is it not?'' the young woman inquired curiously and with surprising civility. ''Ninga and I heard of you, but we made no serious study of the defunct royal court. I did not expect—''

''My great age, you mean? And my timidity?'' Warmly, Clewyn pressed Tamsin's young hand between his two thin, wrinkled ones. ''My dear Queen, do not think it amiss. My longevity in this empire is primarily a result of being meek and inconspicuous, at times practically invisible, especially during the reign of Your Gracious Majesty's heavy-handed predecessor, the late Typhas.

''And yet, now,'' Clewyn went on, ''in the tenure of a more pious and enlightened ruler, and one better loved by her subjects, I find it in my heart to dream that I might once more hold an esteemed place here at the Sargossan court. Dear Queen, on witnessing your regal splendor— and that of your godly protectress, Ninga—I crave nothing more than to bask in your divine radiance and, of course, to serve your empire with the fruits of my travel and experience. Most of all, I wish to spend the last few years that remain to me here in your shadow, in the beloved capital of my youth.''

He spoke frankly, with steady gaze, meanwhile lightly stroking the back of the young queen's hand in his. "I wish this boon, needless to say, only if it affords my adored Queen Tamsin no slightest concern or inconvenience. That is, cherished Empress, I offer and abase myself most humbly and devotedly at your whim . . ."

"Hmmm. Yes, of course, brave Clewyn, if you wish it." Queen Tamsin's reaction was prompt and accepting, if lacking the blush and breathlessness such high flattery might have brought to many another queenly countenance. "There are some, I think, who would not wish to linger in our company. They fear the swift, all-knowing scrutiny of our goddess and her keen, terrible judgments . . . do they not, Ninga?" she coaxed the gourd-doll at her side. "This entreaty of yours, Prince Clewyn, is to your credit . . . and Basifer, your earlier commendation of the prince reflects well on you."

The steward, still subjected to powerful inner tides of feeling, had been reduced to watchful, impassive silence; yet his answer bore in it a surge of conviction. "My sincere thanks, Your Majesty."

"I was just now explaining, my dear Prince, about the unsurpassed value of charms and amulets, at least for those with the spiritual gift to employ them." Taking Clewyn by the hand, she drew him to Basifer's side. "I call your attention to this most unusual piece. Perhaps your worldly knowledge can come to our aid." Reaching out, she took from the steward's slack grip the strangely made medallion. "It is of unfamiliar workmanship. Have you ever seen its like?"

"Why yes, my dear Queen." Clewyn nodded with an

air of uncertainty. "Such work has occasionally been brought here in the past, usually in the stock of traders or as Imperial tribute. But it looks very crude and primitive, held up beside the gems that adorn Your Majesty's most exquisite person."

"Ninga tells me it is very old," Tamsin said. "I, too, sense an elemental power in it, though the goddess has yet to reveal to me how to draw it out." She ran the oval medallion almost sensuously between a red-nailed thumb and forefinger. "It was brought here from the eastern marches, I am told—perhaps part of an ancient trove, or else picked up in trade from the local inhabitants." She draped the ornament over a slender forearm. "It is our intention to scour the land for such rarities, to further enhance the power of our temple."

Clewyn nodded. "There are men—or there formerly were, in the late king's employ—who can mount such an inquiry into any quarter of the empire, however remote."

"That would not surprise me." Tamsin turned to her other retainer. "And you, First Steward . . . can you aid me in such undertakings? Zealously, since I wish it, and without being too chary of expense?"

Basifer sank to one knee, canting his head toward the floor in profound obeisance. "For the sake of Brythunia's queen and the greater glory of her temple, I pledge Your Majesty—I will do anything!"

TWELVE

Savage Destinies

The elk halted in flight, its flanks heaving with exhaustion, its broad nostrils jetting pale vapor into the morning chill. The great head beneath the rack of massively splayed, moss-draped antlers pivoted regally on its shaggy neck, scanning the glade behind for danger. But the narrow expanse of grass was empty, and the farther border of trees and underbrush contained no hint of motion.

Abruptly, somewhere beyond the green curtain, came a movement. Through the leafy screen a long wooden shaft hurtled, shearing off leaves with its razory stone point, skimming low to strike the forest loam between the elk's broad hooves. With a simultaneous spring-taut motion, the animal launched itself into air and vanished, its departure signaled only by the thudding snap of twigs from forest beyond.

"A poor cast, Conan!" Jad called out as he loped forward through the thicket. "You have not yet gained the knack of using the spear-thrower."

"Aye, River-man." Aklak spread his comments out between short breaths as he ran alongside his now-weaponless hunt-mate. "The trees did not allow you enough loft for such range. If you strain your arm too much in attempting long flat throws, you will regret it."

Conan, veering aside through the glade, stooped to grab up his fallen spear. As he pelted along after his four hunt-mates, he couched the weapon ready again the same as the others, its butt resting in the hollow of the crook-ended stick he clutched, with the spearshaft hooked beneath a finger of the same hand that gripped the stick's haft. On an instant's notice, he could heave back his arm, release the spearshaft, and propel the weapon forward at the end of the leverlike extension, farther and faster than a hand-driven spear would fly.

"Here, see, our prey heads northward into the cliff lands," one of the younger hunters called to the others, discovering the scent in a cleft between rocky hills. "I told you so, Aklak! You should have let us stalk ahead and surround the creature before you started it running!"

"Aye, such is the best way," another young stalker, a woman, agreed. "The smartest hunters always lie in wait and let others drive the game onto their spears."

"Aye, yes," Aklak patiently agreed, "but even if you did head it off, could you stand before it? It takes a strong hunter to face a frightened branch-beast—especially one that has not been wearied by a long chase and drained by wounds." Aklak's words came in short, breathy gusts; he could spare the wind to talk only because the band was not running at full speed. They all knew that, while the elk could achieve short bursts of speed, if they kept on its track, they could overtake it. Acting as a team, they further improved their chances.

"Curse this spiteful elk," Jad proclaimed to the others while scrambling up a rock-strewn slope. "It tires us twice! Every step we have to follow it, we must also carry its carcass that much farther back to camp!"

A moment later, Aklak hissed, "Ho, quiet! The prey rests in yonder thicket! It must wait there, else we would have seen it mounting the ridge beyond."

To Conan's silent judgment, Aklak spoke truly. The stony crest along the back of the woody hollow was benched and uneven, but it contained no furrow deep enough to hide the flight of a full-grown branch-beast. Their prey must be sheltering in the copse; it might even decide to turn at bay and fight there.

"Good then, we should spread out and form a circle." The agile young huntress, almost without waiting for her hunt-chief's nod of assent, set out along the edge of the covert. At Aklak's gesture, Jad and the other youthful, impetuous male followed after. Conan and his in-law meanwhile angled the other way, toward the steeper arm of the ridge.

"Be wary, Conan. Allow them time to get into place. And do not cast your spear into the first thing that moves, lest it be one of our reckless friends!"

Advancing in a fluid half-crouch, Aklak led the way silently through the undergrowth. As each new expanse of terrain opened out before him, he would scan it carefully, peering out around a bush or the base of a tree rather than exposing his bushy-haired profile against open sky. Conan stayed some way short of Aklak but used identical skills; he did his best to keep Jad in view so as to complete the circle of hunters. The line straggled out broadly but began to shorten as it converged on a smaller patch of forest.

The stone ridge loomed high through the trees as Conan, with a low, silent wave, caught Aklak's attention. He directed his friend's gaze toward the pair of antlers nodding amid the trees, some fifty paces ahead. The elk was at rest; its red-bearded muzzle browsed quietly on shrubbery, as if the hunt were over.

Conan adjusted his grip on his lance, flexing his arm and drawing it back. Aklak held up a hand and froze—interminably, it seemed, as he waited for some sense of the others' whereabouts. At last he nodded and couched his lance the same as Conan; then he straightened smoothly, commencing a graceful, bounding stride. Conan watched his movements and fell in step with them. An instant later, both spearshafts simultaneously lashed free of their wood slings, sailing between the trees on tightly converging trajectories.

One struck into the grazing animal's flank and lodged there; the other fell short into the turf. As the elk leaped belatedly clear, a third spear hurled by Jad glanced across its back; before falling free, it did some lucky damage, as a spray of blood drops through the air attested.

While the young huntsman pranced and hooted in triumph, the two others converged on the short-fallen weapon. Aklak reached it first.

"My spear," he announced gravely. "Yours was the truer cast, Conan."

223

"Because of your sound teaching, my brother." Conan, meanwhile, picked up Jad's spear and examined its blooded tip; then he slung it sidewise to the young hunter. "I will have to use this," he said, unslinging his ax from its belt loop and replacing it with the now-useless spear-throwing stick.

The three of them loped after the vanished elk. From faint noises in the brush some distance to the side, it was clear that their two younger companions had not managed to hedge in the animal. Their prey's trail was clearer now, from ill-placed hoofmarks and regular dabblings of blood on the leaves and forest litter. At times, too, the animal's hoof-falls, labored and uneven, could plainly be heard from the slope ahead. The spearhead, Conan judged, was not lodged deeply in the elk's side; yet it must be a source of pain and a hindrance. Hefting his ax, he experienced a pang of longing to end the beast's suffering.

"Ki-yaa! Ki-yii!" Baying shrill cries to frighten the prey and summon their fellows, the hunters swarmed up the ridge after the beast. Its blood fell on bare granite now, spattering wide because of its great exertions. Conan took the lead; Aklak came close behind, breathing in deep gasps but still calling out instructions: "When the quarry falters or turns, Conan, remember, do not rush into the way and spoil my spear-cast!"

They came to an open area, a series of rounded granite benches where the elk could clearly be seen. It labored steadily upward, its hooves sliding and faltering on the worn stone, its bony shanks looking as frail and thin as the spearshaft that still dragged from its side. Even so, and before the bounding, baying hunters could come within spear-cast, the trammeled beast hauled itself up over the crest.

Moments later, the Atupans swarmed over the top, their weapons poised for mayhem. They saw . . . nothing. Before them, a broad, steep-rimmed natural amphitheater straddled the ridge, devoid of hiding places and escape paths. At its center lay a shallow puddle, whose rim of drying, flaking mud was untouched, undisturbed. The wounded elk could not possibly have dragged itself out of sight so quickly. Yet, aside from a splatter of wet blood on the rocks before them, there was no sign of their prey.

"I have seen the like of this before." Conan stood over the blood-spoor, intently scanning the hard, stony horizon.

"The hunt is over, so the omens say." Resignedly, Aklak grounded the butt of his spear on the rock. "Some kills are never fated to be made."

"Well . . ." the youngest male hunter forlornly agreed, "if such is the will of the great spirits . . ."

"That may be," Conan said. "But I, for one, intend to get back my spear." He strode away over the rock toward a single blood-drop that glistened on a stone near the upper rim of the amphitheater. "You others can stop here if you want."

"Not I, river-man!" The young female warrior strode after him, brandishing her spear. "I will help you steal back our elk, be it from the Great Badger himself!"

"I, too, will come with you," Jad chimed in. "I have run too far to turn back now. Well, Aklak, what say you? Are you afraid your spear will miss again?"

Aklak frowned, contemplating. "No, I will come," he

declared with sudden resolution. "Let us put an end to this mystery."

Conan, stalking ahead, reached the edge of the amphitheater before the others. He looked out on a level shelf of stone with few bushes and trees, open to the sky. There his gaze settled on a harrowing sight.

A gigantic mountain cat—gray-speckled on silver, with hunched, massive shoulders that made it taller and broader than the elk itself—tore hungrily at the prey's slack body, which it must have caught up in its monstrous jaws and dragged to this spot in a few mighty bounds of its pantherish frame. The bulbous feline head, with its tufted ears, arching eyebrow ridges, gory whiskers, and red-slavering, underslung jaw, bristled with devilish menace. Every feature was vastly oversized, and all centered on a pair of fangs as long and evilly curved as the blades of Zamoran tulwars. The great animal used its huge feline teeth methodically, scissoring away slabs of glistening flesh from the elk's haunches and spilling forth entrails in quivering heaps.

At Conan's arrival, the cat scarcely glanced up from its butchery. Only a horripilation of coarse bristles along the hump of its spine and a slight shift in its feral crouch signaled its awareness of being observed. The creature was not likely to take much interest in humans, after all, since they were too small to make a satisfactory meal or to pose a substantial threat.

Faced with such a vast and godlike . . . or demonlike . . . being, Conan was uncertain of how to proceed. His awe and superstitious dread lasted for several moments—until a spear, deftly and forcefully driven, streaked over his shoulder toward the beast. It was a perfect cast, aimed level and straight at the heart—if the monster, with devilishly quick reflexes, had not flicked up a huge paw and batted the spearshaft aside before it struck.

Hefting his ax, Conan glanced over his shoulder at Aklak, who watched expressionless as his spear shattered to splinters against a boulder. There was something fatalistic in his gaze—and the three younger hunters, who had raised their weapons to cheer, now clutched them defensively, two-handed.

An instant later, the time for reflection was past. The great cat, letting its gory kill fall aside, was among them.

Conan struck first, darting in from the flank, his ax hurtling down on the huge, hideous head. Because of the cat's devilish speed, his weapon struck only glancingly; it sheared away a few tough whiskers but failed to crack, or even to stun, the heavy, bone-ridged skull. Conan was bowled over, his wind knocked out of him, and skin was scraped from his chest and back by the animal's coarse pelt and by rough, bare granite.

As he rolled to his feet, his gut-muscles spasming to recover breath, he saw a demonstration of the monster's fighting prowess. Instead of launching itself through the air to grapple with its prey, rending it with teeth and talons as most cats would do, the beast sidled menacingly into combat. It stalked delicately, ponderously, then lunged with lethal suddenness. Its first adversary—the bold young huntress—it dispatched with one mighty forepaw, brushing aside her spear and catapulting her over backward. The blow undoubtedly broke her neck, leaving her crumpled body lying blood-streaked across a boulder.

The next hunter, Jad, drove in yelling from the side with a vicious spear-thrust at the silver-furred neck. But the giant creature, uncannily swift and supple, ducked beneath the spear. The big cat seemed merely to brush up against its attacker with a toss of its shaggy head; Jad staggered back, dropping his weapon and using both hands, vainly, to try to close the terrible rift in his belly opened by the monster's scything saber-fang.

While Jad shrieked and fell to his knees, the other young hunter met the same fate. Before he could plant his spear, the cat lunged sideward with a flick of its great head, hardly even troubling to open its jaws. Its long, curved incisor laid the youth open more efficiently than a Hyrkanian cavalry knife could have done. It must have struck his heart, for unlike Jad, who knelt sobbing in pain, he crumpled silently in a shower of blood.

Conan, regaining wind and strength, hacked savagely at the nearest part of the cat, the hind leg, lower to earth and less imposing than its massively muscled forepaws. He felt his ax rebound from the tough hamstring, yet the blow must have caused pain; the rough tail lashed his neck almost hard enough to knock him over. As he edged away, the beast turned to swipe at him. Its hooked claws tore through his trailing mane of hair, jerking his neck cruelly and smearing him with gore, which it was hard to be certain was not his own.

As he stumbled in recoil, Jad's gasping screams abruptly halted. Aklak had ended his hunt-brother's hopeless agony, using his heavy stone hatchet, as a good Atupan was sworn to do. He now turned and raised his weapon to meet the saber-cat's rush. There was no feinting or sidling this time, just a straightforward charge. The huntsman's ax flashed high in the sun, chopping down hard on one of the saber-cat's ears. The next moment Aklak's neck was seized in jaws that gaped impossibly wide. They closed, and his head was nipped clean from his body by the huge scissor-fangs.

Conan, half-blind with blood, rage, and anguish, never thought to turn and run. Survival was no eventuality; death was foregone. His only intent as he sprang forward was to do the greatest injury to his foe. He raised the ax two-handed to hew at the cat's lower backbone—but before he could complete the swing, the monster wheeled to confront him with its full, dreadful snarl.

The visage before him gaped terrible, a specter of rage and hideous hunger. Those devil eyes, the bristling, bulging features, and the red-smeared fangs held his soul in a grip as tight and dreadful as the creature's bone-crunching bite. The saber-cat's musty stench engulfed him; its guttural roar beat against his face, while its hot, blood-sweet carrion breath washed over him. As it loomed nearer—intent, as it seemed, on paralyzing and killing him with a mere look—his arm shot out by its own volition, driving his stone axhead upright between the saber-fangs into the beast's bloody, gaping jaws.

The roar became a sputtering cough of rage as the cat tried unsuccessfully to close its mouth. The jaws, wedged open at their widest extent, could not bring their full, terrible strength to bear; the flint ax dug into the ridged pink gums, splintering razor-edged teeth, but did not give. The giant cat raised a paw to swipe at the object lodged in its mouth, but the long fangs at either side were in the way.

The creature shook its massive head, its huge rough tongue bulging and probing to clear away the obstruction.

Conan, meanwhile, groped beside him and found a weapon: his own blood-slimed spear, which had fallen from the gutted carcass of the elk. The haft was slick and difficult to hold, yet he raised it before him just as the saber-cat finally spewed out the axhead, turned, and lunged at him with a shattering roar.

Any retreat was blocked by a boulder—as was the butt of the spear, which caught against its base. The cat, surging forward, took the bloody point in the fur of its chest. Conan slid his grip back down the haft, shrinking low to avoid the fierce, hooking talons; yet he braced the spear-point steady as the monster's weight bore down on it.

The pole bent and twisted in his grasp. Then it snapped, and the cat was upon him. Its writhing, clawing weight crushed him against hard stone, and he felt himself dying.

By the time Conan managed to drag himself from beneath the saber-cat, the sun was low. Once his chest was partially free, enabling him to breathe deeply, his efforts were more successful. Inching clear of the carcass, he saw that the point of his spear must have been driven to the animal's heart as it fell; the broken stub end was flush with the coarse, silvery chest fur.

He found that he could walk, or at least limp. So he did not linger at the site of the carnage to count the dead, or to drive away the circling, feasting vultures, or to determine how much of the gore encrusting his body was his own. If he himself had died, the tragedy could scarcely be greater, and it might have been more just. He was responsible, after all . . . having goaded the others into a fool-hardy attack, and disobeyed his hunt-chief. How could he confess to Songa that he, Conan, had brought about the death of her adored brother?

The way back to camp was hard. He would not stop lest he lose daylight, or find himself unable to crawl back to his feet after a rest. Even so, night set in before he was in familiar territory, and he lost the trail repeatedly between sunset and moonrise. His pain and hardship and the black-ness around him were matched by dark broodings all the way—less dark, however, than what awaited him at camp.

As he approached across the sandy meadow, he saw no fires. The only light was from the half-moon high above the lake, which rippled softly in the chill night-breeze. There was smoke aplenty, though, and the acrid smell of charred wood, hides, and hair. Huts still smoldered dimly, and the avenues between them were strewn with bodies—those of his tribe mates, pierced through with small, tell-tale wounds.

In one of the bodies, that of an elder, the death weapon was broken and had not been retrieved. Conan removed it and examined its two halves in the dim moonlight—a long arrow of passing good craftsmanship. Its fletching was tied on with spun thread, its tip forged of sharp, gleaming steel.

By his count, all, or nearly all, the members of his tribe lay dead, slain by arrowshafts and by keen metal knives. They had been surrounded or tricked, undoubtedly, and massacred with weapons they had never before seen. There lay his mother-in-law, a cudgel still clutched in her slack fist—and lame Glubal, fallen across his hunting-spear, along with two score other men, women, and babes. The

Atupans had fought bravely, or tried to . . . but without success. Markedly absent were any dead attackers or any further hint of their identity.

Also missing was any sign of Songa.

In spite of its dread urgency, the full, gruesome inventory had to wait for morning light, as did any tracking. For the time, he crept with renewed watchfulness into the forest. There he rested, chill and wakeful, bedeviled by grim, silent ghosts.

By dawn's faint light, Songa had not returned, and none lived to answer his calls. Surveying the butchery, he discovered one further, critical fact. Nothing had been taken from the village, except the single possession proudly worn by most adults: scavenged out of the ruined tower, the odd, ancient amulets that Atupans received on becoming hunters—like the ornament that now girdled Conan's waist, gritty and blood-grimed.

For these worthless trinkets, so it seemed, Songa's people and his own had been wiped out. If so, there was no question of where to seek her.

Even if he had not guessed which direction to take, he knew it was impossible to move such a body of men without leaving signs. This was true of men afoot, and especially of civilized ones. In the faint light, their trail was easy to find.

The track they left was slovenly, an insult to the forest and its spirits. They scuffed and dragged their feet, idly defaced trees and plants with their steel, trod carelessly in one another's wastes and tracked them into the wilderness. He could read their callowness in their footsteps; worse, he could smell them, and their stench of civilization soured his nostrils.

Before setting out, he bathed himself in the lake, swiftly and determinedly, washing from his abraded skin the blood of the saber-cat, of his hunt-mates, and of murdered innocents. He daubed himself quickly with colored clay, in the ritual face and chest stripes for a high hunt, and set out at a lope in the sparse costume of his tribe, bearing Songa's stone ax and a heavy, hand-thrown spear. The ruined village, fly-buzzing bodies, and circling carrion birds were best left behind as a warning to other tribes.

The invaders' track led north and west, along ridges flanking the river, toward the Atupans' summer hunting ground. The slayers' progress was rapid and forced, without rests; obviously they guessed they were in danger from survivors or neighboring tribes. The band had a mission, clearly, and a leader's discipline. They gnawed dry figs and oat-cakes as they walked, strewing stems and crumbs in their path. They also hunted along the way—with small success, since the bones cast into their previous night's campfire were few and tiny, the remains of mere vermin.

At a stream crossing, Conan found something more valuable than any diadem: pressed into the damp clay of the bank was a single footprint, shapely and unbloodied. It told him that Songa was alive, that she was being used as guide, as he had hoped, to lead them to the treasure.

Thereafter Conan redoubled his pace. He did not stop to hunt or to glean food, and he forgot his bruises and gashes, sprinting to make up the single day's lead. He sought out shortcuts, pausing only to scale vantage points and scan the country ahead. His speed of overtaking them was aided by several false branches in the trail, where Songa had tried to lead the marchers back upon themselves in a circle.

Their leader was watchful, Conan judged. Doubtless he maltreated Songa to make her obey. Still, she resisted, knowing Conan would follow, and expecting Aklak too, no doubt, along with the rest of the party. Again Conan cursed the fate, or the folly, that had ended his hunt-mates' lives.

At any rate, if he could creep near and rescue his mate, it might be wise to let the rest of the slayers live . . . for a time at least, while he and Songa made good their escape. Songa had friends among the other Atupan tribes; they could raise a war party, obtain their revenge, and then resume their lives together.

But the first need was to overtake her. This unseen commander pressed his murderers harshly indeed, leading them on a cruel forced march. Many of their footprints began to show lameness, and some were blood-spotted by the time Conan overtook the band—near dusk, at the ruined tower that was their goal. The tower's vines now hung dead and brown, rattling dryly in autumn gusts. Brittle fallen leaves lay underfoot, making Conan's approach all the more difficult as he crept toward the low crevice that served as an entry.

Most of the band seemed to have gone inside seeking treasure; only two sentries were posted, one on either flank of the jagged, buckled doorway. They wore no armor or military uniforms. Mere border ruffians, they looked to be, dressed in ill-made hide breeches and loose, woven shirts. One boasted a fur cap and poorly lasted town boots, whose uneven prints had occasionally been visible bringing up the rear of the party; the other one distinguished himself with shapeless buskins and a mangy fur vest, familiar to Conan only because it had shed some of its rotten hair in clumps along the trail.

The two stood motionless, with pike-axes grounded beside them, conversing intermittently in what sounded like coarse Brythunian. They were not in any particular attitude of alertness, but more in subdued dread, or morbid fascination. As Conan crept nearer, he discovered why: before them, in the weeds near the base of the tower, dead bodies were laid in a row.

Two of them, their heads split and shapeless, were ill-dressed ruffians very like the two sentries. The third, pale in the gathering dusk—though darkly stained with blood that had seeped from several arrow wounds—was Songa.

"A regular devil-cat, she," the hatted, booted sentry was saying. "Quiet as a stone monkey she was, the whole way. But tricky . . . ah yes, sly as a vixen cub, you can bet on it!" The fur-hatted sentry was obviously fond of his topic. "But Dolphas, he wouldn't let us touch her."

"Wanted her for himself, you ask me," the other guard muttered.

The first man shrugged. "That may be the way it was. Who'm I to say?"

He shook his fur-capped head and said no more. Conan waited, crouching, for the silence to stop buzzing in his ears.

Impulsively, the first sentry resumed speaking. "Then, finally we get here and the lads want to have sport with her—natural enough. But she, the hellcat, grabs a battle-ax and chops 'em in the noggin!" He shook his head again, his most animated gesture so far, though his voice droned on gloatingly. "Would have chopped a good many more, too, if our bows wasn't strung and ready."

" 'Tis a shame, even so," the other sentry grumbled. "A sorry waste of a woman, you ask me."

"Aye, she would have been something," the fur-hatted one said. "Ferocious, these forest wenches are. 'Tis like having sport with a wild animal." He peered down at the bodies in the gathering dimness. "Even now . . ." He exhaled raggedly. "But Dolphas says not to touch her."

"He still wants her for himself, you ask me."

"What say you, there?" The gruff voice sounded just behind the sentries' shoulders, making both of them start. "Talking on guard duty?" Firelight reflected from inside the archway, growing gradually more visible as sunset waned; now it was partly blocked as a burly form emerged.

"Nay, nothing, Captain Dolphas! Just staying alert."

"Hmmph." The big man's growl was one of suspicion. "What of the forest? Any noises out there?" His gaze swept the trees, passing directly over Conan's crouching form without awareness.

"Nay, Sire, nothing to report."

"Captain," the fur-hatted one asked, "will we have relief to go and eat our supper?"

"Aye, in good time. The kettle is warming." Dolphas climbed out through the broken arch. "No great hurry just now. The jewels have all been gathered up for our return trip." Stepping out between his men, he turned back to look at them. "Remember, you two, any pilfering means death! Report what treasure you find, and you will be paid fairly."

"Aye, Sire."

"Yes, Captain."

"Just you remember it!" The commander strode out toward the tree line, barely glancing aside at the row of bodies. He loosened the front of his trousers, making ready to void into the bushes.

Conan's ax whispered through the air, striking him a glancing blow on the temple. He grunted softly and sagged forward, unconscious. Conan caught him on his free arm, but there was a rustling of leaves as his body sank to earth.

"Captain, what is it?"

"Be you all right, Sire?"

In the darkness, they mistook Conan, striding forward, for their returning captain. The first sentry received Conan's stone speartip in his throat, choking on it with a gargle of blood. The second man started forward, pike raised, only to meet a hurtling stone ax that split both skull and fur hat. Man and weapon dropped to the ground with a clang.

"Dolphas, is that you?" a voice called from within the tower. "Come back in and cast the dice, Captain, before we divide up your winnings!" A shadow loomed dark against fire-lit stone, then receded.

Conan picked up the fallen pike-ax. It was strongly made, with a keen, narrow head and forged-steel haft. A civilized weapon. With this, he could stand outside the tower entry and smite down his enemies one by one as they came forth—until the others climbed to the top and dropped loose stones on his head.

Steel had its uses, some more efficient than others.

Groping in the dimness, he explored the stonework of

the crumbling arch. The lintel, a long, loaf-shaped piece spanning the door's width, lay at chest level. He raised the pike-ax, driving its pointed end into the loose, eroded stonework at one side.

"Hello, Captain? Are you out there?"

Heaving his whole weight against the pike-head, Conan bore it sideways, levering the lintel-stone outward with a heavy, grinding rasp. A dim shape appeared in the doorway; an instant later, as the stone gave way, the man disappeared in a chaos of rubble and dust. Volumes of masonry began to sag into the archway, while high overhead, a grating, rumbling sound commenced.

Snatching up his weapons, Conan whirled and ran for the forest.

Behind him, inside the tower, shouting and screaming began—faint, muffled noises that were quickly drowned out by the thunder of falling stone as the ancient tower fell in on itself.

Later, when the waxing moon rose, it lit a greater desolation than before. The jumble of stone and broken trees lay dusty-pale, motionless now and silent except for faint groans from one edge of the pile.

"Captain Dolphas." Above the wounded man, whose leg and arm were pinned under a battered-down tree trunk, a shadow loomed.

"Who . . . who are you?" the gruff voice rose. One hand slid for a knife-hilt, obviously through long habit, but returned empty.

"Nay, the question is, who are *you*?" The muscular, near-naked man knelt beside the officer.

"You speak Brythunian! You are no savage! Why do you paint yourself like one?"

"I ask. You answer." The questioner loomed closer. "Why are you here? Who sent you?"

"Sent me? Why, no one. I am just an adventurer, an explorer. Are any of my friends yet alive?"

"Enough lies!" The keen edge of a stone spear, sticky with gore, was pressed against the helpless man's throat. "What was your business here?"

"All right, I admit it . . . I am a treasure-seeker!" Rolling his eyes, the captain waved his hand vaguely in the direction of the fallen tower. "Did you know that there is a treasure in yonder ruin? Help me get loose and I will lead you to it . . . a fortune in rare gems!"

"Jewelry, yes." Seizing hold of the gesticulating hand, Conan bent it up to the moonlight. "Like this, perhaps?"

Looped around the middle finger was a metal ring. From the knuckle side it looked to be a mere gold band, but turned inside the hand was a thick escutcheon, deeply graven with a symbol—a gryphon it looked like in the moon's pale beam.

"A seal-ring, is it, then? One that bears the symbol of Imperial Brythunia?"

The ring fit tightly below the knuckle. Conan bent the finger backward, mercilessly, until he heard bone snap. Dolphas let out a quavering, sobbing cry, jerking vainly as the ring came free of his finger.

"Quiet, Dolphas! There are some questions I have for you."

THIRTEEN

Wayfarers

In the stockade town of Shihar, lying on the mountainous eastern frontier of Brythunia, the snow-draped peaks of the north Kezankian chain were everywhere visible. The log walls and coarse-shingled roofs of the town's buildings were low-lying, as were the sharpened timber palings that fenced in the settlement. Even above the smoky battlements of the square-built, sprawling Imperial keep, the lofty Kezankian peaks loomed icy and desolate as seen from any angle of the mud streets.

Little came down out of those mountains, except floods and avalanches at spring-tide. Trails threaded their way upward, to be sure. Worn into the ancient rocks by some former race, they now were used only by gem-finders and trappers, among whom the existence of remoter mountain passes was muttered and legended. It had been long, long past living memory that invading tribes or raiding parties had come over the crags to harry Shihar from the desolate lands to the east. The town's log palisades were raised more to fend off local bandits and rebel factions than to protect against any menace from across the border.

Thus it was that Regnard the Gunderman was surprised to see the lone figure stride down the dewy upper meadow and approach the settlement's eastern gate. There was something different about him, even at a distance and under the morning sun-glare off the peaks. This was no hunter or prospector returning at season's end; he carried strange, rustic weapons, for one thing, and towed no overladen donkey behind him. He wore a heavy cloak that appeared to be formed of a single, silvery bearskin, yet underneath it, he went almost naked, seemingly impervious to the mountain chill.

This, Regnard decided, was a true primitive, a man of the legendary tribes dwelling across the mountains to the east and south. What purpose he had in coming to civilization was hard to guess, but his arrival could mean danger.

It was to greet newcomers that Regnard had stationed himself near the open gate. Small-framed and robust, with the blond, tousled hair and reddish-blond mustache of his clan, he sat basking against a sunny cabin wall, a jug of fragrant, heady cider between his booted feet. He would have been elated indeed to meet a lone hunter or prospector returning from a trek—unwashed and hungry, starved most of all for human companionship, and burdened with tradegoods that would require an able broker to dispose of.

Regnard would have been more than happy to befriend such a man, to offer him a deep draught of cider, take his livestock and cargo in hand, and conduct him to an establishment in town where he could have his hunger, filth, and thirst attended to, along with all of his sublimer human cravings. There would have been easy profit in it for Regnard—more, admittedly, for the buyers of the merchandise and the purveyors of the delights they were liquidated for—but then, that was how the Gunderman made his way through the world. As a drifter, wandering along the coarse fringe of civilization like a flea through the pelt of a dog, he had learned to pander to other drifters and exiles who happened to be less cunning than himself.

This particular newcomer, now—a hill-savage unversed in the ways of a town, much less an empire, and lacking both wealth and understanding—this one did not entirely turn away Regnard's interest. The Gunderman, sipping from his jug, watched contemplatively and patiently as he approached. Here lay a mystery, a challenge, and a possible answer to his longer-term difficulties.

What Regnard wanted most of all was to get out of Shihar. He had come here in high hopes, believing the prospects to be rich indeed. With the provincial administration crippled by the civil war, and the recent surge in the price of mountain gems, combined with the rumored presence in this district of vast gold and jewel mines operated as a crown monopoly, the signs all seemed to point to a gold frenzy, or to downright anarchy—with vast wealth being shaken out through the cracks and healthy profits to be gleaned from below.

Instead, what he had found here was glum and discouraging. The military retained its grip. There was tight secrecy, with a crack, stiff-necked garrison manning the keep and many of the locals borne up in close-mouthed, dangerous doings. If he had been one to face hardship and danger, he might have joined in with them and done tolerably well; but Regnard was a talker more than a fighter.

As far as he could tell, gold and gems were never brokered here, or even transported through the town in any quantity. Imperial discipline under the new queen had proven to be, if anything, stricter than before. The few ragged fortune-hunters who passed through, eking a sparse living from the local mountain valleys, could scarcely sustain a procurer in the rich style to which Regnard aspired. Now, with autumn frosting the air, the prospect of a long, cramped winter in Shihar was one to be avoided at all costs.

As the foreign savage drew near the gate, Regnard heaved himself up and strode out to meet him. "Greetings, stranger!" he called, trying out a pidgin trade-dialect native to the Kezankians and connecting hill ranges. "You must be thirsty from your walk. Will you have a drink from my flask?"

After looking the townsman up and down with a sullen, stony face, the savage finally responded. Shifting his stone-tipped spear from one hand to the other, he reached out and accepted the jug that was offered. As he swigged from the heavy bottle, his bearskin parted wider, and the Gunderman saw how magnificent a figure he was: chest and shoulders broad and massive, with a firm, flat stomach, crisscrossed by scars already stretching to the taut contours of the muscles and fading. His waist was adorned by some kind of rough-jeweled girdle of polished disks that promptly caught Regnard's attention. The loins and legs were bronzed as deeply as were the square face and powerful hands. Amiably, if somewhat guardedly, Regnard watched the rugged features sour at the raw taste of the cider, swirl it about for a moment, then spit it out across the meadow grass in a yellowish spray.

"Strong—good!" Regnard told him, accepting the return of the jug, raising it up to gulp deeply, then offering it back to the newcomer. "Go on, drink some more, and swallow it this time!"

The frowning savage shook his head once, impatiently, with a toss of his square-cut mane and a sideward flick of his hand that must represent some tribal gesture. "Well then, my friend," Regnard said, wanting to keep up the momentum, "you must have traveled a long way. Do you come from across the mountains?"

The foreigner's answer was a nod, accompanied by a faint grunt and an upward flick of his hand.

"What of your people? Do others follow you here?"

A headshake and a curt, frowning syllable: "No."

"Alone, then." Regnard turned slowly, extending an arm to summon his new friend back toward the gate. "It must have been hard traveling so far by yourself. I have heard that men lose themselves in these mountains—even large parties of armed men—and vanish there without a trace."

"Um." The grunt that Regnard's primitive companion offered in reply did not make clear that he understood. But then, it hardly mattered as long as the flow of words was kept up. Walking amiably beside the savage, he conducted him through the gate.

The two Imperial guards did not bother to descend the ladder from their railed lookout. They cast down contemptuous glances at the newcomer but let him retain his rustic spear and stone club. Obviously they cared little about his fate and judged that if he stayed with Regnard, he would pose them no problem.

Within the gate, the town streets were near-deserted, so the uncouth foreigner drew only an occasional, pointed look from a uniformed trooper or an early rising shopman.

"I know a place . . . do you have any trade goods?" The Gunderman peered up at the savage, who was scanning Shihar's smelly, mud-midden streets and ramshackle cabins with a bleak, uninterested gaze. "You know, barter . . . ?" Regnard rubbed thumb against fingers in the universal gesture, eliciting no sign of comprehension. Then he shrugged with elaborate casualness. "No matter. I will stand you to a meal. Come along!"

He led his scowling companion to a broad, low-porched cabin that, aside from its greater size and loftier roof of mossier shingles, was very little different from any of the other town hovels. Inside, it was laid out as a public room, with benches and trencher-boards set around the mud-chinked log walls, and an open space of hard-packed dirt surrounding the firepit at the center. Flourishing an arm overhead and shouting to the bald-headed taverner, Regnard led his guest to one of the trestle tables farthest from the door.

The place was nearly deserted; thus there were few snorts and raised eyebrows at the stranger's uncouth appearance. There were even some murmurs of appreciation, feminine ones that issued from an alcove at one side of the room. At Regnard's urging, his guest surrendered his rough-hewn ax and spear and let them be hung up on a weapons-rack over the table. Wine and cider were offered and refused; at length, the customer accepted a wooden jack of warm, brown Brythunian ale. From it he finally drank—a single sip, which he almost seemed to retain in his mouth as he sat stonily reflecting.

When their feast of salt fish, boiled pork, and sour turnip slaw arrived, the foreigner ate resignedly enough, though Regnard set to work on his own portion with confidence. From his travels about the edges and crevices of the Hyborian world, he was sure he understood the nature of the primitive spirit. This fellow, for instance—for all his deep, inscrutable seriousness, he had the mind of a little child. Such a barbarian, simple and credulous at heart, was bound to understand little about the new world before him. Creatures like this one survived from day to day in the wild, satisfying their coarse urges as luck provided, and worshiping sticks, stones, vermin, and other objects hardly worthy of a five-year-old babe, to improve their meager chances. This stranger looked strong and splendid enough now, coming here from the raw wilderness, but the fellow was all bluff; after a few days in the real, civilized world, without protection and guidance, he would be confused and helpless—sick, stuporous, and penniless—all because of his inborn lack of fitness to survive.

Regnard, however, had no such fate in view for him. Finishing his repast, scraping up the sour gravy with good stiff camp bread that snapped between a man's teeth as he bit into it, he mumbled, "Well now, that was excellent!" Gathering his resources for a moment, he belched cordially. "Now that we have broken fast together . . . tell me, friend, what is your name?"

"Conan," was the other's reply. Having emptied his trencher of food, he sat once again sullen and stoic.

"Well now, Conan, what do you seek here in Shihar? Wisdom, perhaps?" He tapped the side of his head knowingly. "Romance?" He shot a roguish glance across the room to the alcove of women. "Or wealth, such as might be gained by brokering that fine fur cape on your shoulders, and the bauble you wear around your middle?"

In reply, the outlander made not even a grunt, but Regnard interpreted a narrowing of the savage's steel-blue eyes as signifying interest.

"Wild skins command a good price," Regnard explained to him. "Of late, they have grown scarcer in these parts. And such trinkets as you are wearing might be salable too. Do you know, perchance, where any more are to be found?"

To his question, the savage grunted and gave a frowning headshake.

"No? Ah well, 'tis of little matter." The Gunderman amiably smiled. "What, then, of your tribe or kinfolk? Do they know of your wanderings, so far across the Kezankian Mountains?"

Conan regarded him emotionlessly. "My tribe is all dead."

"What? Dead, you say? Of a disease, was it?" Regnard knew from long experience that such brute, uncleanly primitives were highly vulnerable to disease. They often died in droves from ills that were commonplace and lightly regarded in civilized towns.

The savage gazed back at him levelly. "Yes, they died of a disease."

"So. A shame." The Gunderman was not worried; he had little fear of any foreign plague being carried to him that he had not already survived in his travels. "So you have come west to Brythunia, one of the richest of the Hyborian empires, to seek your fortune?"

A grunt and a nod of assent.

"A wise decision. There are comforts here, and rare delights . . ." He gestured across to the tavern women, who now ventured out of their cubbyhole, bantering together in shrill, teasing tones. "This outpost, Shihar, is but nothing, a mere camp. In the greater Brythunian cities there lie wealth and power beyond a man's wildest dreams. But let me tell you—" Regnard leaned across to his guest in a confidential way "—the only safe course in civilized lands is to find a friend, someone you can trust, someone to help you get started. Elsewise, these sly, wily town merchants will outsmart you before you have a chance to learn civilized ways."

At this, the outlander seemed intrigued. "You want to help me?" he asked with a steely blue squint.

The Gunderman hesitated for a moment, then shrugged. "Yes, I suppose so." He smiled and shook his head cannily. "But not unless I, too, can get something out of it. That is how things are done here in the city."

"What do you want out of it?"

Regnard stroked his blond mustache. "What occurs to me is this: what I want most of all—because of the lateness of the season, and my wish to return to more familiar parts—is to get out of Shihar. It strikes me that you, too, would do best to travel into the heart of the kingdom. That way, you will command the best possible price for what you have to offer.''

The Gunderman stepped up the pace of his speech, unsure whether the barbarian understood, but wishing to bear him along nevertheless on the tide of ideas. ''Now, if we were to sell something here immediately—say, that rough hide cape of yours—why, that would bring us enough coin to buy good woven capes with. And there would be enough money left over to travel together to a great city. Once there, we could easily strike our fortunes. You, by selling that jeweled gewgaw of yours, could be set up quite comfortably—''

''What city?'' Conan finally interrupted him.

''What city?'' Regnard mused. ''Well, my mountain friend, why not the greatest of them all? It is only a fortnight's walk from here—Sargossa, the capital of all Brythunia!'' he declared with a flourish.

''Sargossa, yes.'' With a curt nod, the savage stood up from his bench. Untying the plush pelt from around his neck, he laid it on the trestle table.

At this action, sighs and lewd remarks sounded from across the room. The tavern women—four of them, in assorted sizes, shapes, and slatternly costumes—seemed genuinely impressed by the baring of the outlander's husky torso. Two drifted over, cooing with admiration, to stroke the sleek fur of the cape and the sleeker, muscular pelt of its owner. To these intimacies he failed to respond, except with impatient snorts and sullen, dangerous glances that soon drove his admirers to Regnard's side of the table.

The other two wenches, dressed in thinly stretched scraps of blouse and skirtlet, commenced a dance. Carelessly and desultorily, they moved to plinks and plunks from a mandolin in the lap of a bearded, sleepy-looking musician seated against an ale keg. Regnard tried lustily, within the limits of the trade dialect, to point up how they epitomized two very different sorts of feminine beauty then in fashion—the one plump and rounded, with lush, fleshly attributes and the saucy, taunting looks that full-blooded men desire. The other was willowy by comparison, even wispy—a slender phantasm of a girl, scarcely past her twelfth year, and carefully starved, yet nimble and fetching nonetheless. Both girls, moreover, were very fashionably pale, with a powdered, luminous complexion that set off the deep-blue kohl painted around their eyes. The selection was quite good in all, Regnard proclaimed, for a rough border outpost.

Even so, the outlander's failure to take interest in the dancers did not surprise him. These savage woods-dwellers had more crotchets, taboos, and superstitions than a Stygian priest, lacking the first notion of how to relax and enjoy themselves in civilized company. Crude and barbarous as they were, they regarded themselves as haughty noblemen. One had to be careful of offending their rustic dignity if he did not want his skull cracked.

This was all very familiar to Regnard; he must have placated his companion's pride adequately so far, he decided, since the lout did not brain him. In a short time, the uncouth foreigner, with his forbidding snorts and growls, had carved out for himself a safe, dark enclave at the corner of the near-empty tavern. Leaving him brooding over his ale, the Gunderman took up the fur skin and went to trade it away at the local pelt-broker's.

When he returned, a purse jingled comfortably at his belt. He declared, without going into needless detail, that they now had an adequate cash stake for their journey. It was necessary to spend the afternoon provisioning, he said, if they intended to depart the next morning.

Their trek across the heartland of Brythunia was made in mid-autumn, at the height of the country's prosperity. The civil war had ended swiftly enough that it did not lay widespread waste to the land or hinder crop planting; and the victory was recent enough not to have given the common folk a soured opinion of their new queen's wisdom, or their new goddess's favor. Now the harvest was in, and cellars, pantries, and granaries overflowed. Chaff was being burned in the fields, filling the sky with brown, sweetish smoke; fragrant wine grapes were stamped in shallow vats by bare-kneed country girls, and every rural rafter was draped with gourds, cornstalks, and thick ropes of garlic, onion, and sausage. Inns and farm tables set forth lavish meals for the wayfarers; and even in sparsely populated districts where lodgings and victuals were generally scarce, it was not hard for Regnard to buy or beg, and for Conan to hunt or steal, supplies enough to keep them comfortable.

Most typically along the way, the two would be lodged in a rural coach-house. Regnard would be led to a sleeping-stall or a bench near the fire in the Common Room, while Conan, in keeping with his brutish dress and aspect, would be lodged on a hayloft or in a corner of the cattle shed. Food and drink were furnished, in keeping with the travelers' respective stations in the world, at the guest table or outside by the kitchen stoop. Additionally, there might be livelier entertainments, drinking-fests or nightlong revels with customers and wenches of the inn. These were solely Regnard's province, since Conan retained his sullen, solitary demeanor along the route.

Luckily, the savage hunter was strong and uncomplaining, inured enough to hard labor to carry the main share of their supplies and belongings—or the whole lot, on days when the Gunderman was too ill or overhung to manage. Indeed, there were times when Conan almost carried Regnard himself, and defended him as well, from irate inn lords and angry gambling partners. The savage's fighting prowess was amply tested on those occasions when bandits tried to waylay the pair by night or in forest depths. Such brigands departed none the richer—rather the poorer, after accounting for hacked limbs and the spent lives of those of their number they left behind.

On the whole, though, the journey was congenial. Because of the mild, prosperous season and the widespread goodwill arising from the success of the popular rebellion, Regnard—and, to a lesser extent, his savage minion—were cordially received across the breadth of Brythunia. The Gunderman was quick to take advantage of this trust and acceptance, ingratiating himself into the hearts and pockets of the common folk. Conan, however, remained sullen and grim-faced, retreating at every opportunity into broodings and sorrows only he could know.

FOURTEEN

The Small Usurper

Prince Clewyn, bound for his morning visit to Queen Tamsin, wended his laborious way through the palace antechambers. His progress was slowed, not so much by age or infirmity as by the need to stop and exchange gossip and pleasantries with a great many court functionaries as he went. He had come to regard such casual contacts as vital to survival, even when they delayed his engagement at the seat of Imperial authority. He viewed such civility as the grease that made the complex cogs of the palace grind in harmony.

His own uncertain status at court—as a disinherited Imperial relic and sometime-exiled pretender—did not raise him above contact with the lower ranks. On the contrary, his status as the queen's current favorite made it compulsory for almost everyone to seek him out and placate him. Hence, running the gauntlet between his bedchamber and

Queen Tamsin's, he chatted with a wide variety of persons: councillors, eunuchs, courtesans, military officers, priests, attachés, emissaries, even high-ranking attendants and slaves. All such meetings ended cordially, he made sure, for the sake of clinging to power in an ill-defined political turmoil where a single misplaced word could mean banishment or death.

Not that he disliked such undercurrents; he was used to them, navigating them as expertly as a frog in a millrace. Now, once again, he swam near the heart of the maelstrom; after so many years of diplomacy, it was his element. He felt keenly alive here in his birth city, Sargossa, seeking some voice in the destiny of this vast empire.

When finally he found his way to the royal antechamber, he was conducted to a chair by a tribune and told to wait. The uniformed servant, disappearing through the gilded door into the queen's sanctum, returned several moments later and signaled him to rise. The attendant's expression was strange; it hinted at alarm held fearfully in check.

Tamsin's bedchamber was furnished in dark hangings and a high, lace-canopied bedstead of heavy southern wood. Bright daylight poured in through the terrace window, whose satin curtains had been thrown wide. Outside, through open glazed doors and an ornately sculptured balcony rail, spread a view of city roofs and avenues beyond the palace wall.

In the window's glare, some few visitors already waited in respectful attendance. Besides the queen's eunuch guards, several courtiers stood against the walls, including First Steward Basifer. Queen Tamsin lounged abed, her red tresses spread back across the pillows, her pale body half-clad in a scant, filmy nightdress.

In fact, from her languid posture, with her head propped back on the silken bolsters, eyes closed, and mouth poised half-open, the young queen appeared to be sleeping. But that did not explain the voice that issued from the bed.

On nearer inspection, blinking at the reclining figure framed by drawn, draped bed-canopies, Clewyn gained the distinct impression that it was not the queen who spoke. Rather, it was the doll, still clutched in her mistress's slack arm but positioned upright, its poised, painted head waggling in an eerily convincing parody of speech.

"Greetings, Prince Clewyn, and welcome," the shrill, singsong voice rang out. "You are a most fit addition to this party of the faithful—the first group of humans to witness my condescension to your mortal plane of affairs, and to hear in my own accents the decrees and utterances I have customarily passed through the mouth of my High Priestess, here."

"A thousand thanks, Divine Mistress!" Clewyn bowed lavishly, making the obeisance especially slow and deep to conceal his inner dismay. He had encouraged young Tamsin in her conceit of talking to the doll, for the sake of gaining her favor; he credited himself with shrewdness in guessing the way to win the toleration of a powerful sorceress. Yet if the queen was now to lie in a trance, prating her commandments in the voice of her mystical toy, how could there henceforth be any play of reason, or any sane, moderating influence? For once, after a long course of public life, the prince found himself sorely taxed to find words. "I thank you, most sincerely."

"You, Prince," the queen's doll continued, "are, in your newfound authority, the prime implementer of my commands within the palace here at Sargossa. Just as the First Steward, there," Ninga added with an amazingly deft nod of her gourd-head toward Basifer, "is the main prosecutor of my policies beyond, amid the lands and peoples of the broader realm."

In response, the eunuch bowed even more deeply than had the courtly prince. "Thank you, Mistress." Basifer had grown zealously faithful and unquestioning toward his queen and her puppet-goddess. Evidently his subservience was the result of some private arrangement between them, one that defied Clewyn's understanding. Certainly it was not a romantic or carnal attraction, in view of the man's handicap—which, in truth, made his own advanced years seem like no impediment at all. Obviously the young queen felt more comfortable with men who posed no sexual threat; Basifer had even been granted some high appointment in the church, a dual office. Now, in the First Steward's face, the prince read no hint of shock or skepticism, only earnest attentiveness.

"It is indeed a pleasure to make Your Divinity's acquaintance, and to hear your godly voice," the courtly prince ventured at last. "Yet I hope we shall not be deprived of Queen Tamsin's company as well. In recent days, I have grown accustomed to her charming presence."

"No, no, Prince. My oracle and servant will awaken presently, doubtless. She is easily wearied by concerns of state, and by the awkward eminence to which I have raised her at such a tender age." The tiny puppet-voice spoke with an absurd tone of patronage. "That is why I find it needful to inject my own voice into your governmental affairs."

"I understand, Divinity." The prince spoke graciously, trying to gain control of the discussion. "The day-to-day demands of running an empire—"

"Not quite, Sir Prince," the puppet-deity overrode him sharply. "What I have in mind is something more than daily routine. Rather, a revolutionary transformation of the land and faith."

The pronouncement echoed shrill in the silence that followed. "I, ah, would wonder . . ." Clewyn tried to recover. "In truth, Divinity, in the wake of the recent turmoil—"

"Turmoil is a healthy thing," the small goddess declared. "Even chaos, administered wisely, can be a curative measure. But it is important to keep things astir and not let them fall back to their former diseased state. Conditions in Sargossa are grown as slack and corrupt as they were before my arrival."

"Your Divinity," Clewyn temporized, "great Goddess Ninga . . . the Brythunian Empire as a whole has weathered your overthrow of Amalias and Typhas strongly. The health of the state has been maintained—"

"Nay, Clewyn," the puppet corrected him. "After a brief purgation of revolt, the sickness has been restored. The pervasive, creeping rot that bears the false aspect of healthiness continues." The high-pitched voice rang out with surprising vigor. "To look at Brythunia, one would think there had been no revolution at all—that the old, moribund god still rules, that the king still connives here in his privy chambers. What of our sacred mission? What of this glorious union of church and state we have achieved?" The godly puppet, without any apparent aid from the sleeping queen, dashed its misshapen head emphatically toward the open terrace window.

"Look you there, and see! The merchants still shave their coin, the priests nod and prate—though the shapes their lips form are a mite different; and the commoners still grovel and toil, albeit under the gaze of newer idols. Their lives are not transformed, their aims reach no higher, their sense of the sublime and terrible are yet stupidly a-slumber. Can you tell me, Prince, why they have troubled to change masters at all?"

"Divine Ninga, you must know that your subjects are far more content under your benign protection—"

"Precisely, Clewyn, content!" the goddess-head piped, resuming her tirade. "Complacent, dumb, stuporous. Where, I ask you, is the ecstasy, the devotion, the high holy terror? We gods face a sore challenge indeed to mold anything exquisite out of this coarse mortal clay! Yet even so, the labor shall continue forthwith! Through you, my governors, and alike through my priests and armored officers, a new order is decreed. Our followers shall be taken to task for any turpitude or laxness, any fault of thought or deed, the pang being death! And new, harsher demands shall be leveled on them."

Prince Clewyn waited, his furrowed old brow a-tickle with perspiration. "What demands, O Divinity?"

"Why . . . human sacrifice, I think! That is a measure which has enlivened my followers' holy zeal in the past. Each month, every five-hundredth subject in Sargossa and the district capitals shall be honored by slaughter . . . chosen at random from the name rolls. A sacred pyramid of skulls can be established in each main city's temple square.

And catacombs must be hollowed beneath the temples, to hold the bodies of those sacrificed, their heads to be replaced with painted gourds in my image! How does that sound?''

As before, a taut, pervasive silence followed the goddess's words. "It sounds most . . . stringent, Your Divinity," Clewyn managed to choke out.

"Thank you," the goddess said.

"Your will, Immortal Ninga, is our commandment." Basifer's assent followed close on Clewyn's, uttered without hesitation in a voice that resounded firm and manly.

"Aye . . . yes . . . a most sacred duty," came the thin, murmured acknowledgments from the other courtiers in the room. Their faces looked pale in the level daylight.

"Mmm . . . ahhmm." As the frightened subjects stood watching, the young queen stirred in her place. Goddess Ninga had fallen silent; now, with Tamsin's movement, the fetish tipped backward like an ordinary doll.

The girl-queen, meanwhile, opened her eyes. "Oh, my friends are here already!" Unselfconsciously drawing her frail form up against her pillows, she stretched both arms over her head and yawned. "Uumm. I suppose Ninga has been entertaining you all, while I slept. She is such a dear!" She hugged the now-limp doll to her side, kissing its glossy brow, then primped and straightened its garments. Just as casually, she rearranged her own lacy nightdress to cover her bosom.

"The divine Ninga," Prince Clewyn essayed from his place at the foot of the bed, "was speaking to us of certain, ah, modifications regarding the practice of worship in the city temples—"

"Good," Tamsin foreclosed his words. "Excellent! I know she can trust you to carry out all her wishes, whatever they might be." She turned to Basifer, who knelt by her bedside. "Most particularly you, First Steward, in your new office as Priest-Delegate."

"Yes, most surely, Your Highness." The eunuch bent forward and kissed the hem of her bedcover. "I depart this very moment to convey the High Goddess's commandments to her minions—and yours, Gracious Queen—at the temple. All will be carried forward with dispatch."

"Excellent," she said turning from the eunuch-prelate as he bowed his way toward the door. "But you, my dear Prince, you will keep me company while I sup and dress, will you not?" She extended her slender hand to receive Clewyn's dry-lipped kiss. "And you others, morning greetings to you all!"

Servants stood ready with trays of delicate pastry and cozied teapots, which they now brought forward. But the flighty young Tamsin barely sipped and nibbled; in moments, she had slid from her bed, her doll clutched tightly at her side, and summoned dextrous maidservants to clothe and groom both of them before the eyes of her guests. All the while, Clewyn chatted lightly, easefully, with her. Then she led him to a table whereupon were arrayed favorite gems and trinkets from her collection. She showed him each in turn, holding them up to sparkle in the morning light that streamed through the terrace window.

FIFTEEN

Savage Vengeance

It came to pass that one clear morning, with the bite of frost in the air, Conan and Regnard roused themselves from a shabby suburban hostel and approached the walls of fabled Sargossa. The Gunderman had been up late, dicing and drinking with peddlers and smugglers before the kitchen fire, yet this morning he felt brisk and alert, ready to make the most of the good fortune that he was certain lay ahead.

"Here, you, take this," he said, bundling his loose rucksack together with the bulkier one that his savage friend usually slung over his shoulder. "It will look more seemly to the inspectors as we enter town. Remember, we stand on the threshold of a great citadel, where life is richer and grander than anything you have seen. Do not be mazed or frightened at what we encounter. Trust me, stay nearby, and be assured that all will be clear to you in the end."

As they trudged up the road, whose hard-rutted dust soon gave way to cobblestone, it was easy to be impressed by the high city wall. Its broad towers stood out at stately intervals, their battlements gilded bright with dawning eastern sun. The gate to which the High Road led them was splendid, unmarred by the recent war, its pillars inlaid with colored mosaics patterned in ritual symbols—and above the arch, in blazing tile relief, stood forth the rampant gryphon of high Brythunian heraldry.

The great gate was already open and in use, its early traffic watched over by Imperial guardsmen posted both within and without the huge metal door-valves and many-toothed portcullis. Rather than joining the continuous stream of diversely costumed travelers, livestock, and wagons entering the city shadows, Regnard led Conan aside and addressed him.

"You know, the guards would hardly permit you, an unruly-looking savage, to wander the streets of Sargossa on your own. They regard the likes of you as a danger to civil order, unless they are satisfied that someone is taking full responsibility for you. Therefore, we shall resort to a stratagem—a temporary disguise, if you will."

Reaching into his clanking purse, the Gunderman extracted an object other than money: a short, sturdy length of bronze chain with a broad, open clasp at either end.

"If you will wear this, only for the time being, it will appear to the guards that you are a barbarian slave and I your master. That is all the credential you will need to pass through the gate and see the wonders of mighty Sargossa."

Silent and uncomplaining, Conan permitted Regnard to lead him over to the side of the road. There a farrier plied his trade, shoeing country horses with steel for the hard-paved streets of town. Waiting his turn after a sorrel mare and a bay gelding, the Cimmerian stooped obediently and let the craftsman wield hammer and tongs to pound the manacles tight around his wrists.

"Nay, nay—behind the back, my friend!" Regnard insisted, hauling his primitive charge around before the anvil. "That is the way it is done here. But do not worry, Conan. You will still be able to bear your burdens by doubling them over your shoulder, thus. And I can carry these weapons for you."

So it was that the two wayfarers entered Sargossa, with Regnard making a brave show of slave-mastery, shoving Conan along by the shoulder and pummeling him to go faster. Once inside, in narrow, filthy lanes between the tall, leaning tenements, the Gunderman assured Conan they would be better off to continue the charade.

"Here, now, is it not a splendid sight?" he demanded. "Look at the height of those buildings, and see the crowds of people swarming through these streets! All of them plump and richly dressed, too—except for the beggars, whose sores and amputations are truly amazing, a scientific wonder!" He tugged Conan by one manacled arm. "Come here, down this alleyway. As I recall, it will lead us toward the merchants' quarter and the gem market."

Through a maze of twisting streets, rubbing shoulders along the way with peddlers, mendicants, painted trollops, hairless eunuchs, shaven priests, ruffians, uniformed officers, and the thousand other specialized minions of the great city warren, they came at last to a broad bazaar, an open courtyard a half-score paces wide and more than twice as long. The space was, if anything, more crowded than the surrounding streets, jammed with merchants and buyers in all manner of robes and headgear. From its center could be heard an auctioneer's spirited cries, and the chanting out of prices.

"Here we are at last, Conan . . . the one place where you can receive the best price in all Brythunia for your wares." Shoving his companion briskly through the mob, Regnard pressed toward the front of the crowd. "Why should we fatten the purse of some middleman, I ask you, when we can go straight to the source and reap a full, round profit ourselves?"

While shouldering through the bidding customers, the tall outlander was able to see over their heads to the center of the thronging bazaar. There a statuesque, bronze-skinned southern female stepped up onto a stone platform. Standing at her side, a fezzed, wiry-haired Corinthian merchant peeled aside the thin robe that was her only garment, commending her naked charms to the crowd of enthusiastic bidders. Behind those two, a coal-black Kushite waited, festooned with chains far heavier than Conan's. Next in line after him was a Hyperborean lad, fresh from the northern snows, slim and platinum-haired, his wrists bound to a wooden yoke suspended around his neck. Beyond these glum-looking prisoners a pair of burly guards loomed, armed with flails and wearing gold-braided vests and fezzes in the same orange hue as the auctioneer's livery.

"Our next consignment," the dealer was saying, "ripe from the desert oases of the fragrant south, is this fair maid of Zamora, a dancer and fipple-flute player of unexampled beauty. From Shadizar she harks, gentlemen . . . where the nights are warm, the melons grow lush and ripe, and the honeyed fig is luscious to the tongue—''

"Do you really take me for such a fool, Regnard?" Conan murmured at last, a note of grim resignation in his voice. "Here is no gem market—by the Great Badger, you have led me to a slave mart!"

"Now, now, Conan, be not afraid." The Gunderman still prodded his companion forward with the butt of the stone spear. "As I said before, all will be plain to you in time. We may as well put your splendid carcass up on the block, just for now, along with your few possessions; your gems will only make the bidding all the keener. I will collect the money and save it for us. Later on—perhaps this very night—I can creep to your slave den and free you. Both of us will then be wealthy—wait, what are you doing?"

Enthusiastic bidding over the Zamoran wench distracted the buyers on all sides, but Regnard wore a look of alarm. He watched unbelievingly as Conan, working behind his back with all the viselike strength in his hands, pried open the heavy copper manacles and slid them free of his thick, hairy wrists. His motions were swift; as Regnard tried to bolt, he lunged after him. The Gunderman was caught, and sagged nearly to his knees under the weight of the savage grip on his shoulder.

"Now, my good friend, let us see how your own irons fit you—and how long it takes you to pry them open!" As he spoke, his movements swift and ruthless, Conan double-looped the bronze chain around his captor's neck. The wrist-clasps he forced closed on one another, forming two tight, heavy links fastened at Regnard's nape.

The shortness of the manacle did not allow for breath.

In growing panic, Regnard tugged vainly at the heavy fastenings, then at the taut chain, with motions that became a wild clawing at his throat. The noises he emitted were breathless and faint, mere glottal clicks; even so, his lurching frenzy drew notice from the nearby crowd.

"What is it, a stabbing? No, a slave mutiny!"

"Help him, someone, if you can!"

"Nay, fool, to Hades with the foreign trader! Kill that renegade, before he escapes and spreads his madness!"

Retrieving his weapons amid the confusion, Conan lashed out fiercely at the surging, grasping mob. His stone ax struck home once, and again. Blood, spittle, and teeth flew in a maelstrom around him, while choking Regnard writhed and purpled underfoot. As the crowd fell back, the two huge overseers bulled their way forward; but their thin, cruel flails were made for inflicting pain at close range, not for honest fighting. One of them, receiving a light jab in the gut from Conan's spear, sat down on the pavement, bellowing; the other, taking the keen ax-blade across the face, stumbled away blinded with blood.

"Look out, the savage is berserk!"

"He is armed! Call for the city guard!"

The crowd scattered before him, jostling one another in fear, but already Conan heard the clank of guards' armor approaching from a nearby street. Turning in desperation, he rushed the line of slaves awaiting sale and lashed out with his weapons. His ax struck the wooden yoke of the pale-haired Hyperborean, shearing through its knotted thongs. The youth, with an excited cry, freed his hands and began working his neck loose of the poles. Turning from him, Conan hacked through a rope that bound two ragged convicts together, then ran his spear into the city warder who ventured forward to stop their escape.

The Kushite captive, some moments before, had doubled his wrist-chains about the neck of the auctioneer, throttling him till his body hung as limp as a meal sack; now, snatching up the man's key ring and flinging the corpse aside, he plunged forward to hide himself in the crowd. Even the Zamoran woman, bending to steal the dagger from Regnard's now-lifeless, contorted body, tucked the purloined weapon in the bosom of her robe and slipped away, doubtless on some errand of revenge.

The slave revolt and the press of frightened merchants covered Conan's escape. He darted into the least-clogged alleyway, bowling citizens aside and clubbing down those few who stood to oppose him. The city was a cramped, crowded, stench-filled maze to him after his months in the wilderness, but his knowledge of it was swiftly returning. As soon as immediate pursuit was behind him, he bent his steps uphill toward the temple square and the palace, to carry out his high hunt.

It was impossible to pass stealthily. Even in a town as cosmopolitan as Sargossa, with all the broad panoply of costumes and nationalities that peopled its streets, a nearnaked savage, hulking and sun-bronzed, bearing stoneheaded spear and ax into bazaars and residential alleys, was a remarkable sight. Conan could not fail to draw the excited attention of housemaids, peddlers, ragged urchins, and small, yapping dogs.

Accordingly, in place of discretion, he relied on speed. To foil his pursuers and head off encirclement, he loped through the city at a full hunter's gait, using the stamina that had served him so well on long hunts beyond the mountains. As luck would have it, he met with no crowd too dense to be jostled through, no obstacle too large to be upturned or vaulted over, and no Imperial officer too alert and deadly to be beaten down with a single curt weapon-stroke.

So he went, the living image of savagery . . . a swift, darting glimpse of his race's origins, astonishing and unnerving to all those tame urban drones he flickered past. He was the primal hunter, set loose in the city labyrinth: swift and feral, yet surely doomed, stalking who knew what terrible, unconquerable prey?

In time, teeming slums gave way to grand villas and public enclosures, with long, broad avenues running between; this in turn gave the populace more opportunities to scatter at Conan's approach, and to wonder from a distance at his fierce, outlandish aspect. It also gave rise to new dangers—that he might be brought down by arrow-flights from the temple roof, or overridden by mounted troopers. To prevent such disaster, he took action. Spying a wheeled conveyance in the street, he sprang aboard it: a spoked, railed chariot, whose richly robed driver he cast out headlong. It was a light, swift vehicle. Gathering the reins in his ax-fist, he smote the rumps of its two roan coursers with his spearpoint, starting them off at a lively gallop toward the palace gate.

He trusted the beasts to choose their way through the city press, and the citizenry to keep out from under the mounts' sparking, flailing hooves. He would have been uncertain of how to slow their gallop in any case; and he could scarcely steer their headlong rush as it was.

But their speed was a blessing to him, a heady drug.

Perched on the chariot-bed, panting from his exertions, Conan was borne along faster than any possible warning or signal of his coming . . . through the broad, uncrowded temple square, jolting and rumbling toward the main gate of the Imperial Palace.

As it happened, the gate stood open. The guards who moved to bar his way were driven aside by the foaming coursers, who kept up their gallop straight across the inner courtyard. They raced for the double doors of the palace, one huge portal of which gaped wide. When the animals struck the broad, shallow steps leading to the archway, they tried heroically to maintain their speed—but the chariot behind them disintegrated, its frail wheels and axle splintering under the impact. Conan held fast to the rail, riding the slewing wreck until the lathered, panting team could drag it no farther. Then he leaped free, bounding up the remaining stairs toward the palace entry.

"Halt, savage! Advance no nearer, on pain of death!"

A pair of guards moved into the doorway, blocking entry with the hafts of their battle-axes. Conan continued forward, mounting the steps with a weapon leveled in either hand.

"Stop, I say, wild heathen! If you cannot speak as men do, then list ye carefully to my ax—it speaks a language any stinking brute will understand!"

Bounding straight up to the guards, close enough to see the sweat of fear on their faces, Conan abruptly halted. Gathering both his weapons into one fist, he dug a forefinger into his loin-pouch—underneath the jeweled belt that still girdled his hips—and produced a small, shiny object. "Mayhap you can understand this," he told them in coarse

Brythunian. "I have it from one named Dolphas, on the eastern frontier."

Suspiciously the senior guard unclasped one hand from the haft of his battle-ax and accepted the ring, holding it up before his face. "Truly enough, it bears the sigil of the Imperial throne." He glanced sharply at his companion, then back to the intruder. "You really expect us to believe you are one of Dolphas's spies? This is all most irregular!"

Conan glared levelly at him. "I carry an urgent message from Dolphas, for your queen's ears only. Lead me to her at once."

"O-ho. Some savage, this!" Continuing to watch Conan warily, the officer waved away the guards who were closing in on them from the gate. "Come, you will have to wait here for clearance." He shot a look to his companion. "Has Lord Basifer returned?"

"Aye, Captain. He passed within some minutes ago on an errand from the temple."

"So—you, lay down those mock weapons of yours, and wait here." He gestured to a bench situated in an alcove beside the doorway. "Remember to behave yourself. The Imperial Palace is no place for your play-acting!" Retaining the signet ring and shouldering his ax, he turned away, heading for the central stair.

Conan waited under the eyes of the guardsman while another officer came forward from the staircase to take the captain's place. Laying his stone weapons against the wall, the outlander hovered near them, sullenly refusing to be seated. Quietly he sized up his chances to break through into the palace, and found them slight in view of the number of guards lining the broad vestibule. Now was a time for restraint, and for stealth, as on any hunt. First he must get near the quarry, as he had learned from Yugwubwa, by covering himself with the enemy's stink.

From outside, through the lancet window of the guards' alcove, he heard a turmoil at the gate. Likely it signaled the arrival of news from the lower city of his doings there, and of the riot at the slave-mart. Voices were once again raised, and a call went up for the captain of the watch. A mounted civilian officer was admitted through the gate.

More moments passed in the polished dimness. Conan eased himself onto the cold stone bench, within easy reach of his weapons. The two guards had become inattentive to him, gazing through the open door at those bustling toward them from the gate.

All at once, heavy footsteps sounded on the staircase; it was the captain returning in haste. "Come," he said, beckoning to Conan. "The First Steward will see you at once."

"Captain, you are summoned to the gate," the door guard said, glancing uncertainly from the courtyard to his superior. "There appears to have been some kind of trouble in the town—"

"It will have to wait," the officer told him, "for this affair will not!" He turned, and as Conan grabbed his weapons and strode after him, led the way upstairs. "This is a matter of high state import," the captain called back over his shoulder. "Stall off those others until I return, and reveal nothing about our visitor."

Before them unfolded the palace's columned, filigreed interior, a gaudy, impossible stone cage. The clash of the captain's heels on the polished floor made echoes that rang louder than the whisper of Conan's sandals. Rigid-faced guards, servants, and gleaming statues flashed by on either hand, looking as unreal as the phantasms of a fever dream to one whose home was the forest's leafy glades.

But there, just ahead, waited one with real dimension and presence. The watch officer led Conan through a gilded door into a tapestried anteroom, where stood a figure with intensity in his look and restrained menace in his bearing. Wearing the foppish fez and caftan of an eastern eunuch, holding the queen's signet between thumb and forefinger, he paced the ornate tiles, coming abruptly to a halt as the two approached.

"Milord Basifer," the captain announced, "here is the messenger who arrived so indiscreetly—"

"Yes, yes, I can tell." The aristocrat, beside himself with impatience, began his questioning even before Conan fully entered the room. "Well, man, what of Dolphas? Why has he not come himself?" He looked Conan up and down. "You bring me no gems to speak of! Does that mean he has not carried out the queen's command?"

"Dolphas will carry out no more commands." Starting forward at a run inside the archway, Conan raised ax and spear in either hand. "Nor will you and your queen be giving more of them!"

The captain, alert and quick, lunged to intercept him with a sideward sweep of his ax. Conan ducked beneath and came up swinging his own hatchet. Its heavy flint blade slashed crosswise, scraping against the guard's steel helmet and striking sparks from its visor rim. The captain collapsed to the tiles, clutching his face in blood-streaming hands.

"What! You dare violence here? Guards, seize this assassin!" Instead of wheedling for his life or turning to run, the one called Basifer strode indignantly forward—only to take the hurtling point of Conan's spear straight in his breastbone. He made no sound, after the initial grunt of impact, but sank down to his knees, and then sideways onto the polished floor. In spite of his garb, he did not grovel like a eunuch; Conan had to admit that he died a man.

At the far end of the room stood another golden door. It was guarded by two yellow-clad Imperials, who rushed forward at Basifer's outcry. Conan, without time to recover his spear, ran straight forward between their scything blades. One sword missed; the other, striking the hard flint of his ax, snapped off near the hilt. Conan, as he lunged past the broken sword's wielder, cut a leg out from under him by striking at the unarmored back of his knee.

The other swordsman doubled back swiftly. His blade, slashing at the Cimmerian's belly, glanced off his ornamental belt. The blow did no damage, serving only to anger the snarling savage. The swinging ax smote the guardsman on the side of the head, sending the man's cracked steel helmet spinning away across the floor and stretching him out senseless.

The gilded door in the far wall stood ajar. At a kick from Conan's sandaled foot, it shuddered open. Within was a broad chamber lined with dark hangings and lit by bright-burning oil lamps attended by servants. Several courtiers waited around the periphery of the room, while at its center stood two persons in elegant dress: an elderly man, and a pale young woman who clasped in one arm a doll with a painted, misshapen head.

"So," Conan growled, "you are Brythunia's queen, who rules the land by earthquake and volcano, who has set up her toy doll as a god, and who slaughters whole nations to possess their trinkets!''

"What Ninga and I do is our business," the woman answered him readily with a wan, quizzical smile. "In any case, it is idle of you to menace us, for we are proof against mortal weapons. Steel wilts at our touch—" She gestured to a cabinet of charms and ornaments that stood open beside her. "Our trinkets, as you call them, are mightier."

"Tyrant!" Conan shouted, maddened by the sight of the gems. "Do you think to frighten me away with the stink of sorcery?" Raising his ax, he started forward.

Several things occurred at once. Guards from the outer corridor, drawn by the strife and shouting, burst in at the chamber door. The servants, in response to a gesture from Prince Clewyn, smothered their lamps, bringing near-total darkness to the draperied room. And Conan, in the last flicker of lamplight, hurled his stone ax straight at the tall, stately figure of Queen Tamsin where she stood at Clewyn's side.

There were curses then, thumps and shrieks in the darkness, all of which swiftly fell silent as an uncanny radiance was kindled at its center. It was an eerie, bluish-pale glow, streaming up from eggshell-like fragments that lay scattered across the floor.

The light limned, against the room's dark tapestries, the astonished faces of the watchers, as well as one small, forlorn shape. Out of the tumult, the only sound that persisted was that of a little child sobbing.

"Help me. Please, someone, won't you help?" The ragged figure, a thin, towheaded girl, stood in the spot formerly occupied by Queen Tamsin.

"The bad men, they hurt Papa," she cried out piteously.

In one hand she bore a limp rag doll, crudely stitched. Its head—obviously nothing more than a broken gourd—hung shattered, yet it was from those shards that the mystic light emanated. "They came on horses and burned our farm . . . and oh, oh, Mama . . . !" Her childish words gave way to fresh peals of grief as she dropped her broken doll and stood knuckling her eyes, wailing wretchedly.

All movement had ceased in the room. Its occupants gaped at the spectacle, wondering if it bore any reality in the common world of shape and substance. But although the light of the gourd-fragments gradually faded, the child's heartfelt sobbing went on as if it would never cease.

At length, at Clewyn's urging, one of the lamps was rekindled. By its light, the onlookers saw that the savage intruder was gone. He must have slipped away, or else been obliterated by the goddess Ninga's final magic. Of the two guards who had burst in, one lay senseless on the floor, the other sat dazed, massaging a bruised skull. Of certain objects—the assassin's stone ax, the gems and ornaments in Her Holiness's cabinet—and of proud Queen Tamsin herself, there was no earthly sign. But the little orphan child remained, her face a frail cameo-image of the queen, with the same dark red hair and bright green eyes. Without question, she was tangible and alive. Her wails subsiding, she blinked up at the strangers around her in heartbroken bewilderment.

It was Prince Clewyn, his kindly old face crinkling in sympathy, who first found the presence of mind to kneel and comfort the child, hugging her dusty form against his bosom.

"There, there, little one, cry as much as you want. We are here to take care of you."

EPILOGUE:

Encounter by Night

"**H**o, there—you, barbarian! Begone, there is no more ale for you! I am closing shop, and you are the last one here, so haul yourself away . . . before you pass out on my floor and I have to hitch a donkey to your drink-sodden carcass and drag you out! Enough now, go!"

The taverner's manner was less than respectful, it occurred to Conan. He considered whether to take offense, but he decided no, what was the use? A man might rail against the ill fortunes that beset the world—or even take up arms and hurl himself at their source—but in the end, the outcome was always the same. If a mortal tried to seize hold of his own destiny and bolt from the muddy, rutted path the gods had decreed for him, it was in the relentless way of things for him to be cruelly tripped up and tumbled back into the mire.

The drink, at least, was a balm. It kept the toothed shadows at bay, deadened the ache of lost hopes, and sustained a mood of gentle, hushed reminiscence. Impressions came to him, fleeting images that seemed to be reflected from another age, another world—of fir trees shivering in an early morning breeze, the flash of sun on a mountain tarn, soft voices murmuring near a camp fire—

"All right, you hulking northerner, enough weeping in your ale! Here, fellow, I will refill your cup. Take it with you, since I don't doubt you will be back here in the morning! But go now, before I heave you out!"

Glumly, leadenly, after shuffling to the counter to receive the last dregs of the ale-pitcher, Conan turned and trudged up the stone stairs toward the exit. He had a bed to go to— a straw-ticked pad in a bug-ridden tenement flop—assuming he could find the place and rouse up the landlord to let him in at this hour.

His jeweled metal girdle had bought him that much, at least. Sold at the recently inflated prices, it had furnished him his nondescript clothing, the sword-belt that now hugged his middle, passable meals and shelter, and, more important, the flood tide of ale that had borne him up during these past days. After witnessing the witch-queen's strange transformation and making good his escape, he had been quick to sell the gems, change his appearance, and plunge out of sight—into the familiar haunts of the Sargossan underworld, where his absence over the last few months had scarcely been noted.

Amazingly, there did not seem to be much hue and cry. The escapees from the slave-riot were sought, but no call went up for Queen Tamsin's assassin, perhaps because, as a matter of policy, no royal death had been acknowledged.

Instead, the Imperial Brythunian faith had taken a bizarre and rather sentimental turn; the folk of the city and the broader empire were being exhorted to worship a miracle: the birth, or rebirth, of a magical child-Tamsin. She was said to embody a living fusion of their brave queen and the former goddess Ninga. She was described as a benevolent godling who, in her girlish innocence, and ruling the empire under the sage guidance of Prince Clewyn and his councillors, would lead them all to a purer, more harmonious existence. In celebration of her virtues, Ningan priestesses and devout citizens daily donned bright robes and flower garlands to dance through Sargossa's streets, linking hands with passersby and singing childish songs and hymns. The carnage of the late revolution had, miraculously, given way to outpourings of faith and joy.

All of this brought small comfort to Conan in his despondency; it only made him feel more the outsider, more the misfit. As to what had really transpired in the palace with the mad queen—what dire, sorcerous change he had wrought, *or unwrought*—he could not fully judge. For him, revenge had been a simple necessity, not a luxury to be savored and boasted of. It had not eased the pangs of his loss.

The top of the tavern's dim-lit stair corridor stank of retchings and of less mentionable filth. The iron latch was set on the heavy timber door; after Conan shouldered through, the portal swung itself shut with a ragged click. Outside, the alley was dank and obscure. A thin, dusty-bright ribbon of stars zigzagged between ramshackle roofs overhead. Their pale light, mirrored in patches of scummy water pooled among the cobbles, was his only beacon.

Then, in the star-shot darkness, an even darker figure moved with a scrape of bootsole. It loomed momentarily near, then veered away abruptly and slouched off, its retreating movements accented by the muffled clink of weaponry.

"Hold, there! You seem familiar to me!" His drunken haze instantly forgotten, Conan started after the figure—who, in turn, fled all the faster. The way was treacherous, winding past mudholes and half-seen obstacles, so that the race through the nighted streets never accelerated to a run. It ended in a courtyard whose blind recesses created a trap of starlight; there the night-lurker turned at bay, sword drawn, his features visible under the visorless bronze helmet of a city proctor.

"Desist and yield," the fugitive said from his near-cowering stance, putting up a belated show of authority. "Throw down your weapon, in the name of the empire!"

"Ah, yes, that grit-and-cinder voice!" Conan exclaimed. "Now I know you certainly. You are proctor-sergeant hereabouts, are you not?"

"If you know that much, then you know enough to yield to me," the other said, edging forward with renewed confidence. "I tell you what, stranger . . . just go on about your business. I will let you off this time!"

"Indeed." Conan shook his head amiably. "You are fond of lying in wait for late passersby, are you not—you and your uniformed thugs?"

"The town curfew is strictly enforced—" the sergeant began.

"But tonight—" after a quick glance about them, Conan continued in his menacingly pleasant tone "—tonight you are working alone, and not up to facing a quarry that seems too fit.'' He stood easily with hilt in hand, blocking the other's path of escape. ''You rob your drunken victims, clap them into the town dungeon, drug them, and bundle them off to the slave-mines! Such was my fate at your hands, as you may recall.''

''Impossible—none ever returns from the mines!''

''Sergeant, there is only one place from which nobody ever returns. With Crom as my witness, one of us will go there tonight!''

As the Cimmerian spoke, he moved, and the nighted courtyard echoed with the din of swords clashing.